WILLIAM HOWELL

The Art of Shadows

First published by Words of William 2025

This novel is entirely a work of fiction. The names, characters and incidents portrayed in it are the work of the author's imagination. Any resemblance to actual persons, living or dead, events or localities is entirely coincidental.

First edition

ISBN: 979-8-9986031-0-5

*For Leah, whose love steadies every page, and for Lillian, whose wonder reminds me why stories matter.
You are my heart, my home, and my inspiration.*

1

Chapter 1

Amanda Chen stepped out of her black government-issued sedan, heels striking the pavement like gunshots in the early morning calm. The Los Angeles air hung thick with the promise of another scorching day, but the chill taking residence in her chest the past three months was noticeable. She paused, allowing herself five seconds, no more, to breathe before the mask of Special Agent Chen would lock into place. The divorce papers might be filed away, but their edges still cut when she least expected it.

Her ex-husband's parting words echoed through her mind: "You love the job more than anyone could ever love you." The accusation carried the sting of partial truth, which made it all the more painful. Maybe he is right. Maybe that's all she is, married to case files and criminal profiles, sleeping with theories instead of human warmth.

Amanda straightened her navy blazer, fingers lingering over the badge clipped at her waist. The weight of it anchored her to reality when memories threatened to pull her under. Today wasn't about her failed marriage or the empty apartment

1

waiting for her return. Today is about the Eclipse Consortium, shadows and whispers made flesh.

The morning sun caught in her sleek black hair as she crossed the parking lot. She pulled it back into a practical ponytail, a few rebellious strands framing her face. Amanda wore minimal makeup, just enough to mask the shadows beneath her eyes from another night of restless sleep. Her athletic frame moved with deliberate precision, each step measured and controlled, a woman accustomed to commanding respect in rooms dominated by men who underestimated her.

The Los Angeles field office loomed before her, all glass, steel, and bureaucracy. Amanda inhaled deeply, drawing in the scent of concrete warmed by early sun, exhaust fumes from the nearby freeway, and the faintest trace of jasmine from the well-maintained landscaping. The automatic doors slid open with a pneumatic hiss, welcoming her into the air-conditioned interior.

Inside, the office hummed with the controlled chaos that defined federal law enforcement. Phones chirped and rang in competing tones. Keyboards clicked in irregular rhythms. The artificial overhead lighting cast everyone in a sickly pallor, washing out skin tones and highlighting the dark circles that were practically a job requirement.

Amanda moved through the space with practiced ease, her tailored pantsuit lending her an air of authority belying her actual rank. Four years with the Bureau taught her that confidence is as important as competence, sometimes more so. She nodded to agents who glanced up from their work, their eyes showing a deference they might not extend to other women her age.

"Morning, Chen," called Ramirez from the break room.

"Coffee's fresh for once."

"Miracle of miracles," she replied, the corner of her mouth lifting in what passed for a smile these days.

The smell of burnt coffee permeated the air, clinging to fabric and skin like cigarette smoke. The office bouquet, the scent of deadlines, overtime, and stubborn cases that refused to close. Amanda bypassed the break room, coffee could wait. Her desk called to her with the promise of progress, of answers hidden in the chaos of information.

Her workspace stood as an island of organized disorder among the neat stations of her colleagues. Case files fanned out in a pattern that would appear random to anyone but her, a physical manifestation of how her mind worked. Post-it notes in three different colors created a code only she understood. A half-empty cup of yesterday's coffee sat forgotten beside her keyboard, a ring of brown staining the inside of the ceramic.

Amanda slid into her chair, the familiar creak of its hinges greeting her. Her fingers brushed over the top folder of surveillance photos of suspected Eclipse operatives. Each face a puzzle piece, each location a thread in a web stretched across continents. Somewhere in this tangle of information is the path to El Fantasma, the ghost who haunted international law enforcement.

"You look like hell, Chen."

Special Agent Dominic Hayes leaned against her desk, his suit immaculate despite the early hour. His presence carried the scent of expensive aftershave and ambition. They'd been in the same training class at Quantico, and while she outperformed him in almost every area, he advanced faster. The politics of the Bureau were as complex as any criminal organization they investigated.

"Always the charmer, Hayes," she replied, not bothering to raise her eyes up from her files. "What do you want?"

"SAC Darnell is calling a briefing at nine. Eclipse Consortium. Word is, there's movement." He paused, studying her with ever-vigilant eyes. "You've been all over this case for months. Thought you'd want first crack at whatever's come in."

Amanda glanced up, immediately alert. Her heart quickened, though her expression remained neutral. "What kind of movement?"

Hayes shrugged, the gesture too casual to be genuine. "Above my pay grade. But they've pulled in agents from Organized Crime and Art Theft. Must be something big."

He pushed himself off her desk, straightening his tie. "Better pull yourself together, Chen. You know how Darnell feels about people who aren't at their best."

After he walked away, Amanda let out a slow breath. Hayes is an ass, but he wasn't wrong. Special Agent in Charge Darnell has little patience for personal problems interfering with professional obligations. She opened her desk drawer and pulled out her emergency kit, a travel toothbrush, concealer, and a small bottle of eye drops. Five minutes in the bathroom would be enough to erase the visible signs of her sleepless night.

As she stood, her phone buzzed with a text from an unknown number: "Check your case notes from the San Diego port seizure. Not everything was logged."

Amanda froze, staring at the message. Her mind cycled through possibilities, a trap, a leak, a test. She quickly pulled the San Diego file from her stack, flipping to the inventory manifests. The shipping container held priceless artifacts disguised as commercial furniture, a typical Eclipse operation. According to her contact at Customs, there had been whispers of something else, something the official report never mentioned.

She memorized the number before deleting the text. Whoever sent it either possesses inside information or is playing a dangerous game. Either way, it couldn't be ignored.

The office continued its morning routine around her, agents and analysts moving through their days with the steady rhythm of government employees. None of them noticed the slight tremble in her hands as she reorganized her files, preparing for the briefing. Amanda controlled her breathing, in for four counts, hold for seven, out for eight, the technique refined through troubling cases worse than mysterious text messages.

Her eyes fell on a photo clipped to one of the files, a grainy surveillance image of a man entering an upscale Los Angeles gallery. His face was partially obscured, but something about his posture, the confident set of his shoulders, sent a chill down her spine. The photo labeled: "Person of Interest, Possible Eclipse Courier."

Amanda tucked the file into her tablet case. The trembling in her hands stopped, replaced by the steady calm that always came when the hunt began in earnest. This is why she joined the Bureau, not for the politics or the prestige, but for moments like this, when the scattered pieces began to form a picture.

The pain of her divorce, the emptiness of her apartment, the whispers that followed her through the office, none of it mattered now. The only thing that mattered was the case, the pursuit. Hayes is right about one thing: she needed to be at her best today.

Amanda Chen, Special Agent of the FBI, straightened her blazer and headed toward the conference room. Behind her, the ghost of Mandi, the woman she'd been before the badge, before the divorce, faded into the background, a shadow she couldn't afford to acknowledge. Not today. Not when she was so close to catching a ghost of her own.

****

The conference room's glass walls rendered privacy an illusion, a perfect metaphor for the intelligence community. Amanda slipped into a chair at the far end of the polished table, tablet already open to her notes. Around her, colleagues arranged themselves in the unspoken hierarchy of federal law enforcement, senior agents closest to the projection screen, ambitious climbers hovering near them like remoras on sharks, and the rest scattered according to their particular alliances. She remained apart, preferring the unobstructed view her isolation provided.

Special Agent in Charge Darnell entered the room with the contained energy of a career agent, measured steps, watchful eyes, and the permanent furrow between his brows, a souvenir from decades of suspicion. His charcoal suit hung immaculately on his frame, the only indication of his former military service being the precision with which he placed his folder on the table.

"Let's get started," he said, voice like gravel tumbling over bourbon. No pleasantries, no wasted words. Amanda respected that about him, even when his directness cut uncomfortably close to her insecurities.

The lights dimmed as an image appeared on the projection screen, a shipping container being unloaded at the Port of Long Beach, its contents splayed across a warehouse floor.

Antiquities, sculptures, and paintings, each worth more than what most agents made in a year.

"Three days ago, Customs intercepted this shipment. Marked as diplomatic cargo from the Myanmar Consulate, but the seals were forgeries, good ones." Darnell clicked to the next slide. "Lab confirmed the items are authentic, Khmer sculptures from the 12th century, Ming dynasty ceramics, paintings from private European collections that disappeared during World War II."

Amanda's fingers moved across her tablet, recording details and connections. Her mind shuffled through previous Eclipse cases, finding the patterns that others missed.

"Eclipse Consortium," Darnell said, his tone hardening. "They've escalated their operations. This is the third shipment we've intercepted in Los Angeles in two months. According to our intelligence, they're using a network of high-end galleries and private dealers to move the merchandise."

Hayes raised his hand. "Any leads on who's running the local operation?"

"Nothing concrete. But we have reason to believe their leader, code name El Fantasma, will be at the Getty Gala this weekend." Darnell's eyes swept the room, landing on Amanda. "It's a fundraiser for art conservation. Every major dealer, collector, and curator on the West Coast will be there."

A slide showing the Getty Museum lit up at night, elegant and imposing against the Los Angeles skyline. Amanda's chest instinctively contracted. She visited the museum dozens of times, drawn to its quiet halls and the stories captured in oil and stone. Now it would become a hunting ground.

"We need eyes inside," Darnell said. "Agent Chen, your background in art history makes you our best option. You'll attend as a guest of Arthur Whitmore, a benefactor who's agreed to assist us."

Amanda nodded, her face betraying none of the conflicting emotions beneath. Undercover work is always a delicate balance, staying alert while appearing at ease, hunting while pretending to be merely enjoying the evening.

"What about backup?" she asked, her voice steady.

"Hayes and Thompson will be working security. Rivera will be monitoring communications from a vehicle outside." Darnell's tone made it clear this wasn't open for discussion. "The priority is identification only. We need to confirm El Fantasma's presence and potentially identify key members of the network. No arrests, no confrontations."

The briefing continued with technical details, communication protocols, exit strategies, and contingencies. Amanda absorbed it all while part of her mind worked through the implications. The Eclipse Consortium evaded international law enforcement for years. They were methodical, cautious, and ruthlessly efficient. For their leader to risk appearing at a public event, even one as exclusive as the Getty Gala, suggested either supreme confidence or desperate necessity.

As the lights came up, agents began to disperse, their movements accompanied by the shuffling of papers and muted conversations. Amanda remained seated, making additional notes while the room emptied.

"Chen," Darnell said, pausing by her chair. "A word."

She followed him to his office, a glass cube at the corner of the floor that offered views of both the city and the bullpen. He closed the door before speaking.

"You've been tracking Eclipse longer than anyone here," he said, studying her face. "What's your read on this?"

Amanda considered her words carefully. "It's unusual for them to be this active in one location. Three major shipments in two months breaks their pattern. They're either expanding operations or they're under pressure."

"And El Fantasma showing up at the Getty?"

"More unusual. In fifteen years, there hasn't been a confirmed sighting. Either someone's feeding us bad intel, or something significant changed in their organization."

Darnell nodded, his expression unreadable. "Your divorce was finalized recently."

The abrupt change of subject caught her off guard, but she kept her face neutral. "Three months ago. It won't affect my performance."

"I know it won't." His tone softened. "You're our best analyst, Chen. But this operation requires more than analysis. It requires you to be present in ways that go beyond the job."

"I can handle it," she said, the words coming out more defensively than intended.

"I know you can. That's why you're going." He handed her a folder stamped with 'CLASSIFIED'. "Your cover details and background on the key players expected to attend. Memorize it by tomorrow."

Back at her desk, Amanda opened the folder, scanning the documents inside. Arthur Whitmore, her "date" for the evening, was a 68-year-old widower and art collector who occasionally assisted the Bureau. Photographs showed a distinguished man with silver hair and kind eyes. The guest list for the gala read like a Who's Who of the international art world, curators, dealers, collectors, and critics from across the globe.

One name caught her attention: Javier Morales, an art dealer from New York. She pulled up his file on her tablet. His photograph showed a man in his late thirties with olive skin, dark wavy hair, and eyes that seemed to peer through the camera rather than at it. His background included degrees from Columbia and the Courtauld Institute, galleries in New York and Madrid, and clients that included museums and private collectors worldwide.

What it didn't list were any direct connections to the Eclipse Consortium. Yet something about him, perhaps the calculated charm evident even in a static image, or the fact that his name appeared in the periphery of three separate investigations, niggled at her instincts.

Amanda, so absorbed in the file that she almost missed the envelope that had appeared on her desk. Plain white, unmarked, sealed. She glanced around, but no one seemed to be paying attention. With careful fingers, she opened it, extracting a single sheet of paper. The handwriting elegant and precise:

"Watch the art dealer from New York. Getty. Midnight. A Friend."

Her pulse quickened as she read the words again. The message could have referred to any New York dealer, but context and timing suggested Morales. She slipped the note into her pocket, mind racing through possibilities. An informant? A trap? A colleague trying to help outside official channels?

Regardless of the source, the significance of the note remained. Amanda built her career on recognizing patterns, on following instincts honed by education and experience. This didn't feel like a coincidence.

She returned to Morales' file, examining it with renewed intensity. His client list included several individuals with suspected ties to international smuggling operations, though nothing could ever been proven. His travel records showed frequent trips to regions known for both legitimate art trade and black-market antiquities, Turkey, Cambodia, Myanmar, Morocco.

Amanda closed the file and leaned back in her chair, eyes fixed on the ceiling but seeing nothing. Two days until the gala. She'd need a dress, shoes, jewelry, the armor of high society. Before the divorce, she attended enough functions on her ex-husband's arm to know the unspoken rules of such events, the subtle signals of class and refinement.

The thought of him brought a bitter taste to her mouth. He'd never understood why she joined the Bureau, why she traded cocktail parties and charity auctions for stakeouts and case files. "You're wasting your potential," he said during one of their final arguments. "You could be running a gallery or working for Christie's. Instead, you're chasing criminals for government pay."

He'd never understood that for her, the hunt is never about money. It is about justice, about order in a chaotic world. It is about being part of something larger than herself.

Amanda gathered her things, preparing to leave. She had preparations to make a role to craft. But as she stood, her eyes fell once more on the photograph of Javier Morales. Something about him called to her analytical mind, a puzzle wrapped in expensive suits and careful smiles.

"Watch the art dealer from New York," she, committing his face to memory. Midnight at the Getty. She would be there, not just for the Bureau, but for answers that were intensely personal.

As she walked toward the elevator, a familiar sensation

spreading through her chest, the focused anticipation of the hunt. For the first time since signing her divorce papers, she was confident in her own skin. The note might be a lead or a dead end, but it was hers to pursue, a path that belonged to her alone.

***

Amanda stood in front of the full-length mirror in her bedroom, a stranger gazing back at her. The emerald silk gown clung to her athletic frame like water, revealing more than it concealed. She chose it deliberately, the color bold enough to be remembered, the cut classic enough to suggest old money rather than new ambition. The deep V of the back dipped dangerously low, exposing the toned muscles and smooth skin that remained from her competitive swimming days. No one would see the small, puckered scar on her lower left back, a souvenir from a raid gone wrong two years ago. Tonight, all evidence of Special Agent Chen had been erased.

Her fingers traced the delicate silver pendant at her throat, a gift from her mother on her college graduation, before the FBI, before the divorce, before she became someone who chased ghosts through art galleries. The necklace hung like a talisman, a reminder of who she had been and who she still is beneath the silk and subterfuge.

The apartment around her remained sparsely decorated, more way station than home. Fifteen months living here, and still boxes remained unpacked in the spare bedroom. The walls were bare except for a single black and white photograph of San Francisco Bay, her childhood home visible as a tiny dot on the distant shore. Sometimes she wondered if she'd ever feel settled enough to hang more pictures, to claim a space as hers.

Amanda turned, watching how the dress moved with her

body. Her hair fell in soft waves around her shoulders, the normally practical ponytail abandoned for loose femininity. She spent an hour with the curling iron, cursing under her breath as she wrestled her straight locks into submission. The result worth it, soft, touchable, a deliberate vulnerability that would lower defenses and open doors.

The makeup she applied, heavier than her daily minimal routine, but still restrained, smoky eyes that made the dark brown of her irises appear deeper, more mysterious; a touch of blush to warm her complexion; lips painted a shade of muted rose that hinted at desire without screaming desperation. Every element calculated for maximum effect with minimum obviousness.

She slipped her feet into silver heels that added three inches to her height. The shoes were beautiful torture devices, but she trained herself to move in them with the same discipline she'd once devoted to perfecting her butterfly stroke. Pain is temporary. Results were what mattered.

From her clutch, she removed the small listening device disguised as an earring back. She fixed it to her left earring, the weight unnoticeable. The transmitter itself sewn into the lining of her clutch, powerful enough to send signals to the surveillance van but small enough to evade detection by anything short of professional scanning equipment.

"Check, check," she said, testing the connection.

"Reading you five by five," came Rivera's voice in her ear, tinny but clear. "Looking good, Chen."

"You can't see me," she replied, a smile tugging at the corner of her mouth.

"Don't need to. You always look good." The friendly banter is Rivera's way of easing tension before an operation.

"Thompson and Hayes are already in position at the museum. Whitmore will meet you at the main entrance at eight."

Amanda nodded, forgetting momentarily that Rivera couldn't see her. "Understood. Going silent until arrival."

She removed the earpiece, tucking it into her clutch for later. The silence of her apartment enveloped her once more, the soft hum of the refrigerator, the distant wail of a siren somewhere in downtown Los Angeles, the whisper of her own breathing.

In the mirror, her eyes met those of her reflection. You're not here to dazzle anyone, she reminded herself firmly. You're here to hunt a ghost.

Still, doubt flickered beneath the surface of her confidence. What if she misread the signs? What if the mysterious note is a trap? What if El Fantasma recognized her as law enforcement? So many variables, so many ways for the evening to unravel.

She pushed the thoughts away, reaching for the small velvet box on her dresser. Inside lay a pair of diamond stud earrings, real diamonds, not the cubic zirconia most agents would use for an operation like this. They'd been her grandmother's, passed down when she turned twenty-one. Amanda did not often wear them, but tonight authenticity mattered. The wealthy recognized quality almost unconsciously, responded to it on a primal level.

As she fastened the second earring, a memory surfaced, her ex-husband's voice, cutting and dismissive: "You can dress her up, but she's still more comfortable with a gun than a cocktail glass." He said it at a faculty dinner, loud enough for colleagues to hear, passing it off as a joke while she sat frozen beside him, smile fixed in place.

Tonight, would prove him wrong, though he'd never know it. She could move through high society as effortlessly as she moved through a crime scene. Both were just puzzles with human pieces.

Amanda took one final look in the mirror, adjusting a strand of hair, straightening her spine. The woman who looked back at her was elegant, mysterious, and completely in control. Perfect.

The apartment door clicked shut behind her with a sound of finality. The elevator descended, numbers illuminating in sequence like a countdown. In the building's marble lobby, the night doorman nodded appreciatively as she passed. "Have a good evening, Ms. Chen."

"Thank you, Miguel," she replied, the social smile feeling foreign on her lips.

Outside, the hired car waited, a black Audi with darkened windows. The driver held the door as she approached, his eyes professionally averted from the expanse of skin revealed by her backless gown. Amanda settled into the leather seat, arranging the folds of her dress with practiced care.

"The Getty Center, please," she instructed, her voice pitched higher, softer than her normal professional tone. Another piece of the disguise slipping into place.

As the car pulled away from the curb, the city transformed around Amanda. At night, Los Angeles is a different creature from its daytime self, darker, more seductive, its jagged edges softened by distance and darkness. Street lights blurred into streams of gold as they accelerated onto the freeway, the city revealing itself in fragmented glimpses through overpasses and between buildings.

She remembered her first weeks in this city, how alien it felt after San Francisco, the sprawl of it, the way it refused to be contained or understood easily. After she learned its rhythms, the pulse beneath the glamour and grit. Los Angeles is a city of surfaces and secrets, much like the world she was about to enter.

The car turned onto Getty Center Drive, beginning the climb toward the museum complex perched above the city. Through the windows, Amanda caught glimpses of the lights below, a constellation of human ambition spread across the basin. Ahead, the Getty gleamed like a modernist castle, its travertine surfaces transformed to gold by strategic lighting.

"Beautiful, isn't it?" the driver commented, catching her gaze in the rearview mirror.

"Yes," she said, allowing genuine appreciation into her voice. Whatever else happened tonight, the setting would be magnificent.

The car slowed as it approached the museum entrance, joining a procession of luxury vehicles discharging passengers in evening wear. Amanda gathered herself, mentally reviewing key details, names of important guests, background on her "date," the location of exits and security personnel. Her body hummed with the familiar pre-operation tension, adrenaline sharpening her senses.

When the car stopped, she waited for the driver to open her door, using the moments to slip the earpiece back in and activate the connection.

"Arriving now," she said, lips barely moving.

"Copy that," came Rivera's response. "Hayes reports all clear inside. Whitmore is waiting by the main stairs."

Amanda emerged from the car with practiced grace, the evening air cool against her bare back. The scene before her a tableau of wealth and power, women draped in designer gowns and priceless jewelry, men in impeccable tuxedos, all moving through the warm glow of the museum's exterior lighting like actors on a stage.

The Getty Center rose above them, its modern lines softened by night. The travertine stone seemed to capture and amplify the light, creating an otherworldly atmosphere that straddled the boundary between reality and dream. Music drifted from inside, a string quartet playing something classical that Amanda couldn't identify.

She ascended the wide steps, aware of eyes following her progress. The emerald dress had been the right choice, distinctive without being flashy, elegant enough to belong but unique enough to be remembered. Already cataloging faces, matching them against the mental database of suspects and persons of interest.

Near the top of the stairs stood Arthur Whitmore, distinguished in his tuxedo, silver hair catching the light. His eyes brightened as he spotted her, a genuine smile warming his face. Amanda met him during the operation planning, a widower who occasionally assisted the Bureau, finding purpose in his retirement by putting his social connections to use for law enforcement.

"Ms. Chen," he greeted her, taking her hand and brushing his lips across her knuckles. "You look absolutely stunning."

"Thank you, Arthur," she replied, her smile warm and practiced. "And thank you for the invitation. The Getty at night is magical."

He offered his arm, which she took, allowing him to guide her toward the entrance where staff checked invitations and security discreetly scanned for weapons or recording devices. Her clutch contained neither, the listening device sophisticated enough to bypass standard detection.

"I've pointed out a few key people to your colleagues," Whitmore, his voice soft enough that only she could hear. "The Chinese antiquities dealer by the fountain is particularly interesting."

Amanda nodded, letting her gaze drift across the gathering as they passed through the entrance into the museum proper. The central courtyard had been transformed for the evening, tables draped in white linen, flower arrangements creating splashes of color, waiters circulating with champagne and hors d'oeuvres.

The air inside perfumed with flowers and expense, designer fragrances mingling with the scent of lilies and roses from the centerpieces. Conversation rose and fell in waves, punctuated by occasional laughter and the delicate chime of crystal glasses touching in toasts.

Amanda accepted a flute of champagne from a passing waiter, using the moment to scan the room again. Hayes visible near one of the exits, his security uniform allowing him to blend with the museum staff. Thompson would be elsewhere, probably near the main gallery where the most valuable pieces are displayed.

"Shall we mingle?" Whitmore suggested, his eyes twinkling with the excitement of a man playing spy games in his golden years.

"Absolutely," Amanda replied, adjusting the silver pendant at her throat. "I'm particularly interested in meeting some of the New York dealers I've heard so much about."

As they moved deeper into the crowd, there was a subtle shift within herself, part of her mind remaining sharply alert, analyzing and assessing, while another part surrendered to the flow of the evening. She became the woman in the emerald dress completely now, her FBI badge and gun locked away in her apartment safe, as distant as another life.

The hunt began, and somewhere in this glittering crowd is her prey, El Fantasma, the ghost who eluded international law enforcement for over a decade. And perhaps, if the mysterious note was to be believed, an art dealer from New York who might be the key to it all.

Amanda took a sip of champagne, letting the bubbles dance on her tongue as her eyes continued their careful sweep of the room. The night stretched before her, full of possibility and danger in equal measure. Midnight was hours away, but already she could feel time advancing with the inevitability of fate.

Chapter 2

Javier Morales stood before the full-length mirror, his reflection a stark reminder of the duality that defined his existence. The penthouse's warm lighting cast a golden glow on his impeccably tailored suit, emphasizing the sharp lines of his shoulders and the subtle tension that coursed through his body. He adjusted the cuffs of his jacket, the cool fabric brushing against his skin like a whisper of the dangerous world he inhabited.

His fingers moved with practiced precision, smoothing down the lapels and straightening the pocket square. Every detail had to be perfect, a flawless facade to mask the turmoil beneath. Javier's hazel eyes, flecked with gold in the soft light, met their reflection, searching for any hint of the conflict that raged within him.

"You can do this," he said, his voice low and husky. "Another night, another role to play."

But even as the words left his lips, Javier weighed his dual identities, each pressing down on him. He took a deep breath, inhaling the subtle scent of his cologne, a blend of cedar and citrus that spoke of power and sophistication.

His gaze fell to the silk tie draped around his neck, the deep ebony a stark contrast against the crisp white of his shirt. As he began to knot it with practiced ease, Javier's mind wandered to the gala that awaited him.

"The Getty," he thought, picturing the museum's gleaming white travertine walls and the priceless artifacts within. "So much beauty, so much temptation."

His fingers brushed over the silk, smoothing it into place. The familiar motions helped to center him, grounding him in the present moment even as his thoughts raced ahead to the evening's objectives.

Javier closed his eyes, steadying his breathing. In his mind, he rehearsed the persona he would don for the night, charming, confident, with a hint of risk lurking beneath the surface. A role he knew well, one that fit him like a second skin.

"You're not only Javier tonight," he reminded himself, opening his eyes to meet his reflection once more. "You're El Fantasma, the ghost that haunts the dreams of every law enforcement agency in the world."

A small, sardonic smile played at the corners of his lips. If only they knew how close he truly was, how deeply he infiltrated their world. The thought sent a thrill of excitement through him, mingled with a twinge of guilt that he quickly suppressed.

With one last critical look at his reflection, Javier nodded, satisfied that every detail was in place. He was ready to step into the world of glittering facades and hidden agendas, where every smile concealed a secret, and every handshake could be a betrayal.

"Showtime," he whispered, turning away from the mirror

and towards a door that would lead him into the night, into the heart of the Eclipse Consortium's latest operation.

Javier's gaze swept across the opulent penthouse, his mind already racing with the intricacies of the evening ahead. The Getty Museum gala is more than another high-society event; it was a carefully orchestrated dance of power, wealth, and deception. And at its center, a rare artifact that could tip the scales of the Consortium's influence.

"Portrait of a Young Man," Javier, his voice just above a whisper. The name alone sent a shiver of anticipation down his spine. Centuries old, priceless, and rumored to hold secrets that could reshape the art world. And tonight, it would be his.

A smirk tugged at the corner of his lips. "Child's play," he thought, confidence surging through him. Navigating far more treacherous waters than this, was common to him. The gala's security, the watchful eyes of the art world's elite, they were mere obstacles to be deftly maneuvered around.

Yet, beneath that veneer of assurance, a familiar pressure coiled in his gut. The weight of his dual identity pressed down on him, a constant reminder of the razor's edge he walked.

"Another night, another mask," Javier reminded himself, rolling his shoulders to ease the tension. "You've done this a thousand times before."

The sudden vibration of his phone pulled Javier from his reverie. He crossed the room in long, purposeful strides, scooping up the device. Isabel Serrano's name flashed across the screen, accompanied by a brief message:

"Artifact confirmed authentic. All systems go for tonight. Don't keep a lady waiting, Mr. Morales."

Javier's lips curled into a smile, equal parts amusement and admiration. Isabel's expertise was unparalleled, her forgeries so flawless they could fool even the most discerning eye. And tonight, that skill would be put to the ultimate test.

"Wouldn't dream of it, Ms. Serrano," he typed back, his fingers dancing across the screen. "I trust you're ready to dazzle the art world once again?"

As he waited for her reply, Javier's gaze drifted to the city skyline beyond his window. The lights of Los Angeles twinkled like a sea of stars, each one holding the promise of secrets and intrigue.

His phone buzzed again, Isabel's reply flashing across the screen: "Born ready. Now, shall we make history... or rewrite it?"

Javier chuckled, slipping the phone into his pocket. It was time to step into the spotlight, to don the mask of the charming art enthusiast and leave behind the complexities of his true self. For tonight, at least, he would lose himself in the thrill of the heist, in the intricate dance of deception and desire that awaited him at the Getty.

With one last glance at his reflection, Javier Morales, undercover agent, master thief, and man of many faces, strode towards the door, ready to set in motion a plan that would send ripples through the underworld and beyond.

"One small indulgence while I wait for Isabel to arrive," he murmured, reaching for a cut-crystal tumbler. The smooth glass cool against his skin as he poured a finger of dark liquid. The whiskey caught the light, transforming into liquid gold, a mirror to the complexities swirling in Javier's mind.

He lifted the glass. The rich aroma of oak and spice filled his senses, grounding him. As he took a sip, the burn of alcohol traced a path down his throat, a stark reminder of the fire he was playing with.

"To a successful evening," Javier toasted, his thoughts turning to the objectives that lay ahead. The rare painting, the web of deceit he must weave, the delicate balance between his cover and his true self, all hung in the balance of the coming hours.

Javier swirled the whiskey in his glass, watching the liquid create a mesmerizing vortex. His identities pressed heavily upon him, a constant struggle between the Sophisticated smuggler he presented to the world and the dedicated Secret Service Agent he was.

"How long can I keep this up?" he said to his reflection in the window, the city lights twinkling beyond like a thousand judging eyes. The moral compromises he had to make gnawed at his conscience, each lie a small betrayal of the justice he sought to uphold.

He closed his eyes, inhaling. The rich scent of the whiskey mingled with the lingering notes of his cologne, a blend of personas as complex as his own. "It's for the greater good," he reminded himself, but the words were hollow, echoing in the vast emptiness of his penthouse.

Javier's fingers tightened around the glass. "But at what cost?" The question hung in the air, unanswered.

With a sudden, decisive movement, he set the tumbler down on the polished surface of the bar cart. The soft clink of crystal against wood seemed to snap him back to the present. His resolve firmed, jaw set with determination.

"Enough introspection," Javier muttered, striding purposefully towards his desk. He pulled open a drawer, revealing a sleek, state-of-the-art earpiece. As he lifted it, the small device caught the light, a reminder of the technology that both aided and ensnared him.

"Time for metamorphosis," he said to the empty room, his voice resigned and tinged with a mix of resignation and determination. The mask of his criminal persona settled over him like a second skin, familiar and suffocating all at once.

Javier turned, his eyes locking onto the lithe figure of Isabel Serrano as she glided into the room. Her presence brought a shift in the atmosphere, charged with a mixture of professional tension and unspoken familiarity.

"Isabel," he said, his voice a purr. "Are you prepared for tonight's performance?"

She met his gaze, her hazel eyes glinting with a combination of intelligence and mischief. "Javier, darling, when have I ever not been ready?" Her Valencia accent caressed each word, adding layers of depth to her response.

He raised an eyebrow, challenging her bravado.

Isabel's lips curled into a knowing smile. "The Rembrandt will be child's play. My eyes can discern every brushstroke, every hue. The authenticity of the piece won't remain a mystery for long." Isabel's lips slipped from a knowing smile to a devilish grin. "You just worry about your job."

As they moved through the penthouse, Javier's senses heightened, acutely aware of Isabel's proximity and the looming danger of their mission. The plush carpet muffled their footsteps, a stark contrast to the hard, unforgiving world they were about to enter.

"Your confidence is admirable," Javier said, his fingers ghosting over the cool surface of a marble sculpture. "But remember, we're dealing with more than art tonight."

Isabel's laugh was as rich and complex as the finest Spanish wine. "Oh, I'm well aware. The thrill is half the appeal, isn't it?"

Javier didn't respond, instead turning towards the floor-to-ceiling windows. The Los Angeles skyline sprawled before them, a glittering tapestry of lights and shadows. Each pinprick of brightness represented a life, blissfully unaware of the high-stakes game unfolding in their midst.

"Beautiful," Isabel said, joining him at the window. "And utterly oblivious."

Javier felt a pang in his chest, a reminder of the weight of their actions. "Let's keep it that way," he said, more to himself than to Isabel. The city below seemed to pulse with possibility and danger, a reflection of the delicate balance they were about to disrupt.

The private elevator doors slid open with a soft chime, inviting Javier and Isabel into its sleek, mirrored interior. As they stepped inside, Javier caught a glimpse of their reflection, two figures poised on the precipice of danger, wrapped in an illusion of elegance.

"Ready?" he asked, his voice low and controlled.

Isabel's eyes met him in the mirror. "*Por supuesto*," she replied, a hint of challenge in her tone.

The doors closed with a whisper, sealing them in. As the elevator began its descent, anticipation mingling with dread filled his chest.

"You seem tense," Isabel said, her fingers brushing against his arm. "Second thoughts?"

Javier's jaw clenched. "No," he lied. "Focusing on the task at hand."

The elevator hummed softly, its smooth descent a stark contrast to the turbulence of Javier's thoughts. He wondered, not for the first time, how long he could maintain this precarious balance between duty and deception.

"Tell me, Isabel," he said, desperate to distract himself, "what drives you? The art or the thrill?"

She smiled enigmatically. "Both. And neither. It's... *es complicado.*"

The elevator slowed, approaching the ground floor. Javier steeled himself, adjusting his cuffs one last time.

"Complicated," he echoed. "Aren't we all?"

The doors opened, and the change was immediate. Gone was the hushed sanctuary of the penthouse, replaced by the vibrant energy of the lobby. The air buzzed with conversation and anticipation, the upcoming gala casting an electric charge over everything.

Javier stepped out, Isabel close behind. The marble floor gleamed beneath their feet, reflecting the warm glow of crystal chandeliers. He inhaled deeply, catching notes of expensive perfume and polished leather.

"Let's begin," he, offering his arm to Isabel. She took it, her touch light but sure.

As they moved through the lobby, the weight of countless eyes fell upon them. The gala loomed large in his mind, a glittering facade concealing treacherous depths. He allowed himself one last moment of doubt before submerging completely into his role.

"Into the lion's den," Isabel whispered, her lips barely moving.

"We are the lions, *mi preciosa*" Javier grinned ... his transformation nearly complete

As the glass doors of the building slid open, the cool evening air caressed Javier's face, carrying with it the faint scent of jasmine from a nearby garden. The city sprawled before them, a glittering tapestry of lights and shadows, each pinprick of illumination a potential thread in the intricate web of deception they were about to enter.

Javier paused for a moment, his hazel eyes scanning the street, ever vigilant. "Beautiful night," he, his voice smooth. "Almost makes you forget what we're about to do."

Isabel's lips curved into a subtle smile. "The best lies are always wrapped in beauty, Javier. You taught me that."

He chuckled, the sound tinged with a hint of regret. "Did I? Sometimes I wonder if I've taught you too well."

They descended the steps, their footfalls muffled against the plush carpet. A sleek black car idled at the curb, its polished surface reflecting the city lights like a dark mirror. The driver, a silent sentinel, nodded in acknowledgment as they approached.

Javier opened the door for Isabel, his hand brushing against the small of her back as she slipped into the vehicle. The touch was brief, professional, yet charged with an undercurrent of unspoken tension.

As he settled into the leather seat beside her, Javier's mind raced, considering the delicate balance they would need to maintain at the gala. The rare art piece they sought was more than another valuable acquisition; it was a key to unraveling a larger mystery within the Consortium.

"En qué piensas?" Isabel's voice cut through his reverie.

Javier turned to her, his expression a crafted mask of confidence. "Thinking about our performance tonight. The stakes have never been higher."

"You're not getting cold feet, are you?" There was a challenge in her tone, a subtle test of his resolve.

He laughed, the sound rich and warm, belying the tension coiled within him. "Never. But I do wonder, Isabel... how far are you willing to go to get what we need?"

The car pulled away from the curb, merging into the flow of traffic. Through the tinted windows, the city became a blur of light and motion, mirroring the swirling thoughts in Javier's mind.

Isabel's eyes met his, her gaze unflinching. "As far as necessary, Javi. You know that."

3

Chapter 3

Amanda Chen stepped through the towering glass doors of the Getty Museum, the cool air inside washing over her skin like absolution. The evening gown's fabric danced against her body, a second skin she hadn't quite grown into, but her gait remained measured, unhurried. She was a woman accustomed to wearing armor, though usually it came in the form of a blazer and the weight of a badge against her hip, not sapphire silk that whispered with each step across the marble floor.

The grand hall opened before her, a cathedral to wealth and culture. Chandeliers hung from the ceiling like frozen fireworks, their crystal teardrops catching light and fracturing it into countless tiny rainbows. The marble beneath her heels echoed her arrival with every step, each tap a staccato beat that mirrored the rhythm of her heart, measured, but quickening. She breathed in the peculiar scent of old money, subtle perfumes, and champagne.

Men in tuxedos and women draped in couture moved like dancers in a slow, rehearsed ballet. Their laughter floated through the air, effervescent as the bubbles in their crystal flutes. Amanda examined them, a scientist observing specimens, noting the subtle hierarchies in their posture, the territorial way they claimed space, the practiced tilt of a jaw that signaled breeding or its careful imitation.

Her trained eye didn't miss the security personnel stationed at discreet intervals throughout the hall, their alertness disguised as boredom. She noted exits, blind spots, and the paths of least resistance through the crush of bodies. Cataloging details was second nature to her now, a compulsion born of training and the keen edge of survival.

The emerald dress hugged her athletic frame, the color deepening her almond eyes to pools of ink. Her ex-husband's parting words lodged themselves in her psyche like splinters: too angular, too severe, too consumed by the job to be desirable. The memory of them stung afresh as she navigated through women whose curves seemed designed to catch the eyes of men like him.

Amanda paused at the edge of the crowd, allowing herself an instant to appreciate the curved architecture of the museum. The serenity of the arched ceilings and ancient stone offered a strange comfort. Beauty had its place, even in a world full of lies. Her father, with his restaurant in San Francisco's Richmond District, taught her that presentation was everything, whether plating sea bass or presenting oneself to the world. "The eye eats first," he'd say in Cantonese, arranging scallions into a perfect fan. Amanda wondered what he would think of her now, draped in borrowed finery, playing a part in a dangerous game.

She reached for a glass of champagne from a passing server, not to drink but to complete her disguise. The bubbles rose in endless procession, tiny soldiers marching to their demise.

Amanda felt a kinship with them, rising toward a surface that would ultimately dissolve them.

The crowds parted momentarily, offering her a glimpse of the main exhibition area ahead. There, among the mingling guests and priceless art, were the answers she sought. Somewhere in this glittering sea was her target, though she had only fragments to go on: a description, a pattern of behavior, the outline of a crime network that was slithering through law enforcement's grasp for too long.

Amanda's gaze swept the crowd again, more focused this time. She was looking for anomalies, the slight tension in shoulders that suggested concealed weapons, conversations that lasted a beat too long, the telltale signs of deals being made under the guise of social niceties. Her years in behavioral analysis taught her to read these subtle languages, to see the shadows that people cast when they thought no one was looking.

In a glass display case, Amanda caught a fractured reflection of herself: dark hair cascading like breakers across the rocks, cheekbones highlighted by the museum's dramatic lighting, eyes that hold secrets from their owner. For a moment, she didn't recognize herself. The woman staring back was a construction, assembled from pieces of truth and fiction like a collage. Special Agent Amanda Chen disappeared beneath the veneer of a wealthy art patron, a woman whose only concerns were aesthetic and social.

The irony not lost on her. Here she was, surrounded by masterpieces worth millions, and she was perhaps the most carefully crafted fiction in the room.

A man's laugh cut through her thoughts, too loud, too forced. Amanda turned a fraction, tracking the sound to its source. A portly gentleman with a ruddy complexion was entertaining a small group near a Monet. His animated hands moved as he spoke, gold cufflinks flashing. Something about him tugged at her instincts. The way the others deferred to him suggested importance, but his eyes never settled, darting around the room. A man who was afraid of being recognized while desperate to be seen.

Amanda began a casual drift in his direction, reviewing the memorized dossier on the key players in the Consortium. Was he one of them? Or another wealthy patron with something to hide? In her experience, most people in rooms like this had secrets they guarded with ferocity, though few were worth the Bureau's attention.

The scent of another woman's perfume, something expensive with notes of jasmine, wafted past as a couple moved through her path. The woman's diamond earrings caught the light, sending prisms dancing across the wall. The man's hand rested possessively on the small of her back, his watch probably worth more than Amanda's annual salary. They were beautiful together, polished to a high shine, yet she detected the slightest strain in the woman's smile. Amanda wondered, as she often did, about the stories that unfolded behind closed doors, the truths that never made it into case files.

She skirted the edge of a gathering near a display of ancient pottery, her peripheral vision cataloging faces while her posture suggested aimless wandering. The museum's air sagged with the weight of the collective breath of hundreds of guests and the silent exhalation of history from the artifacts around them.

Her training at Quantico prepared her for the physical demands of the job, the endless laps in the pool building an endurance that served her well during stakeouts and pursuits, but no one warned her about this peculiar loneliness., the isolation of being surrounded by people yet separate from them, divided by purpose and knowledge.

A flash of movement at the far end of the hall caught her attention. A man in a well-tailored suit was entering from a side door, his movements fluid, deliberate. Regardless of distance, Amanda could sense something different about him, a particular kind of alertness that mirrored her own. His dark hair swept back from a face that belonged on currency, all clean lines and authority. As he moved through the crowd, people parted for him, like water around a stone.

Something in Amanda's chest tightened, a warning system engaging. Whether it was the agent in her recognizing a potential threat or the woman responding to something more primal, she couldn't immediately tell. But instinct told her with certainty that this man was someone she needed to keep under surveillance.

She turned away before he could catch her staring, refocusing on the portly gentleman from earlier. He moved toward the exhibition room, his small entourage trailing behind. Amanda took a sip of her untouched champagne and began to follow, the game beginning in earnest now.

Senses sharpened to a knife-point, Amanda understood the hunt was on. In this museum of artifacts and illusions, prepared to uncover the truth, whatever mask it wore. Her lips curved into the barest hint of a smile, not from pleasure, but from the cold anticipation of the chase.

***

Javier Morales moved through the exhibition gallery like a man who'd been born into wealth rather than trained to mimic it. His fingers, brushing the stem of a champagne flute, bore no calluses from field training or gun handling, a detail he cultivated through rigorous skincare regimens that amused his handlers. The gallery lights caught the angles of his face in ways that transformed ordinary handsomeness into something magnetic, a quality he weaponized with the precision of someone who understood how attraction could disarm caution.

He laughed at something a silver-haired woman in diamonds said, the sound pitched perfectly, not too loud to be uncouth, not too soft as to be mistaken for indifference. The woman preened under his attention, her wrinkled hand fluttering to his forearm. Javier accepted a fresh glass of champagne from a passing server, his eyes continuing their relentless inventory of the room even as he offered the woman a conspiratorial wink that made her smile tilt wider. He was good at this game, had been playing it so long he sometimes forgot there were other versions of himself deeper down.

His attention drifted to the far corner of the gallery, where a large oil painting hung in majestic solitude. The canvas depicted a Venetian masked ball, figures swirling in silks and velvets, their faces hidden behind ornate disguises. A small cluster of guests gathered before it, murmuring appreciations that were more about being seen appreciating art than about the art itself, Javier thought.

But one figure stood apart from all others, a woman with midnight-dark hair, a deluge of waves framing her face, her emerald dress a deliberate echo of the green tones in the painting. She stood alone, her posture a study in lethal elegance. More importantly, she was watching him. Not with the obvious interest of the other women who tracked his movements throughout the evening, but with something sharper. More clinical. More dangerous.

Intriguing.

Javier took a measured sip of champagne, savoring the bright effervescence on his tongue while he made a decision. He moved toward the painting with unhurried confidence, exchanging pleasantries with a museum board member as he passed, clapping a tech billionaire on the shoulder like they shared secrets. By the time he reached the painting, he positioned himself close enough to the woman in green to make conversation inevitable, far enough that she would have to be the one to initiate it.

Amanda approached the painting, angling her body with precision. She positioned herself beside him, her gaze fixed on the canvas as if absorbed in artistic contemplation. The scent of her perfume reached him, something subtle, nothing overpowering. Nothing that screamed for attention. A scent that required proximity to detect.

"Impressive," she, her voice pitched for his ears alone. "Though I'm not sure the artist meant for the shadows to be more honest than the subjects."

Javier tilted his head toward her, curiosity flaring behind his gaze. Her observation was unexpectedly astute. Most people saw only the surface glamour of the scene, the opulent costumes, the romantic setting, not the darker implications hiding in plain sight.

"Art is nothing if not a mirror," he replied, "and mirrors always lie." He gestured with his glass toward the painting. "Look at the reflection in the water of the canal. The artist reversed the positions of the figures. What appears to be the truth is actually an inversion."

Their eyes met, hers steady and evaluating, his glinting with a touch of danger he didn't bother to disguise. The air between them seemed to tighten, charged with something that wasn't quite suspicion and wasn't quite desire, but contained elements of both.

"You know the artist?" she asked, a slight smile teasing the corners of her lips. The question was casual, but Javier heard the probe beneath it.

"I know how to listen to the silence between brushstrokes," he said, taking another sip of champagne. The bubbles suddenly sharp against his palate. "And you, Miss...?"

"Amanda," she said, offering nothing more. No last name. No explanation of her presence. Just Amanda, like a statement of fact.

"Javier," he said with equal restraint. The abbreviated introduction hung between them, an acknowledgment that they both understood the rules of this particular game.

She turned back to the painting, her profile outlined against the warm gallery light. "The masks are interesting. Not only concealing identity but creating new ones. The wearer becomes whoever the observer wishes them to be."

"Projection is a powerful force," Javier agreed. "We see what we want to see, especially when it's advantageous to our desires." He stepped closer to the canvas, inviting her to follow. "Notice the couple in the corner? The woman's mask is slipping, but no one is looking at her. Everyone is too absorbed in their own performances."

Amanda leaned in, her shoulder nearly touching his. "Careless," she said. "In some circles, that kind of slip could be fatal."

The double meaning not lost on him. Javier's pulse quickened, not from fear, but from recognition. This woman wasn't just beautiful; she was dangerous in ways that resonated with his own artfully constructed facade.

"Fatal seems extreme for a fashion faux pas," he said. "Though I suppose it depends on the circles you frequent."

"Indeed." Her smile remained, but her eyes turned calculating. "What circles do you frequent, Javier? Besides art galleries full of priceless treasures?"

The question skated along the edge of propriety, a bit too direct, a bit too probing for the kind of casual encounter they were pretending to have. Javier welcomed it. Small talk bored him; this verbal fencing was far more entertaining.

"I collect experiences rather than things," he replied. "Art, travel, interesting conversations with intelligent women who ask provocative questions." He turned toward her now. "And you? What brings Amanda No-Last-Name to the Getty on this particular evening?"

"Perhaps I'm also collecting," she said, her gaze unwavering. "Impressions. Insights. Information."

"And what information have you gathered so far tonight?"

Amanda considered him for a long moment, the silence between them stretching taut with unspoken assessments. "That appearances are curated. That wealth speaks its own dialect. That some people move through spaces like this as if they've rehearsed every step."

Javier allowed himself a small, appreciative smile. Most people didn't recognize how he constructed his movements, the deliberate casualness that took years to perfect. "You're very observant for someone enjoying an evening of culture and champagne."

"Observation is a habit," she said. "Hard to break even at

social functions."

"A professional hazard?" he ventured.

"Something like that." She gestured toward the painting. "Speaking of professional hazards, the artist must have understood the risks of duplicity. Look at the figure in the doorway, half in shadow, watching the revelry. Judge, executioner, or a witness?"

"Perhaps all three," Javier said. He shifted, moving imperceptibly closer. "The best observers understand that judgment without knowledge is meaningless."

Amanda's gaze dropped to his hand holding the champagne flute, noting the absence of a wedding ring, the manicured nails, the signet ring on his little finger embossed with a symbol she couldn't quite identify. "And the best performers understand that knowledge can be faked."

Javier felt a flicker of genuine admiration. She was good, the way she cataloged details without seeming to look at them, the subtle probing disguised as idle conversation. accustomed to encounters with law enforcement before, but seldom with this level of finesse.

"Are we still talking about the painting?" he asked, his voice dropping to a more intimate register.

Amanda's lips curved into something too knowing to be called a smile. "Are we ever just talking about the thing we're talking about?"

For a brief moment, Javier allowed himself to imagine a different context for this conversation, one where they were just a man and woman drawn to each other's intelligence, where the heat building between them was less complicated by whatever operation she was running, whatever role he was playing. The fantasy disappeared almost as soon as it formed.

Their reality was far more interesting, if more dangerous.

Amanda noted the crisp precision of his appearance, the barely perceptible accent that colored certain words with just enough foreignness to be intriguing rather than alienating. Everything about him calibrated to an exact degree of appeal, and that calibration itself was a warning flag. Nobody is that perfect without putting extraordinary effort into the illusion.

"You aren't American," she said, a statement rather than a question.

"Not originally," he said, offering nothing more.

"Your accent is interesting. I can't quite place it."

Javier smiled. "Most people can't. It's become a sort of party game, everyone has their theory."

"And you enjoy keeping them guessing."

"Mysteries maintain interest," he said. "Once everything has been discovered, the conversation tends to end."

Amanda took a sip of her champagne, watching him over the rim of her glass. "And you prefer conversations that continue."

"With the right partner." Javier held her gaze for a beat longer than was comfortable, then broke the tension. "The brushwork on this painting is particularly skillful. Look at how the artist captured the quality of light on water, almost appears to move if you watch it long enough."

Amanda allowed the pivot, turning back to the painting. "The technique is impressive. Though I find myself more interested in what's hidden than what's revealed."

"The most valuable things often require a certain... excavation," Javier said.

A waiter appeared at Amanda's elbow, offering canapés from a silver tray. She declined with a slight shake of her head. Javier selected one, the motion smooth and unhurried.

"Not hungry?" he asked.

"I prefer to keep my senses unclouded," she replied.

"Admirable discipline. Though sometimes pleasure enhances perception rather than dulling it." He bit into the canapé, a small act of sensuality not lost on Amanda.

Watching him eat, noting the controlled precision of the movement. Everything about this man was deliberate, which meant everything was a potential clue. Her instincts hummed with warning and interest in equal measure.

"I should continue my tour of the exhibition," Amanda said, though she made no immediate move to leave. "There's much to see tonight."

"There is," Javier said, his gaze traveling over her figure in a way that managed to be appreciative without being crude. "Perhaps our paths will cross again before the evening ends."

"Perhaps," Amanda echoed, a hint of challenge in her tone. "Though in my experience, the most interesting encounters are not left to chance."

Javier's smile deepened, reaching his eyes in a way that transformed his entire face. For a flash, Amanda glimpsed something genuine beneath the polished veneer, a quicksilver moment of real amusement that vanished so quickly she might have imagined it.

"Then I look forward to whatever non-chance brings us together next, Amanda."

She inclined her head a fraction, a gesture of acknowledgment rather than submission, before turning to make her way deeper into the gallery. The weight of his gaze followed her, a tangible pressure between her shoulder blades. She didn't look back, but she didn't need to. She knew he was watching, evaluating, reassessing, just as she was.

Javier Morales was too smooth, too perfect, too calibrated to be anything but dangerous. And yet, she wanted more, more information, more insight, more of whatever electric current sparked between them during their conversation. Her analytical mind registered his potential significance to her investigation even as some more primitive part of her responded to him as a woman to a man.

Dangerous territory, indeed.

***

Amanda moved through the crowd with practiced ease, her posture suggesting idle wandering while her path described a careful spiral that kept Javier Morales within her sightline. She paused to examine a small sculpture, using the moment to recalibrate her assessment of the man. The brief exchange confirmed her initial instinct: Javier wasn't just connected to her case; he might be at its very center.

The gala floor transformed as the evening progressed, the crowd's movements becoming more fluid with each emptied champagne flute. Crystal chandeliers cast fractured light across jewels and silk, transforming the wealthy patrons into constellations of gleaming points that shifted and regrouped. Amanda navigated this human astronomy with practiced detachment, her eyes returning to the one star whose gravity could pull at her.

Javier moved to a different section of the gallery, his attention captured by a series of abstract paintings. She watched him interact with a curator, his head tilted at an angle to suggest deep interest, his hands gesturing with elegant restraint as he asked what appeared to be insightful questions. The curator's posture shifted from professional to fawning, a transformation Amanda witnessed time and time again throughout the evening when people entered Javier's orbit.

She selected a glass of water from a passing server, using the motion to sweep her gaze across the room without drawing attention. The water was cool against her lips, a momentary respite from the warm, perfumed air. Museum galas were always like this, the rarified atmosphere creating a separate reality where wealth and beauty were the only currencies that mattered. It made her FBI field training feel both distant and essential.

Movement at the periphery of her vision caught her attention, a slender man in a tuxedo that didn't quite fit his nervous frame approached the gallery's entrance. His fingers fussed with his bow tie, a gesture that revealed both anxiety and unfamiliarity with formal attire. Amanda recognized him from the case files: Marcus Reingold, a mid-level art dealer with a reputation for acquiring pieces with questionable provenance.

She shifted position, moving behind a large floral arrangement that provided cover while maintaining her view. Reingold scanned the room with darting eyes until they landed on Javier, who stood now with his back to a wall, seeming to examine the room with casual interest.

Something in Javier's posture changed, a subtle tightening, a heightened awareness that would be imperceptible to anyone without Amanda's training. He didn't look directly at Reingold, but he knew the dealer had arrived.

Amanda's pulse quickened. This was it, the connection she'd been waiting for.

Reingold approached Javier with the cautious gait of prey approaching a predator, stopping to greet other guests along the way in what was clearly an attempt at nonchalance. He accepted a drink he didn't sip, laughed at jokes he didn't want to hear. The performance was almost painful, a study in obvious deception.

When Reingold reached Javier, the contrast between them became even more pronounced. The dealer's shoulders hunched, his weight shifting from foot to foot while Javier remained perfectly still, a man who knew how much space he occupied in the world and claimed it without apology.

They spoke, their exchange masked by the ambient noise of the gala. Their body language transparent, reading the power dynamic like text. Reingold gestured toward a painting nearby, offering an observation about the artwork. Javier nodded, his expression neutral, but his eyes, those sharp, assessing eyes, never softened.

Reingold withdrew a program from his jacket's inner pocket. As he handed it to Javier, Amanda noticed the slight tremor in the dealer's fingers, the sheen of perspiration on his upper lip. The program exchanged hands in a motion that appeared casual but executed with the precision of a practiced routine.

A man with graying temples and eyes like flint approached, inserting himself into their conversation. His expensive suit and commanding presence marked him as someone accustomed to deference. Amanda recognized him, too, Richard Harmon, a prominent collector whose name appeared multiple times in the Eclipse Consortium's peripheral dealings, though they'd never established a direct connection.

For a moment, a look passed between Javier and Harmon, fleeting but familiar. A expression of recognition that transcended their careful public personas.

There it is, Amanda thought. Her pulse ticked faster, the familiar rush of discovery flooding her system. This wasn't just a social connection; it was operational. The three men formed a triangle of mutual understanding, exchanging innocuous words that carried meanings beyond their surface.

She angled her body, maintaining her position while continuing to use the trained eye of a hunter to monitor. Reingold's hand trembled as he sipped his champagne, his anxiety almost palpable even at a distance. Harmon spoke with the easy confidence of someone who believed himself untouchable, his gestures expansive and commanding.

Javier, though, was the most fascinating. His face remained pleasant, engaged, listening with apparent interest to Harmon's anecdote. But Amanda caught the tiny muscle twitch at the corner of his mouth when Reingold mentioned a private collection in Singapore. It was nothing, a fraction of a second's tension, but to Amanda, it might as well have been a confession written across the sky.

More telling was the moment when Javier's gaze, while still appearing focused on his companions, flicked toward her. He could feel her gaze. Had probably known all along.

The realization sent a peculiar thrill through her that wasn't professional.

Amanda made her decision, setting her water glass on a nearby table and moving with deliberate grace toward the trio. She would approach, sometimes the most effective cover was no cover at all, just audacity wrapped in silk.

As she drew near, Harmon saw her first, his monologue faltering as his gaze traveled appreciatively over her figure. Reingold followed his gaze, blinking rapidly as if surprised by her appearance. Javier turned last, his movement unhurried, as though he'd been expecting her all along.

"Gentlemen," she said, her voice pitched to suggest apologetic interruption. "I hope I'm not intruding."

"Not at all," Harmon replied, too quickly, "Richard Harmon. And you are...?"

"Amanda," she offered, extending her hand with a smile that suggested men remembered her without needing a last name. Harmon's handshake was firm, his palm damp. Reingold's was brief and tentative, his eyes darting away as soon as they broke contact.

Javier's eyes held hers as he took her hand, his touch neither possessive nor tentative, a perfect balance of warmth and restraint. "We were just discussing the Carravagio exhibit next month," he said. "Are you familiar with his work?"

The question pointed, testing whether she belonged in this conversation of art connoisseurs.

"I know enough to appreciate his mastery of shadows," Amanda replied. "Though I've always been drawn to how he illuminates the faces of common people, thieves, cardsharps, fortune tellers, elevating them to subjects worthy of our attention."

Something flickered in Javier's expression, surprise, perhaps, or reassessment. "An interesting perspective," he said.

Harmon cleared his throat. "If you'll excuse me, I see the museum director and must pay my respects." He departed with a nod that included everyone but suggested he was speaking only to Javier.

Reingold shifted uncomfortably. "I should also, "

"Of course," Javier said. "We'll continue our discussion later."

Left alone with Javier, the air between them was as sharp as a razor, as though the departure of the others removed some buffer that kept their mutual awareness at bay.

"I assume you're not just here for the paintings," Javier said, voice low, his tone a shade more intimate than their brief acquaintance should allow.

Amanda smiled, coy and unreadable. "Aren't we all pretending to be something tonight?"

The question hung between them, charged with meaning. In that moment, standing amid priceless art and wealthier patrons, they recognized each other as players in the same dangerous game, though neither could pinpoint which side the other served.

Javier raised his glass in a silent toast, eyes locked with hers. "To performances that convince even the performers."

Amanda didn't drink, but she inclined her head in acknowledgment. "Your friends seemed... intense."

"Associates," Javier corrected. "And the art world attracts passionate people."

"Passionate about what, I wonder," she said, glancing at the program he still held. "The beauty, the history, or perhaps just the price tag?"

"All of the above, usually." His fingers tapped against the folded paper. "People pursue what they value."

"And what do you value, Javier?" She stepped closer, near enough that his cologne gently reached her nose, something expensive with notes of cedar and bergamot, subtle but distinctive.

"Perception," he said, his gaze unwavering. "The ability to see what others miss."

The double meaning was not lost on Amanda. They were fencing with words, each thrust carrying warnings beneath the surface politeness.

"A useful skill," she said. "Though sometimes what we think

we see is only what we want to find."

As she turned to leave, Amanda let her fingertips brush the edge of the program in Javier's hand. The touch was incidental. The paper, thick, expensive, and too heavy for an ordinary exhibition guide. Her fingertips registered a slight irregularity in the texture, something embedded or attached to the program's inner fold.

She walked away without looking back, heels whispering across the stone floor. The sensation of his gaze burned between her shoulder blades, assessing, admiring, hunting. Let him look, she thought. This isn't over.

The crowds parted before her, conversations ebbing and flowing around her passage like water around a stone. Amanda maintained her pace, neither hurried nor leisurely, while her mind raced through the implications of what she discovered. The program was key, perhaps literally. A data storage device disguised as ordinary paper? A map? Account numbers? The possibilities multiplied with each step she took away from Javier.

From across the room, Javier's eyes followed as she disappeared into the crowd, her emerald dress catching the light before being swallowed by the shifting masses of formal wear. His chest tightened, not from fear, but from the awareness that Amanda Chen was a problem he could not have anticipated, a woman who looked like seduction but moved like strategy.

He'd made his career reading people, separating truth from performance, weakness from strength. Amanda's composition of contradictions refused simple categorization. Her eyes missed nothing while revealing even less. Her questions probed with precision while her smile suggested nothing more than social interest.

She's going to be trouble, he thought, his lips curving into a slow smile as he tucked the program more securely into his jacket's inner pocket. His fingertips lingered where hers had touched, the ghost of her contact still electric against his skin. And he wasn't sure if he wanted to stop her.

Chapter 4

Javier Morales chose his seat with the practiced precision of a man who never left his back exposed. The cafe, with its crushed velvet booths and honey-tinted lighting, offered the perfect balance of privacy and escape routes. He stirred his espresso slowly, the silver spoon making whisper-soft circles against porcelain, while his eyes tracked every entrance and exit as naturally as breathing.

The aroma of fresh-ground coffee beans hung in the air, mingling with the subtler notes from old books lining the cafe's shelves. It was upscale enough to attract Los Angeles' elite but intimate enough to make conversations difficult to overhear, a calculation as precise as everything else in Javier's constructed existence.

Three years undercover, and sometimes he could almost forget which version of himself was real. The Secret Service agent who started this mission seemed like a character from someone else's story now. The faint reflection in the window beside him showed a man with sharp cheekbones and vigilant hazel eyes, dressed in a tailored gray suit that whispered of quiet wealth. A man who belonged in the world of black-market art deals and international crime.

His phone vibrated once. He didn't need to check it to know she arrived.

Ginevra Sforza entered the cafe like she was walking onto a runway, her presence causing a subtle ripple through the room. Tall and statuesque, she wore a black leather jacket over a silk blouse the color of aged cognac. Her dark hair fell in a sleek curtain past her shoulders, and her eyes scanned the room with predatory efficiency before settling on him.

Her lips curved into a smile lacking any warmth. As she approached, Javier noted the details a casual observers would miss, the almost imperceptible weight of her handbag where it concealed a ceramic knife, the slight rigidity in her gait suggesting a second weapon strapped to her thigh.

"Darling," she purred, bending to brush her lips against his cheek. Her perfume was exotic and expensive. "Sorry I'm late."

"Worth the wait," he replied, the words practiced, the tone perfect. He rose politely as she slid into the booth across from him, her movements liquid and deliberate.

A server appeared almost immediately. Ginevra ordered an espresso macchiato without looking at the menu, her Italian accent making the simple order sound like poetry. When they were alone again, she studied him, her head tilted to the right.

"You look tired, Javier," she said, her voice carrying genuine concern he learned not to trust completely. "Trouble sleeping?"

He offered a smile that revealed nothing. "Just busy. The Brentwood event went longer than expected."

"Mmm." Her fingers drummed once on the table, nails

painted a deep burgundy reminding him of dried blood. "And how was our little soiree at the Getty? Productive?"

Javier took a sip of his espresso, using the moment to arrange his thoughts. "Reingold is compromised," he said. "Too nervous. He nearly dropped his champagne when he approached me."

Ginevra's expression didn't change, but something coldly amused flickered in her eyes. "Some men aren't built for our line of work. Should I arrange a more... permanent retirement package for him?"

"Not yet," Javier replied, keeping his tone even. "He still has connections we need. But we should limit his involvement going forward."

Her espresso arrived, and she added a precise half-spoon of sugar, stirring slowly. "And what about our other potential issue from last night? The woman who caught your attention?"

The question was casual, almost disinterested, but Javier recognized the dangerous undercurrent. Ginevra missed nothing, especially when it came to his behavior. It was part of what made her valuable to the Consortium, and dangerous to everyone else.

"She was... unexpected," he said, swirling the spoon once more before setting it down. "Elegant, but sharp. Asked good questions. And her eyes, they were looking for something. Not like the others."

Ginevra leaned in, lips curved in a half-smirk. "Sounds like someone left an impression."

Javier didn't rise to the bait. His mind flashed to Amanda Chen, the controlled intensity in her dark eyes, the way she appreciated the paintings with actual understanding rather than social obligation. The slight tension in her shoulders spoke of someone more accustomed to action than cocktail parties.

"She's dangerous," he replied. "Or curious. Maybe both."

"Mm." Ginevra tilted her head, the light catching the perfect angles of her face. "Do we need to worry?"

"She didn't recognize me," Javier said, the statement true but incomplete. What he didn't say was, he recognized her. Not personally, but professionally.

"Or if she did," he added, "she played it well."

Ginevra reached across the table, letting her fingers graze his wrist, more possessive than affectionate. Her touch was cool, deliberate. "You're slipping, Javier," she said. "You used to be better at keeping your interests strictly professional."

His jaw tightened almost imperceptibly. "She's just a variable."

"Variables get people killed." The words hung between them, Ginevra's tone conversational despite the threat curling beneath the surface. She leaned back in her chair, legs crossing with feline grace. "Still... if you're bored, I can give you something far more satisfying to tangle with."

The suggestion was laden with meaning, evoking memories of Madrid two years ago, Paris last summer, their bodies entwined in hotel sheets, a dangerous indulgence he allowed himself to maintain his cover. Sex and violence were Ginevra's currencies, and she spent both with elegant precision.

Javier's gaze flicked over her, appreciating but unmoved. "We have a mission, Ginevra. Stay focused."

Her smile never faltered. "Always." She took a sip of her espresso. "Speaking of which, El Fantasma is pleased with the Caravaggio acquisition. The buyer in Hong Kong has already transferred the first payment."

El Fantasma, The Ghost. Javier spent three years trying to identify the Eclipse Consortium's shadowy leader, known only by this alias. Every trail he followed turning cold, every informant disappearing. Whoever ran the organization was meticulous about operational security and ruthless about loose ends.

"And the Vermeer?" he asked.

"In transit. It will arrive at the safe house in Malibu tomorrow. You'll need to authenticate it before we contact the Russian."

Javier nodded, mentally filing the information away. Another piece for his handlers, another breadcrumb on the trail he was building toward the heart of the Consortium. "What about the museum director?"

"Uncooperative, unfortunately." Ginevra's expression shifted to one of theatrical regret. "I had to be rather firm with him. He won't be returning to work." She sighed, as if discussing a minor inconvenience rather than murder. "Such delicate hands he had. But ultimately, not very useful."

A familiar cold weight settled in Javier's stomach. Another death he couldn't prevent without blowing his cover. Another name to add to the ledger of collateral damage growing longer with each passing month. He learned to hide his reactions early on, to compartmentalize the guilt until it was almost indistinguishable from the constant low-grade anxiety of living undercover.

"We'll need another contact at the museum," he said, his voice betraying nothing.

Ginevra smiled, the expression making her look younger, almost innocent. "Already arranged. The assistant curator is far more amenable to financial persuasion. And she has quite the gambling debt to leverage if persuasion isn't enough."

She reached for her handbag, extracting a slim envelope which she slid across the table. "Your new passport and the details for next week's auction in Vancouver. The target is the Degas. Small enough to transport easily, distinctive enough to be worth eight figures to our collector in Dubai."

Javier took the envelope without opening it, tucking it inside his jacket. "And the FBI? Any problems?"

"Our friend in the FBI continues to be invaluable," Ginevra replied. "He's redirecting their investigation toward the Mexican cartels. By the time they realize they're on the wrong track, we'll have moved to other endeavors."

Javier kept his expression neutral despite the surge of adrenaline her words triggered. At last, confirmation of his suspicion, the Consortium had someone inside the FBI's Art Crime Team. Information that could save his operation, but also information that could get him killed if Ginevra suspected he wasn't who he claimed to be.

"Clever," he commented. "Though I've never liked relying on those we can't directly control."

Ginevra laughed, the sound musical and chilling. "Oh, darling. None of us are beyond control when the right pressure is applied." Her fingers drummed once more on the table. "Which brings me back to your mysterious woman from the gala. Should I make inquiries?"

The question loaded. Ginevra's "inquiries" typically ended with disposed bodies and police reports citing tragic accidents.

"No," Javier said, more quickly than he intended. He modulated his tone, adding, "If she's law enforcement, any attention might trigger scrutiny we don't need. I'll handle it."

"How generous of you to volunteer," Ginevra's smile was

knowing, amused. "Just be careful your 'handling' doesn't become... complicated."

"When have I ever been anything but professional?" he countered.

Ginevra stood, smoothing her blouse with a practiced gesture. "Not since," she hesitated "Florence, but I forgive you for that." She bent and pressed her lips against his cheek, lingering a moment too long. "You're usually so controlled, Javier. So perfect. But even you can break under the right pressure... like you did in that hotel room. I still get damp thinking about how your eyes changed when I took you that night" Her voice dropped to a whisper. "I sometimes wonder which version of you is real."

She straightened, dropping cash on the table to cover both their drinks, a casual display of dominance in their dynamic. "The Malibu house, tomorrow at nine. Don't be late."

The straight line of her back, the confident swagger in her step his reward for his eyes as they followed her. Only when she disappeared through the door did he allow himself to exhale slowly, the tension in his shoulders easing fractionally.

Javier remained at the table for precisely twelve minutes, long enough to ensure Ginevra wasn't waiting to see if he met with someone else, not long enough to appear suspicious to the cafe staff. He left a additional tip, nodded to the barista, and stepped into the late afternoon sunlight.

As he walked to his car, his mind circled back to Amanda Chen. He recognized the name when he ran it through his sources this morning. FBI Special Agent, assigned to the Los Angeles Field Office. Specialization in art crimes and human trafficking cases. An impressive record. A potential threat. He knew they would send someone to the gala, but he never imagined she would be so alluring.

A complication he didn't need.

Yet he couldn't shake the image of her at the gala, the intelligence in her dark eyes, the understated confidence in her posture, the way she saw through his carefully cultivated art dealer persona enough to be suspicious.

Dangerous, yes. But also something else, something making him question, for the first time in three years, whether the lines he crossed for this mission took him too far from the man he'd once been.

Javier slid into his car, pushing the thought away. Sentiment was a luxury he couldn't afford. Not when he was this close to identifying El Fantasma. Not when everything he sacrificed would be for nothing if he failed now.

He started the engine, already planning how much information to feed Amanda Chen, enough to earn her trust, not enough to expose himself or jeopardize his mission. A delicate balance, like everything in his double life.

As he pulled into traffic, Javier glanced at his reflection in the rear view mirror. Sometimes, he barely recognized the man looking back.

***

As he drove his mind was brought back to his first encounter with Ginevra.

The villa perched on the Tuscan hillside like a secret whispered among the cypress trees. As dusk bled across the sky, Javier Morales stood by the marble-topped bar, his reflection fractured in the crystal tumbler between his fingers. The liquid caught the light from the antique sconces, gold against gold, while the last notes of a mournful jazz piece curled through the air like forgotten promises.

57

Outside, the hills unfurled in waves of deep green and purple shadow, dotted with the lights of distant farms. Inside, wealth dripped from every surface, from the hand-carved walnut panels to the Renaissance paintings that graced the walls with their solemn faces. Most were genuine. Three were not. Those three had made the Eclipse Consortium fifteen million euros richer.

The last of the buyers stumbled out the door, a portly German collector whose knowledge of art was inversely proportional to the size of his wallet. Javier watched him go, then took another burning sip of whiskey. The alcohol traced a familiar path of fire down his throat, but did nothing to quiet the low, persistent hum of disgust, his constant companion.

Six months undercover, and he was still getting used to it, the visceral revulsion followed every "success." His hands were steady, his expression impassive, but beneath the surface, something writhed and twisted. Another operation completed. Another step closer to bringing down the Consortium. Another night of being Javier Morales, trusted lieutenant, instead of the Secret Service agent who had once believed in something as simple as right and wrong.

The quiet click of the front door closing left him alone with the ghosts of his conscience. Almost alone.

"Celebrating alone? How tragically American of you."

The voice slid into his awareness like silk over skin. Javier didn't turn immediately. He didn't need to. Her presence announced itself in other ways, the whisper of expensive fabric, the subtle shift in the air's chemistry, the faint scent of perfume and something darker beneath it.

When he looked up, Ginevra Sforza stood in the archway between the salon and the bar, barefoot on the marble floor.

Her black gown clung to her body like a shadow, the slit revealing an expanse of leg that ended somewhere beyond propriety. Her dark hair tumbled in artful disarray around her shoulders, as though she'd emerged from a lover's bed, or was about to enter one.

"The champagne's better," she said, lifting her flute in a lazy salute. The liquid caught the light, turning briefly to liquid gold before disappearing between her lips.

"I'm not in a celebratory mood," Javier replied, his voice flat.

Ginevra pushed away from the doorframe and drifted toward him, each step a study in controlled grace. An assassin's grace. The kind belonging to someone who consciously moved through the world without disturbing it, until the moment she chose to strike.

"You should be happier," she purred, stopping close enough that he could see the flecks of gold in her dark eyes. "You played your part beautifully. Even I almost believed your little speech about the Modigliani's provenance."

A muscle in his jaw tightened. "Just doing my job."

"Your job." the word like fine wine, savoring it. "Always so serious about your work. That's what makes you so... effective." Her lips curved into a half-smile that always set his nerves alight, warning signals flaring in his mind. "And so delicious."

She was dangerous, he understood that from the moment they met in Milan last spring. Ginevra Sforza, art historian by day, contract killer by necessity. The Consortium used her expertise to authenticate their forgeries, her connections to move their merchandise, and her other talents when a problem needed permanent resolution.

"You never answered my question," she said, setting her champagne flute on the bar, inches from his hand. Her fingertips lingered on the crystal stem. "Why so tense? The operation was flawless."

"Just tired," he lied. The truth, each successful operation for the Consortium drove another nail into his soul, wasn't something he could share. Not with her. Not with anyone.

"Liar," she said, but her tone was almost affectionate. "You're always watching, calculating, measuring. Even now.

Her hand rose to his collar, one perfectly manicured finger tracing the edge where fabric met skin. The touch was feather-light, yet it burned like a brand.

"I'm thinking about the next shipment," he said, forcing his voice to remain steady as her finger continued its leisurely exploration down his chest. "The Japanese buyer wants, "

"The Japanese buyer can wait." Her palm flattened against his heart, as if testing its rhythm. "Tonight is for satisfaction. Don't you think we've earned that?"

Javier set his glass down with deliberate care. "Mixing business and pleasure is dangerous."

"Everything worth doing is dangerous." Her smile deepened, revealing a glimpse of white teeth. "That's what makes it worth doing."

Her scent enveloped him, primal and breathtaking. He allowed himself one moment of weakness, letting his gaze drop to the curve of her throat, the shadow between her breasts.

"You're too tense," she said, pressing closer until the silk of her dress whispered against his suit. Her hand traveled lower, toying with a button on his shirt. "Let me help you with that."

The invitation hung between them, weighted with promise

and peril in equal measure. Javier's mind raced through the possibilities, the risks, the potential damage to his cover and his mission if he refused her, and the damage to something deeper if he didn't.

His hands came up to circle her wrists, neither pushing her away nor pulling her closer. A holding pattern. A moment of decision.

"What exactly are you offering, Ginevra?" His voice had dropped to a dangerous register, rough-edged with something that wasn't completely feigned.

Her laugh was soft, intimate. "Nothing you haven't thought about since Milan." She leaned in, her breath warm against his ear. "I've seen how you watch me. How you keep your distance. Tonight, I'm tired of distance."

His hands were numb, but the warmth in his chest rose unbidden, an uncomfortable heat he recognized as guilt, and beneath it, a hunger having nothing to do with his mission and everything to do with the woman before him.

She was the enemy. A killer. A liar.

She was also, in this moment, irresistible.

"If we do this," he said, his fingers tightening slightly around her wrists, "we do it my way."

Her smile widened, eyes gleaming with triumph. "Of course," she said, voice silk-smooth. But the gleam in her eyes said what her words did not, Ginevra Sforza had already chosen her own path. She always did.

When she pulled away, extending her hand in silent invitation, Javier took it. His decision was part calculation, part surrender, the perfect cover for getting closer to one of the Consortium's most valuable assets, he would later tell himself. The perfect excuse for following her down the corridor toward her bedroom, where the moonlight painted silver paths across the floor and the night waited to claim them both.

***

The bedroom door closed with a soft click that seemed to sever Javier's last tether to reason. Moonlight spilled through gauzy curtains, painting silver streaks across Ginevra's bedroom, a temple of luxury where even the shadows came across as expensive. The air hung heavy with anticipation, thick enough to taste. As she turned to face him, her silhouette outlined against the window, Javier felt the ground shift beneath him, the familiar sensation of falling into a role he hadn't finished prepared for.

The room whispered of forbidden indulgence. Plush velvet drapes framed tall windows that overlooked the slumbering Tuscan countryside. Antique mirrors in gilt frames multiplied the space, creating infinite reflections of the massive bed with its black silk sheets and mountain of pillows. Everywhere, touches of gold caught the moonlight, the filigree on the bedposts, the ornate handles on the armoire, the delicate chains of hanging lamps that cast honeyed pools of light across the parquet floor.

Ginevra stood in one such pool, her skin luminous, her eyes dark and knowing. She reached behind her neck, a simple gesture that made her spine arch slightly, and unclasped something that Javier couldn't see. The sound of a zipper followed, whisper-soft in the quiet room.

The black silk gown slipped from her shoulders with agonizing slowness, revealing the elegant curve of her collarbone, the swell of her breasts, the taut plane of her stomach. It pooled at her feet like spilled ink, leaving her nude except for a thin gold chain around her waist that gleamed against her olive skin.

No underwear. No pretense. Only the stark, breathtaking reality of her body, all dangerous curves and deliberate grace, like a weapon crafted for pleasure.

"Nothing to say?" She tilted her head, studying him with the patient curiosity of a cat watching a cornered mouse. "That's unusual for you, Javier. You always have something clever to say."

His mouth was dry. His clever words, his practiced charm, his careful control, all abandoned him in the face of her naked confidence. He remained dressed, yet somehow he was more exposed than she was.

"I'm reconsidering my life choices," he said, aiming for lightness but landing somewhere closer to truth.

Her laugh was low and rich, like aged bourbon. "A bit late for that."

She crossed the room toward him, each step measured and unhurried. Her bare feet made no sound on the floor. The moonlight sliding over her body revealed a map of subtle scars, a thin line across her ribs, a small, puckered mark on her shoulder, testimony to a life lived dangerously. These imperfections only heightened her beauty, making her real in a way that was almost unbearable.

Javier remained motionless as she approached, caught between the training that told him to control every situation and the raw, human need that urged him to yield to this one.

"Still brooding?" She stopped before him, close enough that he was struck by the heat radiating from her skin. Her hands came to rest on his chest, a deceptively gentle touch that nonetheless burned through the fabric of his shirt. "Or are you ready to give up control for just one night?"

Without waiting for his answer, she began unbuttoning his

shirt with practiced ease, her eyes never leaving his. Her fingers brushed against his skin with each button, small electric shocks that traveled straight to his core.

"In my experience," she continued, her voice a velvet murmur, "men like you find it... liberating... to lose control in the right circumstances." She pushed his shirt open, exposing his chest to the cool air and her hungry gaze. "With the right person."

Javier caught her wrists, a reflexive assertion of control and her smile widen. "And you think you're the right person?"

"I know I am." She twisted her wrists free with a dancer's grace and placed her palms flat against his chest, walking him backward toward the bed. "Because I understand what you need better than you do."

When the backs of his knees hit the edge of the mattress, she gave him a gentle push. He sat, looking up at her standing between his legs, her body haloed by moonlight. With her above him, the power dynamic between them shifted palpably.

She leaned down, her hair falling forward to create a dark curtain around their faces and pressed her lips to his.

The kiss wasn't gentle. It wasn't sweet. It was an invasion, a claiming, a declaration of intent. Her mouth moved against his with confident hunger, her tongue tracing the seam of his lips until they parted for her. She tasted of lust and femininity, desires he kept locked away behind duty and discipline.

Javier's hands came up to grip her hips, desperate for anchor against the storm of sensation she unleashed. Her skin was silk beneath his palms, warm and alive. For one moment, he tried to guide her, to assert some semblance of control.

She broke the kiss, pulling back enough to look into his eyes. "No," she said, and the single word held both command and promise. Her hand slid up to cup his jaw, thumb brushing across his lower lip in a gesture both tender and possessive. "Tonight, you do not lead. Tonight, you do not carry the weight. Tonight, you give in to me."

She pushed him back onto the bed and followed him down, her body moving over his with sinuous grace. Her thighs bracketed his hips as she settled atop him, the pressure of her against his still-clothed arousal drawing a low sound from his throat.

"That's better," she purred, rolling her hips in a slow, deliberate motion that made his breath catch. "Stop thinking, give in to me."

Her hands were everywhere, unbuckling his belt, pushing fabric aside, exposing him inch by inch to her touch and her gaze. When she had him as naked as she was, she sat back to admire her work.

"Beautiful," she said, trailing her fingers down his chest, over the ridges of muscle, following the dark line of hair that narrowed below his navel. "So much power, contained in such perfect form."

Through half-lidded eyes, caught in a undertow of desire so strong it threatened to drown his better judgment. This wasn't just sex, it was primal, and some part of him recognized the danger. But when her hand wrapped around him, warm and sure, that part fell silent, overwhelmed by more immediate concerns.

She leaned down to kiss him again, her breasts brushing against his chest, skin to skin. "No rules tonight," she whispered against his mouth.

What followed was a masterclass in pleasurable torment. Ginevra moved over him like a conquering goddess, her mouth and hands mapping his body with devastating precision. She found every sensitive spot, every hidden trigger of pleasure, as though she'd studied him for years rather than moments. When she took him into her mouth, the wet heat of it nearly undid him, but she sensed his approaching edge and pulled away, denying him release with a wicked smile.

"Not yet," she said, voice husky with her own desire. "I'm not finished with you."

She kissed her way back up his body, nipping at his skin, soothing the small hurts with her tongue. By the time she straddled him again, Javier was breathing hard, his control in tatters, wanting nothing more than to flip her onto her back and drive into her until they both forgot who and what they were.

As if reading his thoughts, she pinned his wrists to the mattress. "Surrender, Javier," she commanded. "Let go."

And then she sank down onto him in one fluid motion, taking him deep, and the world contracted to this single point of connection. Her heat enveloped him, tight and perfect, drawing a groan from somewhere deep in his chest.

She began to move, setting a rhythm that was exquisitely slow. Each rise and fall of her hips was a study in controlled pleasure, designed to keep him on the edge without tipping over. Her head fell back, exposing the elegant line of her throat, her lips parted on silent gasps as she took her own pleasure from his body.

Javier's hands moved to her thighs, her waist, her breasts, touching, grasping, trying to exert some influence over the pace. But Ginevra caught his hands and interlaced their fingers, using the leverage to pin him more firmly as she increased her tempo.

"You feel it now, don't you?" she said, her voice thick with pleasure. "The freedom in surrender."

And he did. With each thrust, each gasp, each moment of exquisite friction, something in Javier unraveled. The constant vigilance, the careful maintenance of his cover, the weight of his mission, all of it fell away, leaving only sensation, only the present moment, only the woman who rode him with such determined grace.

Her rhythm became more urgent, her breathing more ragged. She released his hands to brace herself against his chest, her nails digging half-moons into his skin. The slight pain only heightened his pleasure, pushing him closer to the edge he'd been hovering near since she first touched him.

"Look at me," she nearly shouted, and he did, opening eyes he and focusing on her beautifully savage expression.

Their gazes locked as she drove them both toward climax. In her eyes, Javier saw something unexpected, vulnerability beneath the dominance, need beneath the control. For one unguarded moment, as pleasure built between them like a gathering storm, he glimpsed the woman beneath the assassin's mask.

That glimpse, more than anything, was his undoing.

Release crashed through him with stunning force, tearing a hoarse cry from his throat as his body arched beneath hers. Ginevra followed him over the edge seconds later, her inner muscles clenching around him as she shuddered and gasped, her composure shattered.

For several long moments, they remained joined, breathing hard in the moonlit darkness. Sweat cooled on their skin. Reality began its slow, unwelcome return.

When Ginevra lifted herself off him and rolled to the side, her mask was back in place, the satisfied smile, the hooded eyes, the casual confidence that revealed nothing of the woman he glimpsed in that moment of shared vulnerability.

"See?" she said, trailing fingertips across his damp chest. "Wasn't that worth surrendering for?"

Javier didn't answer. He couldn't. Because the truth, that for a few precious minutes, he forgot who he was supposed to be and simply existed as himself, was too dangerous to acknowledge, even in the sanctuary of his own mind.

Instead, he turned his head to look at her, taking in the tumble of her dark hair against the black silk sheets, the curve of her hip in the moonlight, the lazy satisfaction in her eyes. She was beautiful and deadly and for tonight, at least, she was his, or perhaps more accurately, he was hers.

The thought should have disturbed him more than it did.

Ginevra smiled, as if reading his confusion, and leaned over to press a surprisingly gentle kiss to his shoulder. "Don't think so much," she said against his skin. "Morning will come soon enough."

She settled beside him, one leg draped possessively over his, her head on his chest. Her breathing gradually slowed and deepened, but Javier didn't underestimate the lethal beauty beside him, even in sleep.

He stared at the ceiling, listening to her breathe, the weight of her body against his a constant reminder. This encounter had changed something fundamental between them, shifted the balance in ways he couldn't yet comprehend. He revealed more of himself tonight than was safe, and that the woman curled against him saw more than he intended to show, and that was dangerous.

The mission, his cover, the careful dance of deception he'd

been performing for months, all of it suddenly more complex, more precarious. More personal.

Sleep, when it claimed him, brought no resolution, only a temporary respite from the questions that would demand answers with the coming dawn.

***

Dawn crept across the Tuscan hills like a thief, stealing the night's secrets one by one. Javier sat perched on the edge of the bed, his bare back to Ginevra, shoulders rigid with a tension that had nothing to do with physical exertion. The sheet pooled around his waist, and the first golden rays of morning painted his skin in shades of bronze. Beyond the windows, birds began their chorus, oblivious to the silent war raging within him.

The villa was quiet now, purged of guests and music, leaving only the aftermath of celebration, and indiscretion. The air in the bedroom still carried traces of their night together: the faint musk of sex, the lingering notes of jasmine from her skin, the whisper of sheets against flesh. Memories that would be impossible to forget, no matter how much professional distance he tried to rebuild.

Behind him, Ginevra lay sprawled across the black silk sheets, her breathing deep and measured. He didn't need to turn to know she was awake, her gaze on his back as palpable as her finger tracing the contours of muscle.

Javier ran a hand over his face, the stubble rasped against his palm. Six hours ago, he'd been the consummate professional, shepherding art collectors through the auction, ensuring every detail was perfect. Now he was... what? Another conquest? A momentary diversion? Or something worse, compromised.

His training prepared him for many risks of undercover work. The possibility of violence. The isolation. The constant vigilance against slipping up. But they hadn't adequately warned him about this, the danger of connection, of vulnerability, of revealing too much of his true self in moments of abandoned control.

Last night had been a mistake. Not because Ginevra was a target, an asset to be investigated and eventually brought down with the rest of the Consortium. But because for brief, shattering moments in her arms, he forgot he was playing a role. He'd been simply himself, raw, unguarded, real. And that lapse could cost him everything.

"Your thoughts are so loud they're keeping me awake," Ginevra said, her voice husky with sleep and satisfaction.

Javier didn't turn. "Sorry," he said, the word terse, inadequate.

The sheets rustled as she moved, and then her hand was on his back, fingers tracing idle patterns across his skin. Each touch sent conflicting signals through his nervous system, pleasure and warning, desire and dread.

"Regrets already?" she said, a smile in her voice. "That was fast, for an American."

Her hair was a tangle of black vines across the pillow, her lips a crooked line that suggested both disinterest and amusement.

The sheet fell away from her body, revealing the elegant slope of her breasts, the curve of her hip, the long line of her thigh. She made no move to cover herself, comfortable in her nakedness in a way that spoke of complete self-possession.

"Not regret," he lied, reaching for his discarded boxer briefs. "Just thinking about the day ahead."

"Liar," she said, but there was no heat in the accusation. "You're wondering if you made a tactical error. If I'll use this against you somehow." Her smile deepened. "If I'll tell El Fantasma that his new favorite lieutenant has a weakness after all."

Javier stilled, caught in the act of standing. The mention of the Consortium's shadowy leader sent ice down his spine. "Will you?"

Ginevra stretched like a cat, all languid grace and predatory satisfaction. "Now why would I do that?" she asked. "What happened between us..." She gestured to the rumpled bed. "This was between us. No one else."

He stood, pulling on his underwear before reaching for his trousers. Each article of clothing he donned felt like armor being reassembled, piece by piece, reconstructing the persona he needed to wear. Javier Morales, trusted lieutenant. Not the man crying out her name in the darkness.

"Besides," she continued, watching him dress with open appreciation, "everyone has their... indulgences. Even El

Fantasma." She sat up, letting the sheet fall away completely. "Especially El Fantasma."

There was something in her tone that made Javier pause as he buttoned his shirt. A hint of something personal, intimate. Did she know the Consortium's leader beyond professional association? Was she more than a simple asset to their organization? The possibility added another layer of complication to an already complex situation.

"What is your relationship with El Fantasma?" he asked, the question casual, as though making conversation while he threaded his belt through the loops of his trousers.

Her laugh was low and knowing. "Careful, Javier. Your jealousy is showing."

"Not jealousy. Professional curiosity."

"Of course." She slid from the bed and walked naked to the window, parting the curtains to gaze out at the Tuscan morning. The sunlight gilded her body, turning her into a Renaissance painting come to life. "Let's just say we understand each other. We each have our uses, our talents." She glanced over her shoulder at him. "Our secrets."

The implication hung in the air between them. Did she suspect something about his true identity? Was this whole night a elaborate play to test his loyalty? Javier's mind raced through the possibilities, each more alarming than the last.

He finished dressing in silence, using the routine to center himself, to push down the chaos of emotion and calculation. When he turned to face her, his expression was once again the constructed mask he wore for the Consortium, confident, slightly amused, revealing nothing of consequence.

"I should go," he said. "We have the meeting with the Japanese buyers at two."

"Yes," she agreed, making no move to dress herself. "Business calls." She tilted her head, studying him with those penetrating eyes that saw too much. "But before you go, tell me something, Javier."

He paused, one hand on the doorknob. "What's that?"

"Last night... when you came to my room." Her voice was soft, almost gentle, but with a razor's edge beneath. "Was it really just about pleasure? Or were you hoping to... extract information from me?"

The question hit its mark. Because it contained a kernel of truth, when he followed her to her room, part of him rationalized it as an opportunity to get closer to someone with intimate knowledge of the Consortium. To gain her trust. To learn her secrets.

But inside he knew it became something else.

"Does it matter?" he asked, deflecting rather than lying outright.

"It might." She moved away from the window, approaching him with that same unhurried grace that captivated him the night before. "Next time," she said softly, reaching up to adjust his collar with intimate familiarity, "don't pretend you came here just to interrogate me."

Her words struck him like a physical blow. Not because of their content, but because of what they revealed, she saw through him, at least partially. She knew he had ulterior motives yet allowed the night to unfold anyway. For her own reasons. For her own game.

Javier said nothing. There was nothing to say that wouldn't either reveal too much or add another layer of deception between them. Instead, he opened the door and stepped into the hallway, the cool morning air a shock against his skin after the heated intimacy of her bedroom.

The door shut behind him with quiet finality. He stood for a moment in the empty corridor, gathering the scattered pieces of his professional demeanor. With each step away from her room, his resolve strengthened. This had been a mistake, a momentary lapse, a complication he couldn't afford. It wouldn't happen again.

But as he thought it, Javier knew the truth. He hadn't fallen into bed with Ginevra Sforza by accident or momentary weakness. He'd been drawn to her from their first meeting to her danger, her intelligence, the shadows that danced behind her eyes. He could still taste her on his lips, feel the imprint of her body against his. Her breathless moan echoed in his mind, the low, raw sound she made when pleasure claimed her. There was no going back now. He'd crossed the line, and it was branded into him.

He would be back. Despite his training, despite the risk to his mission, despite knowing better. Something shifted between them, something fundamental and irreversible. She saw parts of him no one in the Consortium was meant to see, and he had glimpsed something in her that went beyond her role as the organization's elegant assassin.

He'd fallen into her trap. And somewhere deep down, he knew...

Resigned he would be back.

Chapter 5

Amanda stood beneath the gallery's soft lighting, her gaze sifting through the crowd with practiced indifference. The contemporary paintings hung like expensive afterthoughts against pristine walls, bold splashes of color framed in gilded edges matched the champagne flutes and polished smiles of Los Angeles' art scene elite. She adjusted the thin strap of her clutch, a casual gesture that allowed her to scan the room once more, searching for Marcus Reingold among the sea of black ties and designer dresses.

The art was contemporary, expensive, and perfectly forgettable, splashes of emotion without substance, or perhaps substance hidden beneath too many layers of pretense. Much like the people admiring them. Amanda understood the game. She wore it herself tonight: a sleek black dress whispered against her athletic frame, hair swept up near the delicate slope of her neck.

Dominic shifted beside her, his posture relaxed in a way that seemed deliberate rather than natural. "See anything interesting?" he asked, swirling liquid in a crystal tumbler.

"Besides overpriced displays of existential crises?" Amanda kept her voice light, but something in Dominic's expression, or lack thereof, intensified the unease which had been building since their last briefing. His face remained passive, unreadable, like a mask.

"You know what I mean, Chen." His eyes never left the crowd, scanning with the same practiced nonchalance as hers. "Reingold should be here any minute."

"I know my job," she replied, softer than intended. The words hung between them, unnecessary and revealing. Dominic had always been a competent partner, if somewhat distant. But lately, his distance came across as intentional rather than professional. Small inconsistencies in reports, missing minutes in debriefs, calls undocumented. Tiny threads that, when pulled, might unravel something significant.

"Of course you do," he said, offering a smile that didn't quite offer reassurance. "That's why we're here."

Amanda nodded, taking a sip from her untouched champagne. The bubbles fizzed against her tongue, sharp and expensive. A waste, she thought, when all she really wanted was coffee with a splash of cream. Something honest.

The gallery's main doors opened, and the room shifted, not obviously, not dramatically, but like a slow current changing direction. Heads turned, conversations paused mid-sentence. Amanda sensed it before she saw it, a presence altered the air pressure in the room.

Javier Morales entered with the quiet confidence of someone who belonged everywhere and nowhere. His charcoal suit hung from broad shoulders with bespoke precision, the fabric catching light as he moved. His dark hair swept back, revealing sharp cheekbones and those hazel eyes absorbed everything while revealing nothing.

Amanda's pulse stumbled before her training caught it. *Not now. Not here.* But it was already too late. Her body recognized him before her mind processed the implications of his presence. The man who had now appeared at two separate events connected to the Eclipse Consortium in the past month. The man whose file was noticeably thin despite his apparent connections to art dealers and collectors across Europe and Asia. The man whose smile lingered in her thoughts despite her best efforts.

He greeted the gallery owner with familiar ease, accepting a drink with a gracious nod. His eyes scanned the room, and Amanda recognized the exact moment he spotted her, his gaze paused, hardened for a heartbeat, then softened into something almost like amusement.

"I need to circulate," she murmured to Dominic, who was now watching Marcus Reingold enter through a side door. "Keep an eye on Reingold. I'm going to test a theory."

Dominic gave a curt nod, already drifting toward his target. Amanda smoothed a hand down her side, composed her features into something less analytical, and began making her way across the gallery floor. Her heels tapped a steady rhythm against the polished concrete, a counterpoint to the erratic beat of her heart.

She approached Javier, stopping to admire a large abstract canvas of blues and blacks that reminded her of the ocean at midnight. Her skin announced his arrival before she heard him, a subtle shift in the air at her back.

"Looking for meaning in the meaningless?" His voice was gentle, tinged with an accent deepening when he whispered. "Or admiring the price tag?"

Amanda turned, her lips curving into a smile more genuine than intended. "You again," she said, voice light, tone just teasing enough. "Do you haunt every gallery in Los Angeles, or is this just a very curated coincidence?"

Javier's mouth lifted at one corner, a lazy, knowing smile that suggested he held secrets just beyond her reach. "I could ask you the same, Amanda." Her name in his mouth sounded different, like it belonged to someone else, someone less cautious, perhaps.

"I appreciate art," she replied, gesturing to the canvas. "Though I'll admit, some of it escapes me."

"What escapes you?" His eyes never left her face. "The technical skill or the emotional intent?"

"The value, perhaps." She turned back to the painting. "Two hundred thousand dollars for something that looks like the artist had a vivid nightmare about drowning."

Javier laughed, a warm sound that drew glances from nearby patrons. "You have a refreshing perspective. Most people here wouldn't dare admit they don't understand why a canvas of black and blue costs more than their car."

"I'm not most people," Amanda said, meeting his gaze directly.

"No," he said, something like respect flickering in his eyes. "You're not."

They moved through the gallery together, a careful dance of proximity without closeness. Amanda noted how he steered their path away from certain groups, how his eyes lingered on security cameras with a professional's assessment rather than casual observation.

"You seem to know your way around," she commented as they paused before a sculpture of twisted metal.

"I travel in these circles," he replied, vague in a way that felt deliberate. "Art has always been a passion."

"Art, or the business of art?" She kept her tone curious rather than accusatory.

His eyes narrowed. "Both have their merits. Their dangers, too."

"Dangers? In art?" She arched an eyebrow. "Beyond pretentious critics and overpriced wine?"

"The art world is built on authenticity and provenance, on what's real and what's merely an illusion." He stepped closer, his voice dropping. "It attracts those who appreciate the difference, and those who exploit it."

The hair on Amanda's arm began to raise. His words carried weight beyond their surface meaning, and she wondered if he was warning her or testing her. "Like forgers?"

"Among others." His eyes drifted past her shoulder, focusing on something, or someone, behind her. "Some collect art for beauty, others for status. But some collect for power, for what art can hide or reveal."

She followed his gaze to where Dominic now stood with Marcus Reingold, their heads bent in conversation that appeared casual.. Reingold's fingers tapped nervously against his drink, his eyes darting toward a secured door at the back of the gallery.

"You have given this a lot of thought," Amanda said, turning back to Javier.

"I'm an observer by nature." He took a sip of his drink, the movement drawing her attention to the strong line of his throat. "Like you."

The statement hung between them, neither accusation nor compliment, only acknowledgment. Their eyes met, held.

Something electric and dangerous stretched taut in the space between their bodies.

"What do you think you've observed about me?" she asked, voice steadier than she her nerves would admit.

"That you're not here for the art." His gaze was direct, unapologetic. "That you're looking for something, or someone, with an intensity that has nothing to do with aesthetic appreciation."

Amanda's pulse quickened. "Perhaps I'm thorough in my interests."

"Perhaps." He smiled again, that same knowing smile that suggested he was privy to a joke she never heard. "Or perhaps Agent Chen, you find yourself drawn to mysteries that might be better left unsolved."

The use of her title should have shocked her, should have triggered immediate defensive protocols. Instead, it settled over her like an expected revelation. "You've done your homework."

"As have you, I'm sure." He gestured toward Dominic with a subtle tilt of his head. "Though I wonder if your research has been as thorough as you believe."

Before she could respond, a woman in a crimson dress approached, whispering something in Javier's ear. His expression shifted, hardened into something flinty and focused. He nodded once, then turned back to Amanda.

"Duty calls," he said, the warmth in his voice replaced by professional courtesy. "Until next time, Agent Chen. Do be careful, art galleries can be treacherous places. All those sharp edges and fragile pieces, waiting to shatter."

He moved away, the crowd parting for him like water around a stone. Amanda as he left, the warning in his words settling like lead in her stomach. She caught Dominic watching her, his expression unreadable.

She turned away, pretending to study a nearby painting while her mind raced. Javier knew who she was, and why she was here. And instead of avoiding her, he sought her out, engaged her in this dangerous verbal dance. Why?

The painting before her was all hard lines and soft colors, a contradiction that somehow worked despite itself. Much like the man who had just left her side. A contradiction wrapped in expensive fabric and knowing smiles. A mystery she couldn't afford to be distracted by, yet couldn't ignore.

Amanda straightened her shoulders and moved toward the bar, already planning her next approach to Reingold. But even as she focused on the mission, on the evidence they needed, on the careful construction of her cover identity, Javier's presence reached across the room like a physical touch.

Their paths would cross again. The certainty of it thrummed through her veins, equal parts warning and anticipation. Next time, she promised herself, she would be better prepared for the way his eyes saw through her facades. Next time, she would remember that attraction was another weapon in the arsenal of deception.

But for now, she had a job to do, and a growing suspicion that Dominic Hayes was not the ally she thought he was.

***

A single desk lamp cast long shadows across Isabel Serrano's studio, bathing the space in pools of ambient light and ink-black darkness. The lamp's glow caught on open paint pots and half-squeezed tubes, on brushes standing like soldiers in cloudy water, on canvases that leaned against every available surface like sleeping ghosts. Isabel hunched over her work, her spine curved in the particular posture of someone who forgot their body existed, her entire being concentrated in the delicate stroke of her brush against canvas.

The painting before her, a near-perfect recreation of a lesser-known Caravaggio, breathed with life beneath her skilled hands. Three hundred years collapsed into nothing as she mixed pigments with the same meticulous care as the master himself might have done, her fingers dancing between palette and canvas with the precision of a surgeon. The original hung in a private collection in Milan, but tomorrow this flawless copy would be authenticated by experts who prided themselves on their discerning eye, then sold to a collector whose hunger for prestige outweighed his concern for provenance.

Isabel leaned back, narrowing her eyes at the tiny imperfection in the corner of the canvas, a shadow that fell too heavy, interrupting the delicate balance of the composition. Her mouth thinned to a determined line as she lifted her brush again, dabbing it in a mixture of burnt umber and the faintest touch of Payne's gray. The correction took mere seconds, a whisper of pigment applied with the lightest touch, but the difference transformed the entire piece from impressive to extraordinary.

"There," she said, her voice disturbing the silence of the studio. Her shoulders relaxed for the first time in hours as she set down her brush and flexed her cramping fingers.

Only then did she see the blue glow of her burner phone, half-hidden beneath a rag stained with oils and turpentine. She silenced it earlier, she always did while working, but the screen showed three missed messages, all from Javier. She wiped her hands on a clean cloth before picking up the device.

The most recent message was terse, urgent: "FBI watching.

Be careful."

Isabel read it once, then again, the words sinking through layers of concentration until they pierced the artistic fugue that enveloped her for the past six hours. Javier had always been protective, sometimes more than she wanted, sometimes more than she deserved. Their connection spanned years, continents, varying degrees of legality. He moved through the world with an elegance that made crime seem like performance art, his charm a smoke screen that concealed sharp edges and calculated intentions.

She tucked the phone behind a hollowed-out copy of "Art and Illusion" on her bookshelf, a hiding place that amused her with its literal symbolism. Her studio, tucked into the back of a seemingly abandoned warehouse in downtown Los Angeles, was a monument to deception, a forgery itself, with its exterior of neglect concealing the precision workshop within.

Isabel's mind drifted to the gala last month where Javier had first mentioned the FBI agent. She'd been there too, working as a consultant for the museum's authentication committee, her legitimate cover that made her forgeries all the more valuable. The woman had been striking in an understated way, moving through the crowd with alert eyes that missed nothing. Isabel noticed her immediately, not for her beauty but for her attention, the way she cataloged faces, exits, and interactions. The way her gaze lingered on Javier longer than casual interest would warrant.

"Beautiful psycho," Isabel muttered, reaching for the glass of water that remained untouched during her hours of work. But she didn't mean the FBI agent. Her thoughts shifted to Ginevra Sforza, whose elegant presence haunted the periphery of their operation like an exquisite threat. Ginevra, whose family name carried centuries of power and whose hands carried blood more recent than yesterday's newspaper. Ginevra, who collected art, and lovers with the same passion she collected lives.

Isabel met her only twice but once was enough to recognize the danger coiled beneath the surface of that statuesque beauty. Ginevra's eyes missed nothing, judged everything. Her cultivated warmth, and her charm carried the subtle edge of a blade wrapped in gossamer. If Ginevra discovered any misstep, any threat to the Consortium's operations, her response would be as precise and artful as it would be lethal.

Isabel turned back to her canvas, studying the forgery with renewed critical focus. Her work was flawless, it had to be. Not for the payment, substantial as it was, but for her survival. The Consortium tolerated nothing less than perfection, and Ginevra was their most exacting critic.

The painting before her would pass any expert's scrutiny. The artificially aged varnish, the careful crackling of the surface, the pigments mixed according to historical formulas she spent years perfecting, every detail was a testament to her skill and obsession with authenticity, even in deception.

Isabel's path to forgery began legitimately enough. Her training in art restoration at Madrid's prestigious Instituto del Patrimonio Cultural de España gave her the technical foundation. Her eidetic memory for color and brushwork made her exceptional. But it was her father's gambling debts that eventually pushing her toward the first forgery, a minor Dutch master, recreated from memory after months spent restoring the original.

She'd been approached afterward by a collector who recognized not just her skill but her potential. The money had been enough to save her father, to keep their family home. The rush of successfully deceiving experts had been intoxicating. By the time Javier entered her life three years later, Isabel was already well established in certain circles as the most technically proficient forger in Europe.

"Just one more job," she told herself then, as she told herself now, the familiar lie comfortable as an old sweater. She knew she would never stop. Not for Javier's warnings, not for the mounting danger, not even for her own increasingly complicated feelings about what her art enabled.

Her hands were steady as she made the final touch to the canvas, not to the painting itself, but to the aged frame that would complete the illusion. An uncomfortable heat rose in her chest, she recognized as guilt, quickly suppressed beneath layers of rationalization. Art belonged to everyone, she told herself. Her forgeries democratized beauty that would otherwise remain locked in private collections or museum storage.

The fact that they also funded arms deals and human trafficking was a truth she kept separated from her work, locked away like toxic paint in a cabinet she never opened.

Isabel stood, stretching muscles that protested after hours of stillness. Dawn would break soon, and with it would come the courier, a faceless man who would deliver the painting to its authentication appointment and return with payment that would appear, after passing through several offshore accounts, as a legitimate consulting fee.

She glanced again at the shelf where her phone lay hidden, thinking of Javier's warning. FBI watching. She should move locations, change her routine. Yet a part of her, the part that craved recognition even in anonymity, whispered that no FBI agent would ever detect her work. Her forgeries fooled experts with decades of experience and technologies designed to catch fakes.

Still, Javier had never been overcautious. If he sensed danger, it existed.

Isabel began methodically cleaning her brushes, a ritual that marked the completion of each project. The soft bristles yielded their colors to turpentine and soap, returning to their original state as she would return to her public persona, the respected art restorer whose name appeared on scholarly articles and museum consultation lists.

As she worked, she considered the woman from the gala, the FBI agent who caught Javier's attention. Not professional attention, Isabel worked with him long enough to recognize when his interest ran deeper. She saw it in the subtle shift of his posture when he spoke about her, in the careful way he avoided saying her name too often. Early on she hoped those devastating hazel eyes would turn on her and the attention would be hers to revel in.

Isabel dried her brushes and arranged them with precision in their holder. If this agent had Javier tangled up enough to send warnings at three in the morning, she was either great at her job or dangerous to his. Possibly both.

Either way, Isabel would need to be more careful. Her fingers traced the edge of the forgery one last time, appreciating the perfect deception she created. Tomorrow it would hang in some collector's home, admired as a lost masterpiece. Tonight, it was still hers, her creation, her secret, her guilt and pride intertwined.

She reached for the small bottle of signature varnish, the final layer that would protect her work and complete the aging process. As she brushed it over the surface, she wondered which was the greater forgery, the painting, or the life she constructed around it.

***

The gallery hummed with practiced conversation and the gentle clink of glasses against teeth. Amanda moved through the space with renewed purpose, her encounter with Javier still burning beneath her skin like a fever. She tucked away the lingering heat of their conversation, filing it alongside other dangerous distractions to be examined later. Right now, her focus sharpened on Marcus Reingold, his fingers drumming an anxious rhythm against his thigh as he spoke with potential buyers.

Amanda cataloged each detail with methodical thoroughness. Years of training taught her to look for patterns in mundane, to find meaning in gestures and glances that others might dismiss as incidental. And there were patterns here, a gallery assistant who checked her watch too frequently, patrons who exchanged business cards with a specific orientation, Marcus Reingold's left hand repeatedly brushing against the inside of his jacket.

She set her empty glass on a passing server's tray and moved closer to where Reingold now stood alone, pretending to study a large abstract canvas. His profile showed beads of sweat at his temple despite the gallery's carefully controlled climate. He pulled a small black notebook from his inner jacket pocket, consulted it , then returned it with anxious precision, Amanda catalogued every movement.

Amanda's pulse quickened. After weeks of surveillance, of combing through financial records and import manifests, this might be the first tangible evidence connecting Reingold to

88

the Eclipse Consortium. She needed to see that notebook.

She glanced around, locating Dominic across the room in conversation with the gallery owner. His posture relaxed, but something in the set of his shoulders suggested tension. She caught his eye, gave an imperceptible shake of her head, *stay there*, then turned her attention back to Reingold.

Pickpocketing had never been part of the FBI training curriculum, but three months embedded with a ring of art thieves in Venice taught her more than standard fieldcraft. Amanda adjusted her dress, released her hair from where it was tucked behind her ear, and adopted the unfocused expression of someone who enjoyed one too many glasses of champagne.

She moved toward Reingold with deliberate casualness, allowing her path to weave as though unsteady. Her target was now speaking with a young couple, his hands gesturing animatedly as he described the painting before them. Perfect.

Amanda timed her approach to coincide with Reingold's step backward, angling her trajectory to ensure collision. Their bodies met with calculated force, enough to seem accidental, enough to create the momentary confusion she needed.

"Oh!" she exclaimed, stumbling against him. Her right hand caught his arm for balance while her left slipped inside his jacket with practiced precision. "I'm so sorry, these heels are ridiculous on this floor."

Reingold steadied her reflexively, his face shifting from surprise to forced politeness. "No harm done," he said, his voice higher than she expected. "Are you alright?"

"Embarrassed more than anything," Amanda laughed, sliding the notebook into the bodice of her dress in one smooth motion. She straightened, tucking her hair behind her ear again, a gesture of flustered recovery that drew his eyes away from her other hand. "I should probably switch to water."

He smiled, already turning back to his prospective clients. "Perhaps a wise choice."

Amanda moved away, heart drumming against her ribs. The notebook felt heavy against her breast, a physical manifestation of weeks of investigation. She made her way to a quieter corner of the gallery, positioning herself before a small sculpture that allowed her to partially shield her actions from view.

With practiced casualness, she opened her clutch and slipped the notebook inside, extracting a compact mirror in the same motion as though checking her makeup. A quick glance confirmed the notebook was filled with what appeared to be coded notations, columns of numbers and letters arranged in no pattern recognizable to the casual observer. But Amanda recognized the format without much thought. It matched fragments of communications they intercepted from suspected Eclipse operatives over the past six months.

It's them. It's Eclipse. It has to be.

She snapped the compact shut, adrenaline singing through her veins. This could be the breakthrough they'd been waiting for. The first solid connection between Reingold's legitimate art business and the shadowy network of smugglers and dealers that comprised the Consortium.

"Anything?" Dominic's voice startled her, though she managed not to show it. He approached silently, his footsteps absorbed by the gallery's ambient noise.

Amanda composed her features into a wry smirk, dropping the compact back into her clutch and securing it closed over the stolen notebook. "Only overpriced paintings and uncomfortable shoes."

He chuckled, the sound practiced and hollow. "Let me know if that changes."

He walked away, the unease in her stomach intensifying. Dominic had always been professional, competent if somewhat distant. But lately, his distance seemed to be weighted with something else, purpose rather than personality. Small inconsistencies in mission reports, unexplained absences during surveillance shifts, phone calls with no logs. Nothing substantial enough to warrant an official inquiry, but enough to raise her internal alarms.

Across the room, the physical touch of Javier's gaze caressed her. She didn't need to look to know he was watching her, had been watching her, likely since her collision with Reingold. The weight of his attention pressed against her skin, raising goosebumps along her arms despite the gallery's careful climate control

When she allowed herself to meet his eyes, his expression was unreadable. But there was something in the set of his jaw, the slight tension around his mouth, that suggested concern rather than suspicion. He held her gaze for three heartbeats, then extracted his phone and typed something brief. A warning? A threat?

Amanda looked away first, forcing herself to circulate through the gallery as though nothing had changed. She accepted another glass of champagne that she had no intention of drinking, engaged in meaningless conversation with a woman wearing excessive diamonds, and made her way toward the exit.

The notebook pressed against her side like a brand. She needed to get it somewhere secure, somewhere she could examine it properly without Dominic or anyone else looking over her shoulder. Her apartment, with its specialized encryption equipment disguised as ordinary electronics, would be safe enough for tonight.

She was nearly to the door when she sensed movement behind her, the displacement of air that signaled someone approaching. She turned, expecting Dominic or perhaps Reingold, who might have discovered his loss by now.

Instead, she found Javier, his expression neutral as he reached past her to open the gallery door. "Leaving so soon?" he asked, his voice pitched low enough that only she could hear. "The night is still young."

"Some of us have early mornings," she replied, matching his tone. Up close, the scent of his cologne, something woody and subtle, mingled with the warmth of his skin.

"And some of us have dangerous evenings," he countered, his eyes dropping to her clutch before returning to her face. "Be careful with what you've collected tonight, Agent Chen. Some things are more volatile than they appear."

The warning, delivered in the same tone one might use to comment on the weather, sent a chill down her spine. He knew. Of course he knew. He'd been watching when she bumped into Reingold, had likely seen the slight shift in her posture as she secured the notebook.

"I always am," she said, stepping through the door he held open. Their fingers brushed as she passed, and sparks arced between them, static from the dry air, but it jolted them nonetheless. Or perhaps it was something else, something more dangerous than electricity.

"Until next time," Javier said, the words hanging between them like a promise or a threat.

Amanda nodded once, then turned away, stepping into the

cool Los Angeles night. Streetlights streaked gold across her skin as she walked toward her car, the sound of her heels sharp against the pavement. She resisted the urge to look back, to see if he was still watching from the doorway. Of course he would.

The night air cleared her head, washing away the lingering scent of expensive perfume and champagne. But it couldn't erase the memory of Javier's eyes, the knowing glint in them as he warned her about her stolen evidence. Nor could it silence the questions multiplying in her mind: Who was he, really? What was his connection to the Consortium? And why warn her unless he had some stake in her safety?

Amanda reached her car and slipped inside, locking the doors. She extracted the notebook from her clutch and placed it in the hidden compartment beneath her center console, secure enough until she reached home. As she started the engine, her thoughts drifted back to Javier, to the enigma of his presence and his warning.

The notebook hidden beneath her console might provide answers about the Eclipse Consortium. But she suspected the real mysteries, the ones that might prove most dangerous, had only just begun to unfold.

Chapter 6

The cafe door swung open with a whisper of cold air, and Amanda Chen slipped inside like she was entering a crime scene rather than meeting a friend for coffee. Her eyes performed their habitual sweep, exits, cameras, faces that lingered too long on phones or newspapers, before settling on Sarah in the corner booth. Amanda's shoulders, which had been rigid beneath her charcoal blazer, softened. A friend was a luxury in her line of work, a small island of truth in a sea of necessary deception.

The bell above the door chimed, its gentle tone almost drowned beneath the symphony of steaming milk, clinking mugs, and the muted conversation of strangers sharing secrets in public. Amanda wove through the maze of tables, her steps measured and quiet. The scent of freshly ground coffee beans and buttery pastries enveloped her, but it failed to soften the edges of her thoughts.

Sarah Hansen looked up, her smile cracking through the professional mask Amanda came to recognize in most of her acquaintances. Ten years of friendship had survived law school, FBI training, and Sarah's move to the private sector. She was one of the few people who knew Amanda before the badge, before the walls.

"You're only seven minutes late," Sarah said, pushing a second mug across the table. "That's early for you these days."

Amanda shrugged off her coat with more force than necessary, the weight of it oppressive in the warm cafe. "Nice to see your schedule's less of a disaster than mine," she replied dryly, sliding into the booth.

Sarah's knowing smile was a familiar comfort. "It's not. I like pretending I have balance."

They shared a brief laugh that dissolved quickly, leaving behind the unspoken weight Amanda carried through the door. She wrapped her fingers around the mug, cream, no sugar, still hot, and stared into its depths as if it might offer clarity.

"So," Sarah said, leaning forward on her elbows, "how's the world of federal crime-fighting? Still saving democracy one fingerprint at a time?"

Amanda's lips quirked upward. "Classified," she said, the word their long-standing joke. Then, taking a sip of coffee, she said, "Well, it's been... complicated."

"Complicated how? The usual bad-guys-with-guns complicated, or the bureaucratic-nightmare complicated?"

"Neither. Or both." Amanda's fingers drummed against the ceramic mug. "The Eclipse Consortium case is heating up. We have solid intel they're moving art and antiquities through high-end galleries on the west coast."

Sarah nodded, knowing enough about Amanda's work to follow without needing details that would cross professional lines. "And that's complicated because...?"

Amanda hesitated, her gaze drifting to the window where

raindrops began to trace lazy paths down the glass. "We're close. Closer than we've ever been. But there's someone..." She trailed off, unsure how to continue.

"Someone interfering with the investigation?"

"No." Amanda's voice dropped lower. "Someone who might be connected to the case. Or might not be. I can't tell yet."

Sarah's eyebrows rose in question. "Okay, now I'm intrigued. Who is this mystery someone?"

Amanda took another sip of coffee, using the moment to organize her thoughts. "I need a sanity check," she said, setting down her mug with deliberate care. "There's a man. Smooth, charming, suspiciously knowledgeable about baroque landscapes and espionage-level eye contact. Name's Javier Morales. And I can't decide if I want to interrogate him or... kiss him."

The confession hung in the air between them, more revealing than Amanda intended. Sarah's expression shifted from surprise to something softer, a look that made Amanda immediately regret her candor.

"Don't give me that face," Amanda said. "This isn't some romantic comedy. He's either connected to the Consortium or he's not. Either way, I shouldn't be thinking about him like... that."

"Like what?" Sarah pressed not wanting to anger her friend.

Amanda's jaw tightened. "Like someone who doesn't make me feel like I'm always on the job. Like someone who sees past Special Agent Chen to... whoever I used to be before."

"You mean Amanda? The human being? Heaven forbid." Sarah's teasing tone softened the blow of her words.

"You know what I mean," Amanda sighed. "I met him at an art auction last month, one we were monitoring for Consortium activity. He outbid everyone on a minor Caravaggio landscape, then we spent twenty minutes discussing artistic intricacies, all the while my panties melted into a puddle beneath me."

"Sounds terribly boring," Sarah said, her eyes sparkling with amusement.

"It wasn't. That's the problem." Amanda couldn't help the small smile that formed at the memory. "He talked about light and shadow like they were living things. And he kept looking at me like..."

"Like?"

"Like he could see right through me." Amanda's voice grew quieter. "Two encounters since then. Always at events connected to our case. Always just... there. Watching me. Talking to people we're investigating. Moving through those spaces like he belongs."

"And does he belong?" Sarah asked. "What do you know about him?"

Amanda's professional instincts reasserted themselves. "On paper? He's clean. He apparently collects art and attends charity galas. But there's something off. Something in his eyes sometimes, like he's calculating everything."

"Says the woman who just performed a threat assessment on a coffee shop."

"That's different. It's my job."

"Maybe it's his job too," Sarah said. "If he thinks like you and has the same habits you do. Maybe there is some law enforcement in his background."

Amanda's fingers traced the rim of her mug. "Maybe. But my gut says there's more. When we talk, it's like... a dance. He reveals something, then steps back. I advance, he counters.

It's maddening and exhilarating at the same time."

"So, he's an enigma. A puzzle." Sarah's smile was knowing. "And you've never been able to resist puzzles."

"This isn't about intellectual curiosity," Amanda protested, though the flush creeping up her neck suggested otherwise.

"Isn't it? The great FBI agent, meeting someone she can't quite figure out?" Sarah leaned closer. "When was the last time someone surprised you, Mandi?"

The nickname, hardly ever used now, struck a chord. Amanda looked away, her reflection in the window fragmenting through the raindrops. Her ex-husband had been an open book, predictable in his betrayal. Her colleagues were types rather than individuals, dedicated, ambitious, by-the-book. But Javier defied categorization.

"He has these hands," Amanda said, the words escaping before she could reconsider. "Artist's hands, but with calluses that don't match. Like someone who knows both beauty and violence intimately." She stopped, embarrassed by her own observation.

"Oh," Sarah cooed. "Oh, you're in trouble."

"I'm not, it's not," Amanda fumbled for denial. "It's professional interest."

"Is that what they're calling it these days?"

Amanda shot her a warning look. "You're not helping."

"What kind of help are you looking for? Permission to pursue this man? Or reasons to stay away?"

The question hung between them, cutting to the heart of Amanda's conflict. She ran a hand through her sleek black hair, loosening a few strands from her practical ponytail.

"I don't know," she said. "When I'm with him, I forget to be suspicious. When I'm away from him, all I can think about are the inconsistencies. The way his smile doesn't always match his intensity. How he sometimes touches his left wrist when discussing certain people, a tell of some kind."

"You're profiling him," Sarah said as one eyebrow raised with the hint of accusation.

"I can't help it."

"Have you considered that might be why you're attracted to him? Because he's a puzzle within your puzzle? The Consortium case wrapped inside an enigmatic man?"

Amanda shifted. "That would be incredibly unprofessional."

"Also, incredibly human." Sarah reached across the table, her fingers touching Amanda's. "Not everything has to be a case to solve, you know."

From across the room, Ginevra Sforza lifted her delicate teacup without a sound. Her legs crossed at the ankle, her posture perfect, a study in refined stillness. Her golden eyes, cool and unblinking, never left the two women in the corner booth. The cafe's ambient noise washed over her without penetrating the bubble of concentration she created. Her red-painted lips parted as she caught fragments of their conversation, enough to confirm her suspicions.

Agent Chen was indeed a problem. A problem with a weakness.

In the corner booth, oblivious to the observation, Amanda rubbed her forehead. "So what do I do? Follow the attraction and risk compromising the case? Or shut it down and chance missing a valuable source of information?"

"Those aren't your only options," Sarah said. "You're assuming an either/or scenario when reality is messier. Keep your eyes open. Trust your instincts, both the professional and the personal ones. They're part of the same brain, after all."

Amanda nodded, a decision forming. "I'll see him as sure as the sun will rise tomorrow. The Consortium has connections all over this town, and he keeps popping up every time we lift a stone."

"And if you don't?" Sarah asked, her voice gentle. "If he's just a man who makes your heart beat faster when he talks about baroque brushwork?"

Amanda lifted her coffee in a small salute, a rare smile playing at her lips. "Then maybe I'll learn what baroque brushwork is supposed to looks like."

They both laughed, tension breaking for a moment. The knot in Amanda's chest loosening enough to breathe.

Across the room, Ginevra set down her cup and slipped a phone from her designer purse. Her fingers moved across the screen, a brief message taking shape: "Agent Chen. Emotionally compromised. Approaching tonight." She sent the text, then returned the phone to her purse in one fluid motion.

The rain tapped harder against the windows as shadows lengthened across the cafe floor. Amanda checked her watch. "I should go. Need to prepare for tonight."

Sarah nodded. "Be careful. With the case and with your heart."

"Always am," Amanda replied, though they both understood it wasn't the whole truth.

As Amanda gathered her coat, her FBI-trained senses failed to notice the elegant woman who had already slipped out the door, vanishing into the rainy afternoon like she had never been there at all.

***

The park emptied as evening approached, abandoned to

100

lengthening shadows and the occasional whisper of wind through nearly bare branches. Javier Morales sat on a bench worn smooth by years of anonymous bodies, his posture relaxed in a way that required constant effort. To any passerby, he might have appeared to be enjoying a moment of solitude, perhaps reading something on the phone he held in one hand. They wouldn't catch how his eyes scanned the perimeter, how his breathing remained measured and shallow, how the muscles in his jaw flexed with each distant sound that disrupted the precarious silence.

Above him, a skeletal tree stretched its bare limbs against the darkening sky, its few remaining leaves trembling in the breeze like nervous witnesses. November stripped the park of its softness, leaving behind only structure and shadow, an apt metaphor for what his life had become, Javier thought wryly. The distant hum of traffic provided a constant reminder that beyond this momentary isolation, the city continued its relentless momentum, oblivious to the quiet conversations that redirected lives.

A figure appeared on the path, moving with deliberate casualness that Javier recognized at once. The hood of a gray jacket obscured the face, but Javier recognized the walk, the rolling gait of someone accustomed to carrying concealed weight. His handler had arrived.

Javier didn't look as the figure settled beside him on the bench, leaving eighteen inches of empty wood between them. No greeting, no acknowledgment. Just two strangers sharing a bench at dusk.

"You're late," Javier said , his voice barely carrying over the rustle of leaves.

"Precautions," the handler replied, voice pitched low.

"You're being watched more closely now."

Javier allowed himself a small smile that contained no humor. "I'm always being watched. That's the point."

The handler remained still, face angled away from Javier's as if contemplating the empty playground thirty yards ahead. "How deep are you in?" The question came clipped, professional.

"Deep," Javier replied, scrolling through his phone as he spoke. Anyone watching would see two men ignoring each other, nothing more. "Reingold confirmed shipments coming through the gallery. Isabel's verifying authenticity. The FBI's getting close..." He paused, the name catching in his throat before he pushed it out. "Agent Chen is watching too."

There was a beat. A breath. The handler shifted minutely.

"Chen?" The word carried a sharp edge of concern. "The one from the gala?"

Javier hesitated, his finger hovering over his phone screen. "Yes."

The silence that followed stretched between them, taut with implication. A distant siren wailed, rose, and faded, like a warning.

"You're not getting attached." It wasn't a question.

Javier's jaw clenched. "No." The lie tasted bitter on his tongue.

"You can't afford it," the handler continued, voice harder now. "Don't forget what happened in Buenos Aires."

The mention of Buenos Aires sent a cold ripple across Javier's shoulders. His hands were leaden, fingers stiff around his phone. Three years passed, but the wound remained fresh, a phantom pain that flared with every reminder.

"Buenos Aires was different," he said.

"Was it?" The handler shifted again, hood turning enough for Javier to glimpse the profile beneath, sharp, weathered, uncompromising. "You got emotionally involved. Someone died."

Javier's chest tightened. Elena Vasquez. Twenty-seven years old. Artist. Confidential informant. His asset. His responsibility. His failure. Her blood had been warm against his hands as he tried desperately to stem the flow from the bullet wound meant for him. Her eyes had been warm too, until they weren't.

"I remember," Javier said, the words scraping his throat.

"Then remember this: Agent Chen isn't your ally. She's FBI. Her job is to take down the Consortium and everyone connected to it, including the man she believes you to be."

Javier nodded, eyes fixed on the gathering darkness. "I know who she is."

"Do you? Because your face changes when you talk about her."

The observation struck him like a physical blow. Had he become so transparent? Or was his handler simply that observant? Either possibility was dangerous.

"I'm playing my role," Javier said. "Getting close to potential threats is part of that."

"Getting close is one thing. Letting her get close to you is another." The handler paused, then said with deliberate precision, "She's investigating Isabel Serrano. The forger's been careless. Left a trail that Chen is following."

Javier absorbed this information, recalibrating. Isabel was a key piece in the Consortium's operation, brilliant, meticulous, and embedded in the Getty's restoration department. If Amanda was closing in on Isabel, the entire operation could unravel.

"I'll warn Isabel," he said. "She can clean up whatever trail she's left."

"No." The word was sharp. "Let Chen continue investigating Isabel. We need to know what the FBI has. You'll monitor Chen, report her movements, but do not interfere with her investigation yet."

Javier's eyes narrowed. "You want to use Chen to identify our vulnerabilities."

"Exactly. And then we'll use those vulnerabilities to feed her false information."

The plan made tactical sense, but something about it settled uneasily in Javier's stomach. Using Amanda, manipulating her investigation, meant drawing her deeper into danger she couldn't see coming. If the Consortium realized they were being investigated...

The handler stood, adjusting the hood to better shadow his face. "Remember your position, Morales. Three years undercover. Too many resources invested. Too many lives at stake." A pause, then: "If your cover is blown, we can't extract you. We won't even try."

The words hung in the chill air like fog. Javier had always known the terms but hearing them stated so plainly reinforced the precariousness of his situation. He was alone on the razor's edge, and the slightest misstep would draw blood.

"One more thing," the handler said, beginning to walk away. "If it comes to a choice between maintaining your cover and protecting Agent Chen... there is no choice."

Javier remained motionless on the bench, not watching as the hooded figure retreated along the path and disappeared among the trees. The park grew darker, the temperature dropping with the sun. A harsh gust of wind shook loose a flurry of dead leaves, sending them skittering across the ground like frightened animals.

His hands were cold, fingers still wrapped around the phone that now displayed nothing but a black screen. Yet in his chest, a persistent warmth grew, an uncomfortable heat that he recognized as guilt, anticipatory and corrosive.

Amanda Chen. Her name in his thoughts produced a complex response, tension and release, caution and anticipation. When he'd first encountered her at the auction, he approached her as a tactical move. The FBI agent investigating the Consortium needed to be assessed, perhaps misdirected. He hadn't expected her quiet intensity, the way her analytical mind worked behind those expressive eyes, how her rare, genuine smile transformed her face.

He didn't expect to find himself thinking about her when there was no tactical advantage in doing so.

Javier stood, slipping the phone into his pocket. The cold seeped into his muscles, making movement a conscious effort. Or perhaps it was the weight of his thoughts that made each step deliberate as he walked toward the park exit.

Buenos Aires taught him the cost of attachment. Elena's death had been his fault, not because he pulled the trigger, but because he allowed his feelings to cloud his judgment. He missed the signs, ignored the warnings, convinced himself that he could protect her while maintaining his cover. He'd been wrong in the worst possible way.

He couldn't make the same mistake with Amanda. She was too smart, too dedicated, too principled. And unlike Elena, she had no idea who he really was. To Amanda, he was Javier Morales, art collector with suspicious connections, a potential criminal worthy of her professional attention and nothing more.

Except there had been moments, brief, electric moments, when something more passed between them. A look held too long. A conversation that veered from professional to personal. The slight catch in her breath when their hands had accidentally touched over a champagne flute.

These were dangerous indulgences, Javier knew. Yet he found himself anticipating seeing her again at the gala tonight, planning what he might say, how he might navigate the delicate space between truth and deception. And this anticipation itself was perhaps the most dangerous sign of all.

As he reached the street, lights from passing cars intermittently illuminated his face, revealing the conflict that he otherwise kept hidden. Tonight, at the Getty, he would see Amanda again. Ginevra would be watching. The Consortium would be listening. And somewhere in the choreographed dance of appearance and reality, Javier would need to find a way to protect Amanda without revealing who he really was.

Buenos Aires taught him that such protection was an illusion. Yet he couldn't help but reach for it anyway, like a man trying to catch smoke with his bare hands.

The cafe grew more crowded as the afternoon stretched on, the rising volume of conversation creating a blanket of white noise that wrapped around their booth. Amanda stared into her half-empty coffee mug, the liquid now cooling, much like her professional resolve whenever she thought about Javier. Sarah sat, her with the patient expertise of someone who had witnessed Amanda's walls being built brick by brick over the years and could point out which loose stones to wiggle.

"So," Sarah said, leaning forward on her elbows, "you like him."

Amanda rolled her eyes, the gesture as defensive as a shield. "I'm not thirteen, Sarah."

"But you do." Sarah's voice held no question, only gentle certainty.

The afternoon light filtering through the rain-streaked windows cast shifting patterns across their table, like thoughts too restless to settle. Amanda traced one finger along the rim of her mug, weighing silence against confession. Outside, pedestrians hurried past, huddled against the chill, strangers with their own secrets, their own complications.

"It doesn't matter if I do," Amanda said. "The case comes first. Always."

Sarah tilted her head, studying her friend with the attentiveness that made her a formidable prosecutor before she moved to private practice. "Amanda Chen, hiding behind her badge. Never saw that coming."

"I'm not hiding."

"Aren't you? How long has it been since you've allowed yourself to feel something for someone? Really feel something, not just... whatever calculated dating app experiment you tried last year."

Amanda's jaw tightened. "That's not fair."

"Maybe not," Sarah conceded. "But it's true. Ever since David,"

"Don't." Amanda's voice cut sharp through the cafe noise. "This has nothing to do with him."

"Doesn't it?" Sarah's tone softened. "He left four years ago, Mandi. And you've been building walls ever since."

The mention of her ex-husband sent a familiar dull ache

through Amanda's chest. David, with his easy smile and easier betrayal. David, who looked at her one morning over breakfast and said he'd fallen in love with someone else, a colleague with flowing blonde hair and curves that Amanda's athletic frame couldn't replicate. David, who made her feel, for the first time since childhood, that being herself wasn't enough.

"This is different," Amanda said. "David was... personal. Javier is connected to my case. There are professional ethics involved. Lines that can't be crossed."

"And if he wasn't connected to your case? If you met him at a coffee shop or a bookstore? Would the walls still be quite so high?"

Amanda exhaled, running a hand through her hair. "I don't trust him. I shouldn't trust him. But when I look at him, it's like he sees something in me no one else does. Something I forgot was there."

The confession hung between them, more vulnerable than Amanda intended. Sarah's expression softened, her eyes warming with understanding rather than the judgment Amanda had half-expected.

"Maybe he does," Sarah said. "Maybe your instincts aren't just about the case."

Amanda stared into her coffee, watching the light play across its surface. Her armor was cracking, enough for the draft to be felt. She thought of Javier, his voice like rough velvet, the way his eyes held hers as if memorizing something precious, how his touch during their brief encounters felt both calculated and genuine. Her thoughts tangled around him, the remembered scent of his cologne, the careful precision of his words, the way he made her both seen and hunted all at once.

"There's something about him that doesn't add up,"

Amanda said, her analytical mind refusing to be silenced. "The way he moves through rooms, always aware of exits and sightlines. How he can charm anyone in seconds but keeps real connection at arm's length. His knowledge of art is extensive, but sometimes he says things that suggest experiences he shouldn't have had with his background."

"So he's complicated," Sarah shrugged. "Find me someone worth knowing who isn't."

"Complicated is fine. Deceptive is a problem."

"And you're sure it's deception, not just... layers? Complexities that take time to understand?"

Amanda hesitated. Her training taught her to trust her instincts, to follow the evidence where it led. But those same instincts pulled her in contradictory directions when it came to Javier Morales. The professional in her sensed shadows and inconsistencies. The woman in her sensed something else, a recognition, a possibility, a door unlocking.

"I want to trust what I feel around him," she said. "But my feelings have been wrong before."

"With David, you mean."

Amanda nodded. "I thought I knew him. I built a life on that knowledge. And I was wrong."

"You were married to David for three years, Amanda. You've had what, two encounters with Javier? Maybe your judgment isn't the problem. Maybe you need more information."

"That's the FBI agent's solution too," Amanda said with a small smile. "Gather more evidence."

"See? Your personal and professional instincts can align." Sarah leaned back, her expression growing more serious. "But can I ask you something? When you're with him, analyzing every word and gesture, are you looking for reasons to trust him, or reasons not to?"

The question struck Amanda with unexpected force. She spent years building a fortress around her heart, telling herself it was professionalism, duty, caution. But maybe it was fear, fear of being wrong again, of being vulnerable, of being left.

"I don't know," she said after a moment's thought.

"Well, that's at least a start, admitting you don't know everything." Sarah's smile took any sting from her words. "Your whole life is about certainty, Amanda. Evidence, facts, profiles, patterns. Maybe this is about allowing space for uncertainty. For possibility."

Amanda's fingers tightened around her mug. "When we talk, it's like... we're having two conversations at once. The words we're saying, and something else underneath. I've never experienced anything like it."

"It is. And exhilarating." Amanda's cheeks warmed. "Last time, at the gallery, we were discussing a painting, some pastoral scene with mythological figures, and he said something about how the real story was happening in the shadows, beyond what the artist wanted us to see. The way he looked at me when he said it..." She trailed off, the memory still vivid.

"Like he wasn't talking about the painting at all," Sarah finished for her.

"Exactly." Amanda took a deep breath. "And I keep thinking, what if that's genuine? What if, underneath whatever game we're playing, there's something real? And what if I miss it because I'm too afraid to look beyond my case?"

Sarah reached out, fingers brushing Amanda's. "You'll make the right call. Just don't ignore what your gut's telling you because your fear's louder than your truth."

The touch was brief but grounding, pulling Amanda back

from the spiral of her thoughts. Her gaze drifted to the window where early evening began to settle over the city, lights blinking on in office buildings, headlights cutting through the lingering rain.

Sarah smiled. "My professional opinion is that you should stop asking for opinions and trust yourself. My friend opinion is that you should wear that caramel dress the next time you think you are going to meet him, the one with the subtle draping that makes your shoulders look amazing."

Amanda laughed, the sound surprising her with its lightness. "Who said anything about a dress?"

Sarah raised her near empty mug in a small toast. "To following the evidence wherever it leads, even if it leads to actually feeling something."

Amanda raised her own mug in response, the gesture half-ironic, half-sincere. "To feeling something," she echoed, as if testing the words.

Outside, the rain had stopped, leaving the streets glistening under the emerging city lights. Amanda sensed the night stretching before her, filled with unknowns and possibilities. For once, the uncertainty wasn't a problem to solve, but a story unfolding, one where she wasn't just the investigator, but also a participant.

With Javier Morales waiting somewhere in those evening shadows, nothing was certain. But for the first time in years, uncertainty and hope were mingling in her mind.

***

Twilight deepened into full darkness by the time the handler returned, materializing from the shadows like a thought given form. Javier hadn't moved from the bench, partly strategic, partly because of his earlier conversation anchored him to

111

the spot. The temperature dropped further, sending a chill through his jacket, but he didn't register the cold. Physical discomforts were background noise, easily filtered out when necessary. The approaching footsteps, however, cut through his thoughts with precision.

The park, empty now, abandoned to night creatures and clandestine meetings. Distant streetlights cast elongated shadows across the path, transforming familiar shapes into something more sinister. A fitting backdrop, Javier thought, for decisions that lived in moral twilight.

The handler didn't sit this time, instead remaining standing several feet away, face still obscured by the hood. The posture spoke of urgency, of information too volatile to be delivered sitting down.

"New intel," the handler said without preamble, extending a thin folder toward Javier. "The Consortium's next shipment is in motion. Port of Long Beach, three days. You'll intercept, quietly. Chen can't know yet."

Javier took the folder, the exchange brief and practiced. His fingers didn't tremble, his expression revealed nothing beyond professional interest as he flipped it open. Inside, thermal imaging photos showed a cargo container being loaded onto a ship in Shanghai, along with manifest documents that listed art supplies and reproduction frames as the contents. To most eyes, the paperwork would appear legitimate. To trained ones, the discrepancies were subtle but present, weights that didn't match declared contents, routing anomalies that suggested possible stops not on the official itinerary.

"Tucker will be handling the customs clearance personally," Javier said, scanning the documents. "That's unusual."

"The contents are high-value," the handler replied. "Consortium leadership is taking a direct interest."

Javier nodded, calculating what this meant. Aaron Tucker, ostensibly a respected customs broker, was a key figure in the Consortium's West Coast operation. His personal involvement suggested the shipment contained something beyond the usual stolen antiquities or forged masterpieces.

"What am I looking for?" he asked, closing the folder.

"Intelligence suggests original manuscript pages from the Vatican archives. Fifteenth century. The Consortium has a buyer already lined up, private collector in Dubai."

Javier kept his expression neutral even as his mind processed the implications. Manuscript pages from the Vatican would be impossible to forge convincingly. This was likely straight theft, which meant someone inside the Vatican had been compromised. The Consortium's reach was expanding.

"Your role is observation only," the handler said. "Confirm the delivery, track the hand off, identify the courier. We need to map the entire network before moving in."

"And Chen?" Javier asked, the name slipping out before he could reconsider.

The handler's posture stiffened almost imperceptibly. "The Bureau has resources at the port. They're watching for something, but they don't know what or when. Keep Chen distracted. Feed her something small if necessary, enough to convince her that she's making progress without compromising our operation."

"She's smart," Javier said. "If I give her something too obvious, she'll suspect it's misdirection."

"Then be subtle," the handler replied with menace. "That's your specialty, isn't it? Getting close to people, making them trust you?"

The barb found its mark, though Javier's face revealed nothing. Madrid again, the ghost that haunted every conversation, every decision, every moment of hesitation.

"I'll handle it," he said, sliding the folder into his jacket's inner pocket.

The handler stepped closer, voice dropping lower. "Your cover's holding. But if it breaks, you won't have time to explain to her who you are. She'll be the one putting a bullet in your chest."

The words painted a vivid image, Amanda's face hardening with betrayal, her service weapon raised, her finger steady on the trigger. It wasn't mere hyperbole. If his cover was blown, if Amanda discovered him in the wrong context, her training would take over. She would do her job, just as he was doing his.

The handler melted back into the darkness, footsteps fading until they were indistinguishable from the night sounds of the park.

Alone again, Javier closed the folder, jaw set. The paper, unnaturally heavy in his hands, weighted with implications and consequences. Amanda's face flashed in his mind, sharp, beautiful, dangerous. Her eyes, always watching, analyzing, seeking truth. Her rare smile, like a crack in professional armor, revealing something genuine and unguarded beneath.

He didn't want to lie to her anymore. But he would. Because he had to.

The thought settled like frost across his shoulders as he stood, muscles stiff from the cold and the tension he'd been holding. Three years undercover taught him to compartmentalize, to separate the man he was from the man he pretended to be. Usually, the divisions were clear, actions taken for the mission belonged in one mental box, true feelings in another, never to mix.

But Amanda Chen had somehow slipped between those barriers. When he thought of her now, he couldn't distinguish between the professional assessment (smart, dedicated, dangerous to his cover) and the personal recognition (perceptive, complex, increasingly important).

This meeting with his handler should have reinforced the divisions, reminded him of his purpose and the risks of deviation. Instead, it had only highlighted the growing fracture in his resolve. The prospect of seeing Amanda at the Getty gala tonight should have been a tactical consideration. Instead, he found himself thinking of how the museum lights would catch in her dark hair, how her analytical mind would engage with the art, how her eyes might soften when they met his across a crowded room.

Dangerous thoughts. Potentially fatal ones.

***

The cafe's warmth lingered on Amanda's skin for a mere three steps before the evening chill reclaimed her. She tugged her coat closer, buttoning it against the wind that tunneled between buildings and seemed to seek out every vulnerability. Beside her, Sarah adjusted her scarf, her breath forming small clouds that dissolved into the darkening sky. The streetlights had just begun to flicker on, casting everything in that peculiar glow that made the familiar seem altered, as if the world shifted a few degrees while they'd been talking.

Behind them, the cafe's windows glowed, framing the silhouettes of people living ordinary moments, leaning toward conversations, laughing over steaming mugs, absorbed in private worlds of their own making. Their reflections in a parked car's window allowed Amanda a view, struck by how she could identify those who were alone by choice and those who carried their solitude like an unwanted gift.

"I should get going," Sarah said, checking her watch. "Court tomorrow morning, and Judge Abernathy doesn't appreciate creative interpretations of punctuality."

Amanda nodded, still half-lost in her thoughts. "Thanks," she said. "For not judging me."

Sarah's smile was gentle, her eyes knowing. "That's what friends are for. Judgment-free zones and occasional brutal honesty." She hesitated, then said, "Just don't let him make the decisions for you. Whatever happens with Javier, you decide what it means, what you want it to be."

They embraced, Then Sarah was stepping back, raising her hand in a small wave before turning toward the subway entrance half a block away. Her friend disappeared down the steps, swallowed by the city's underground arteries.

Then she was alone on the sidewalk, surrounded by the anonymous current of passersby. She began walking, her stride purposeful despite the uncertainty that followed her like a shadow. The city was alive around her, honking cars navigating the early evening traffic, storefronts bleeding light onto the sidewalks, people laughing in passing shadows or hurrying toward their next destinations.

The caramel dress hung in her closet, unworn since a fundraiser last spring. She'd almost forgotten its existence until Sarah mentioned it. Now she could picture it clearly, the subtle draping that followed the lines of her body without clinging, the way the color deepened her skin tone and made her eyes appear almost black in certain light. It was elegant but restrained, professional enough for work yet undeniably feminine.

Would Javier notice? The thought slipped through her defenses before she could stop it.

Three blocks from the cafe, Amanda turned right onto a quieter street. The buildings here were older, their facades textured with decades of history and renovation. Her apartment was another twelve minutes away, a third-floor walk-up in a pre-war building that resisted gentrification through some administrative oversight. The rent was reasonable, the location convenient, the security adequate, all she needed.

What she wanted was a different question, one she hesitated before allowing herself to consider.

Her senses were dialed up, footsteps behind her, the shift of wind against brick, the flicker of headlights as cars turned onto the narrow street. Nothing triggered her professional alarms, yet something prickled at the base of her neck, that peculiar awareness that sometimes preceded discovery in her cases, a subconscious recognition of patterns not yet consciously identified.

From across the street, Ginevra Sforza matched Amanda's pace with fluid grace. Her movements measured and efficient, never drawing attention yet never losing sight of her target. Her heeled boots made no sound on the pavement, a skill acquired through years of practice and several thousand euros spent on specially modified footwear. The evening wind caught her coat, revealing glimpses of the tailored outfit beneath, charcoal gray and expertly cut to allow freedom of movement while maintaining an elegant silhouette.

Ginevra's gaze locked on Amanda's back, studying the FBI agent's unconscious habits, how she favored her right side when turning corners, how her hand brushed against her hip where her service weapon was undoubtedly holstered, how she maintained awareness of her surroundings without appearing vigilant. Every detail was mentally cataloged, each potential vulnerability noted.

Unlike the men who typically conducted surveillance, Ginevra didn't need technical devices or constant communication with a team. Her memory was impeccable, her patience legendary. She had once spent fourteen days observing a target without ever being noticed, learning his habits so thoroughly that when she finally approached him, knowing which vulnerabilities to exploit.

The light changed, and Amanda crossed the street, her stride lengthening. The sidewalk narrowed as she turned onto a street lined with trees that had long since shed their leaves. Their bare branches created skeletal patterns against the night sky, beautiful in their stark simplicity. Like truth, Amanda thought, often stark, rarely comfortable, but possessing its own austere beauty.

Ginevra maintained her distance, pausing to examine a storefront or check her phone, movements calculated to appear natural while keeping Amanda within sight. Her eyes revealed nothing of her thoughts, her expression a perfect mask of casual indifference.

But beneath that mask, Ginevra's mind was busy constructing a profile of Special Agent Amanda Chen. Disciplined. Observant, but with blind spots. Physically capable, based on her posture and movement. Potentially dangerous in a fight. But also, and this was most useful, distracted. The agent's thoughts were elsewhere, creating opportunities for mistakes.

The Consortium had been clear in their instructions: assess the FBI agent, determine what she knew about the operation, identify her weaknesses. They did not specify what actions to take afterward, but Ginevra understood the implications. People who threatened the Consortium's interests never remained in positions to do so for long.

Amanda turned onto her street, familiar buildings rising on either side. The neighborhood was neither fashionable nor neglected, a place where people minded their own business and expected others to do the same. Perfect for someone who valued privacy. Her building appeared ahead, its brick facade distinguished from its neighbors only by the more ornate cornice and the recently replaced front door.

Safe inside, Amanda leaned against the wall for a moment, eyes closed. The conversation with Sarah, thoughts of Javier, the upcoming gala, all of it swirled in her mind like leaves caught in an eddy. She had decisions to make, preparations to complete. The midnight blue dress waited upstairs. So did her case files, her service weapon, her professional obligations.

Only her eyes betrayed her true nature, cold and calculating as she composed the approach she would make later that evening.

Behind her, the city swallowed Ginevra whole, the evening crowds absorbing her presence until she was nothing more than another shadow moving through the gathering darkness.

Chapter 7

The elevator hummed a metallic lullaby as Amanda Chen leaned against the brushed steel wall, her eyelids weighted with the day's exhaustion. The case files she memorized flickered behind her closed eyes like phantom projections, faces, locations, connections, a mental web that refused to disconnect as the numbers ticked upward on the digital display. Her body ached not from exertion but from the perpetual state of readiness, muscles primed for action that never came in the tedious surveillance work that consumed her week.

Four... five... six.

Her eyes snapped open at the soft ding, pupils contracting against the stark fluorescent hallway lighting. The corridor stretched before her, empty and silent, the kind of quiet that made her skin prickle. Too quiet. The neighbors in 612, an elderly couple with a television always tuned to game shows, should have been audible through their thin door. Amanda's fingers tightened around her keys, thumb brushing the jagged edge of the apartment key as she approached her door.

She paused, gaze dropping to the nearly invisible strip of

clear tape she always placed at the corner where door met frame that morning. Intact. Either no one entered while she was away or someone knew her methods. Amanda had grown accustomed to paranoia; in her line of work, it wasn't paranoia if they really were watching.

The lock surrendered with a familiar click, the sound comforting in the tomblike hallway. She stepped inside, throwing the deadbolt with a practiced flick. The darkness of her apartment welcomed her, and she didn't reach for the light switch. Instead, she let the shadows settle around her, listening to the apartment's breath, the soft hum of the refrigerator, the barely perceptible whir of her laptop in sleep mode on the coffee table, the irregular drip from the bathroom faucet she'd been meaning to fix for three weeks.

Amanda moved through the dark with certainty, having memorized every dimension, every potential obstacle. Her hand reached for her throat, kneading the tension that wound itself like copper wire beneath her collarbone. The day sat on her shoulders, eight hours of sifting through surveillance footage from the Getty, cross-referencing faces against known Eclipse Consortium affiliates.

You need to let this go. At least for one night.

But Sarah's voice floated through the static of her thoughts: "Maybe your instincts are right. Maybe you don't always have to doubt them." Sarah, with her endless optimism and unfailing belief in Amanda's "gut feelings." Sarah, who didn't understand that instincts were patterns of recognition masquerading as intuition, and patterns could be misleading.

Amanda exhaled, her breath mingling with the apartment's still air as she tugged her shirt over her head. The motion of undressing became a ritual of surrender, the suit jacket first, then the blouse that smelled of the coffee she spilled that morning, finally the slacks that grew tight around the knees after hours of crouching in the surveillance van. Her clothes formed a trail behind her like breadcrumbs, marking her passage through the living room toward the bathroom.

Javier Morales

The name ambushed her thoughts again, refusing to be filed away with the day's other observations. It had taken up residence in her mind over the past week, echoing through her consciousness more than her ex-husband's voice had during the worst days of their divorce. Javier was a puzzle with mismatched edges, charm that seemed effortless but practiced, eyes that noticed emergency exits before the artwork in a gallery, hands that moved with the precision of someone who understood how quickly circumstances could change.

And the way he looked at her at the gala last weekend, not with the transparent hunger she grew accustomed to from men assessing her value, not with the clinical calculation of a predator measuring prey, but with something else. Like recognition. Like he found something he didn't realized he was searching for.

Stop. Focus. He's either a threat or a mirage.

The bathroom transformed into a foggy sanctuary as she turned the shower to its hottest setting. Steam curled around her like a living entity, obscuring her reflection in the mirror, a mercy she she needed until the glass clouded over. Amanda stepped under the spray, and the heat struck her skin like a welcome slap, sharp and purifying.

She braced her palms against the slick tile wall, dropping her head beneath the stream, letting water pound against her scalp and cascade through her hair. The tension in her shoulders began to loosen, knots unraveling beneath the persistent heat. Her thoughts, too, began to untangle as the water sluiced away the day's accumulated strain.

Then it hit her, not a thought so much as a memory flashing with sudden clarity.

Javier at the museum three days ago, always positioning himself near exits. The waiter's tray clattering to the marble floor. Javier's hand twitching toward his side without thought, a motion so swift and automatic most people would miss it. But Amanda wasn't most people, and that movement wasn't the reaction of an art dealer or collector.

It was the movement of someone accustomed to carrying a weapon.

Her breath caught, suspended in the steamy air. Law enforcement. The answer crystallized with stunning simplicity. Maybe even undercover.

She blinked, water clinging to her lashes like tiny prisms. How hadn't she seen it before? It wasn't his posture or his awareness of his surroundings. It was his knowledge of the Getty's security protocols, the way he guided her away from the main gallery moments before the security sweep, his offhand comment about the surveillance blind spot near the east wing.

What if he's not hiding from me... but from them?

Her pulse quickened, its rhythm no longer dulled by the shower's white noise. She rolled the idea through her mind, testing its angles and dimensions. Javier Morales: charming art collector with connections to the Eclipse Consortium's smuggling operation... or a ghost-level operative embedded within their organization?

The pieces aligned with unsettling precision. His knowledge

of the players was too intimate, his anticipation of their movements too accurate. And there had been that moment, a fraction of a second when their eyes met across the crowded gallery, when something like recognition passed between them, a current of understanding, neither acknowledged.

If he's undercover, if he's on our side, why hasn't he said anything?

The question pulsed in her mind as she turned off the faucet. Water droplets chased each other down her back as she stood motionless in the steam-thick air. The silence was different now, expectant, weighted. She reached for her towel, hanging just beyond the shower door.

And froze.

Something changed. The air pressure, perhaps. Or a subtle shift in the ambient sounds of her apartment. The kind of change prey animals sense before predators emerge from tall grass. Her hand remained suspended in mid-reach, water droplets gathering at her fingertips before falling to the shower floor with tiny, percussive sounds that were suddenly too loud.

Amanda's body tensed, switching to a state of heightened awareness. Her breathing slowed, her senses extending beyond the bathroom's confines. She listened, searching for disruptions in the apartment's familiar symphony of sounds.

***

The air shifted. A molecular change, like the sudden drop in barometric pressure before a storm. Before Amanda could process the sensation, a hand, gloved, firm, practiced, clamped over her mouth. The cold kiss of metal pressed against the hollow of her throat, not hard enough to break skin but with enough pressure to communicate intent. Amanda didn't scream. She didn't flinch. Her training crystallized into perfect stillness, as she cataloged her disadvantages: naked, wet, weaponless, alone.

Her first instinct was to twist. Break the wrist. Disarm. But the angle was wrong, her feet slick beneath her, her heart hammering too fast to fake calm.

"Shhh..." A sultry voice purred against her ear, accented and smooth as aged whiskey. "We're going to have a little chat. Woman to woman."

Ginevra

Amanda didn't need to see her. The calculated calm in her voice, was pure elegance sharpened into a weapon.

"Don't move," Ginevra said, her voice dark silk. "No matter how good you think you are, I am better."

She wasn't here to kill Amanda. Not yet. Amanda felt it in the measured pressure of the blade, not quite breaking the skin. A warning.

"Okay. What are your options?" Amanda's thoughts a whirl.

The sink was two steps away. Her sidearm, out of reach. The glass shower door, fragile, but useless without momentum. She catalogued every item in the bathroom: towel bar, hair dryer cord, tile ledge, perfume bottle.

She needed a distraction. A shift in weight. She needed ...

Click, Click.

The unmistakable ratchet of her own handcuffs locking around her wrists behind her.

"I thought you might be more hospitable after a nice warm shower, Agent Chen." Ginevra said.

Amanda's stomach contracted, muscles pulling tight against her spine. The blade never left her throat as she was drug backwards, her bare feet skidding against the damp tile, then catching on the carpet's rough fibers. The bathroom's lingering steam clung to her skin while the cooler air of the bedroom raised goosebumps along her arms and legs. Her nakedness was another weapon being used against her, vulnerability by design.

It wasn't until they reached the bedroom that Amanda was allowed to turn, just enough to catch her reflection in the full-length mirror she inherited from her mother. The image was jarring, her own naked body, water still tracking rivulets down her shoulders and back, and behind her, Ginevra Sforza in perfect, predatory composure. The woman wore a black silk blouse that clung like a second skin, tailored leather pants, and heels that should have announced her presence but somehow made no sound on Amanda's hardwood floors.

The cold metal dug into her skin, not tight enough to cut circulation but secure enough to eliminate any possibility of slipping free. Amanda said nothing, reaction was information, and she wasn't ready to give Ginevra anything yet.

A firm hand between her shoulder blades propelled Amanda forward, forcing her to sit on the edge of the bed. The duvet was cool against her bare thighs, a tactile reminder of her exposure. Ginevra stepped back, studying her captive with the clinical interest of an artist assessing a canvas. Then, with unhurried confidence, she crossed the room and settled into Amanda's reading chair, crossing one long leg over the other.

The streetlight painted stripes across Ginevra's face through the half-closed blinds, highlighting cheekbones sharp enough to draw blood, lips stained a deep crimson, almost black in the dim light, the cold intelligence eyes of a predator who enjoyed playing with her food before consuming it.

"You're stunning I must admit," Ginevra said, her head tilting as she studied Amanda. "I almost envy him."

Amanda blinked. "Who?"

The question hung in the air, unanswered. Ginevra's gaze traveled slowly over Amanda's body, neither lascivious nor vulgar, but assessing, like a surgeon plotting incision points.

Ginevra didn't answer, just smiled, slow and mean. "He is taken by you. I see it in the way he watches you. Like he doesn't know whether to kiss you or kill you."

Javier

Amanda said nothing.

"You know," Ginevra said conversationally, "most agents would be begging by now. Or threatening. Empty words about backup and protocols." She said never taking her eyes from Amanda's. "But not you. You're quite remarkable, Agent Chen."

Ginevra rose again, not pouncing, but prowling. She stood on the edge of the bed, looking down on Amanda her dominance on full display.

Without warning, Ginevra settled onto Amanda's lap, straddling her with practiced ease. The leather of her pants was cool against Amanda's bare thighs, the weight of the woman distributed to maintain balance while limiting Amanda's movement options. It was an intimate position, a violation of personal space, designed to disorient and intimidate.

Amanda's breath caught, not from fear but from the calculation required. Each potential movement, each response, needed evaluation. Fight now? Wait? Gather information? The knife reappeared, not touching her skin but hovering nearby, a silver promise in Ginevra's right hand.

"Let's talk about your case," Ginevra said, using her free hand to drag a damp strand of hair away from Amanda's face with surprising gentleness. "Let's talk about what you know..."

Her blade tracing a lazy pattern just above Amanda's heart, "...and who you're starting to trust."

"And let's talk," Ginevra said, her lips close enough to Amanda's ear they startled her, "about what happens to people who get too close to El Fantasma."

"I don't know what you're talking about," Amanda said, her voice steady despite the knife hovering near her ribs.

Ginevra's laugh was soft and musical, genuinely amused. "Of course you don't." She shifted her weight, creating space between them only to close it again. "You also do not know that your handsome Javier Morales has been critical in our planning."

Amanda's pulse jumped, a betrayal she hoped wasn't visible. Javier. So he is connected. But connected how? And why was Ginevra revealing this?

"He's not mine," Amanda replied, keeping her tone flat, uninterested.

"You're wondering if he's on your side. Or mine," Ginevra said, her breath hot against Amanda's temple. "Wondering if he's a consortium member, a mask we use, or whether he could be of use to you. Maybe you even think he is an ally."

Amanda's muscles coiled, calculating. Her knees could pivot to throw Ginevra off. But not with her hands bound. Not without risking the knife.

"Don't flatter yourself," Amanda said, voice flat.

"Oh, amore mia." Ginevra leaned in, her lips brushing Amanda's cheek. "I don't need to. You're doing that all on your own."

Her free hand moved to Amanda's throat, fingers wrapping around it without applying pressure, yet. "I admire competent women, Agent Chen. Truly I do. Which is why I'm here, a warning, a bullet, it makes little difference to me."

Amanda maintained eye contact, refusing to be the first to look away. "You broke into a federal agent's apartment to deliver a warning? Seems pretty far fetched."

"Believable or not," Ginevra replied, her thumb brushing the pulse point in Amanda's neck. "Sometimes the message is in the method. You are being watched, no, *studied*, by people who could have eliminated you a dozen times already."

Her grip tightened fractionally. "El Fantasma knows your morning coffee order. Knows about your swimming routine at 5 AM. Knows about the scar on your lower back." As if to emphasize this last point, the tip of the knife traced a line above where Amanda's handcuffed wrists rested against her spine, where the bullet wound from three years ago left its permanent mark.

The details were more chilling than the blade. Amanda's personnel file was classified. Her shooting had been kept quiet, the records sealed. This wasn't information the Consortium should have.

"What do you want?" Amanda said, her voice lower now, controlled.

Ginevra's expression softened into something almost resembling kindness. "Distance yourself from the Morales investigation. Request reassignment. Take a vacation, I hear Portugal is lovely this time of year."

"Or?"

Amanda's phone buzzed on the nightstand. The sound broke the stillness like a gunshot. Ginevra's head snapped toward it, her eyes narrowing, and in that flicker of distraction, Amanda saw something else.

Jealousy. Real. Raw.

"She's calling again," Ginevra said, almost to herself. "Your little lawyer friend. Sarah."

Amanda's breath hitched. A mistake.

Ginevra smiled. "I could make her scream. I'm told I have that effect."

Amanda's voice was low, dangerous. "You touch her, and I'll burn the whole Consortium to the ground."

Ginevra's knife grazed upward again, pausing at Amanda's pulse point. "Oh good. I was hoping for fire."

But she stood.

Ginevra's eyes bored into Amanda's, her smile fading to something darker. "Tell your mystery man he's mine."

Amanda's jaw tensed. "If you touch him,"

"What?" Ginevra cut her off. "You'll what? Lock me up? Pull the trigger? He will not see it coming if I decide he's more useful dead than distracted." She leaned closer, and for one harrowing second, Amanda thought she might kiss her or slit her throat.

Instead, she whispered against her temple: "Do you know what haunts a man like him? Not failure. Not death. Regret." A beat. A breath. "And I'll make sure you're his biggest one."

She straightened, unhurried. Then slid the blade back into the seam of her blouse like it belonged there.

And with that, she vanished. The door shut with a hush, more terrifying than a slam.

Only when she was certain she was alone did Amanda allow herself a shaky exhale. Her body trembled, not with fear but with delayed adrenaline. Her mind, however, remained analytical, processing each fragment of information Ginevra revealed, intended or not.

This wasn't intimidation. It wasn't a simple warning.

It was war. And somehow, Javier Morales was at the center of it.

8

Chapter 8

The unfinished forgery caught the studio's dim light in ways the original never would. Javier traced its contours with his eyes, admiring Isabel's mastery. While incomplete, the painting breathed deception, the brushstrokes perfect lies that would fool the most discerning collectors. His hands were steady as he approached it, but his mind raced with jagged thoughts, each one cutting deeper than the last. The plan was fraying at the edges, like his conscience.

Isabel's studio occupied the converted attic of a pre-war building in downtown Los Angeles, a space where sunlight filtered through skylights during the day, illuminating dust motes swirling like microscopic galaxies. Now, in the evening hours, strategically placed lamps cast pools of warm yellow across the wooden floorboards. The sharp bite of turpentine mingled with linseed oil and the earthy perfume of pigments, creating an atmosphere both intoxicating and cloying, not unlike the double life Javier had been leading.

He circled the easel where the forgery rested. It was a lesser-known Vermeer, one which hadn't been exhibited in decades.

Isabel captured the master's luminous quality, the way light generated from within the subjects rather than fall upon them. Three more days of work, and the Getty's best curators would sign affidavits to its authenticity.

"Beautiful and dangerous," he said to the empty room. "Like everything else in this mess."

Isabel was gone for the evening, a calculated absence he arranged through untraceable channels. The Consortium thought he was here to check on their investment. His handlers at the Secret Service believed he was gathering intelligence. Neither was aware he was about to risk everything on a gamble with one FBI agent's life in the balance.

Javier reached into his tailored jacket, the fabric rustling against his silk shirt. He withdrew a small piece of paper, folded into a tight square no larger than a postage stamp. On it, written in a cipher that only those with specific training could decode, was the proof the FBI had to be connected to the Eclipse Consortium's American operations. One piece of evidence with the potential unravel years of careful criminal enterprise or get Amanda Chen killed if she trusted the wrong person.

His fingertips tingled as he held the paper, a physical manifestation of the risk he was taking. He moved to the ornate frame leaning against the wall, waiting to embrace Isabel's forgery once it was complete. With precise movements, he slipped the folded paper into a hairline crack where the wooden backing met the frame's edge. Invisible unless you knew where to look. A breadcrumb on a trail that would lead Amanda to safety, or disaster.

For a moment, he rested his palm against the frame, as if in benediction. His hands were cold, but an uncomfortable heat sat in his chest, he recognized as guilt. She didn't deserve to be pulled into this. Didn't deserve the danger he was placing her in. But he saw how close she was getting, too close to the truth without the protection of knowing who to trust.

Javier withdrew his phone, the screen's blue glow harsh against the studio's warm tones. He tapped out a message, anonymous and untraceable:

"Check the warehouse on 9th. West side entrance. Midnight."

His thumb hovered over the send button for three heartbeats before pressing down. The message disappeared into the digital ether, bound for Amanda Chen's encrypted phone. There was no going back now.

As he slipped toward the door, Javier paused to look back at the studio. In another life, this could have been a place of creation rather than deception, of beauty rather than betrayal. The thought clung to him like the scent of paint that followed him down the narrow staircase and into the night.

***

The abandoned warehouse loomed against the moonless sky, a hulking shadow cut from darkness itself. Amanda killed her headlights a block away, parking her government-issue sedan where it wouldn't attract attention. The gentle hum of the cooling engine seemed to echo in the empty industrial district.

"Remind me why we're not waiting for backup?" Dominic asked, his voice carrying that particular blend of casualness Amanda had long ago learned to distrust. It wasn't the question of a nervous agent; it was the question of someone testing waters.

"Anonymous tip. Unverified source. Might be nothing," she

replied, checking her service weapon before tucking it into her shoulder holster. "Or it might be what we've been looking for. Either way, I'm not risking scaring them off with a parade of agents."

Dominic nodded, his features arranged in what appeared to be thoughtful consideration. "Smart play."

Something in his tone made the fine hairs at the nape of Amanda's neck rise. She spent enough years studying the micro-expressions of liars and killers to recognize when something was off, even if she couldn't pinpoint what. Dominic Hayes had always been polished. His rise through the FBI ranks had been meteoric, his case closure rate impressive. Yet there was something about him that never quite settled right in her analytical mind.

They approached the warehouse on foot, sticking to the shadows. The night air carried the briny scent of the distant harbor mixed with motor oil and neglect. Their footsteps unnaturally loud on the cracked pavement, each sound creating tiny fractures in the midnight silence.

The west side entrance was where the message indicated, a rusted door set into corrugated metal siding, partially concealed by overgrown weeds that pushed through the concrete years ago. Nature reclaiming what industry abandoned.

"Someone's been here recently," Amanda said, crouching to examine the disturbed vegetation. Fresh breaks in the stems, green rather than brown. Someone came through within the last few hours.

"You think our tipster left us more than just a message?" Dominic asked, moving toward the door.

Amanda straightened, watching him with calculated neutrality. "Maybe. Or maybe we're walking into something else entirely."

The door groaned as Dominic pulled it open, the sound amplified in the empty night. Beyond it lay darkness so complete it may has well been solid. Amanda withdrew her flashlight, its beam cutting through the gloom like a knife, illuminating swirls of dust suspended in the stagnant air.

"Creepy enough for you?" Dominic asked, his voice oddly casual for the situation.

"Don't need it to be creepy," Amanda said, sweeping her light across cracked walls and the skeletal remains of machinery. "Just need it to be real."

They stepped inside, the concrete floor gritty beneath their boots. Amanda's mind cataloged each detail automatically, footprints in the dust showing at least two different tread patterns, both recent; crates stacked against the far wall in too orderly a fashion for an abandoned building; the faint but distinctive odor of gun oil beneath the mustiness.

Her flashlight beam danced across an empty space, revealing the bones of what had once been a thriving manufacturing facility. Conveyor belts sat motionless, frozen in time. Office partitions had collapsed inward, their contents long ago looted or decayed. Yet something felt deliberate about the disorder, as if it had been arranged rather than abandoned.

"Bureau's been watching this place for months," Dominic offered as they moved deeper into the building. "Nothing ever panned out."

Amanda absorbed this information without comment. If the Bureau had been monitoring the warehouse, why hadn't Dominic mentioned this when she received the tip? Why come at all if previous surveillance yielded nothing?

The silence pressed against them as they moved forward,

broken only by their footsteps and the occasional skitter of rodents in the walls. Amanda's senses strained against the darkness, picking up currents in the air suggesting larger spaces ahead, the subtle change in acoustics indicated a shift in the building's architecture.

"There," Dominic said, stopping short. His flashlight fixed on a section of wall that seemed unremarkable at first glance. But as Amanda moved closer, she saw what drew his attention, the dust pattern was different, disturbed in a perfect rectangle. The wall itself looked cleaner, more deliberate than its surroundings.

Dominic knelt, running his fingers along what appeared to be a seamless junction with the floor. His touch revealed a narrow gap, wide enough to be a door. "Looks like someone didn't want this found," he murmured, a note of something unidentifiable in his voice.

Amanda stepped beside him, her mind working through probabilities and scenarios. If this was an active Consortium site, it should be guarded. If it was abandoned, why the hidden door? And how had Dominic spotted it so quickly in the darkness?

"Ready?" he asked, looking up at her with an expression both eager and guarded.

Amanda nodded, one hand moving instinctively closer to her weapon. Together, they pressed against the hidden panel, resistance giving way as it gave way with a soft click.

The door swung inward, revealing a rectangle of faint golden light beyond, a maw opening into secrets that might devour them both.

***

Golden light spilled from the hidden room like morning

sunshine through a thick fog, slow, rich, and somehow threatening. Amanda stepped through the threshold, the air inside noticeably different: warmer, tinged with the distinct scent of canvas sizing and the metallic whisper of expensive security systems powered down. This was no abandoned storage space. This was a vault disguised as neglect, a treasury masquerading as trash.

The room stretched deeper than she expected, perhaps twenty feet square, its walls lined with industrial metal shelving. Low-voltage track lighting cast a protective glow over the contents: wooden crates with foreign markings, stretched canvases turned to face the wall, and half-finished works on portable easels. In the center stood a large table bearing the tools of an art forger's trade, specialized brushes, period-appropriate pigments in glass jars, magnifying equipment, and reference materials.

"Jackpot," Dominic said, but the word held none of the excitement it should have carried. His tone was flat, observational. Too controlled.

Amanda moved forward with measured steps, her FBI training manifesting in the precise way she scanned the room, left to right, top to bottom, cataloging details with machine-like efficiency. Her fingertips tingled with the electric recognition of importance. This wasn't any forgery operation; this was high-level, professional, the kind that infiltrates major museums and private collections without detection.

"These aren't street-level fakes," she admired, approaching one of the canvases. With gloved hands, she carefully turned it to face them.

A Caravaggio. Or rather, a forgery of such exquisite quality that it made her breath catch. The dramatic chiaroscuro, the psychological intensity of the figures, the masterful rendering of flesh tones, all executed with a technical perfection that spoke of years of study and practice.

"Someone has institutional knowledge," she said, examining the edge of the canvas without touching it. "The aging techniques are museum-quality. This isn't skill; this is insider information."

Dominic circled the room with an unusual lack of investigative energy, his attention seeming to drift rather than focus. "Looks like we stumbled onto something bigger than expected."

Amanda's response died in her throat as her eyes fell on a painting leaning against the far wall. Unlike the others, this one was completely finished, framed in an ornate period-appropriate setting. It was a Flemish landscape, the same obscure painting Javier discussed with casual expertise at the gallery opening what seemed like a lifetime ago. A piece so specific, so niche that fewer than a dozen experts worldwide could properly authenticate it.

Her heart performed a complicated maneuver in her chest, part sinking, part racing. Javier Morales. The man whose smile both irritated and intrigued her in equal measure. Whose intelligence matched her own in ways that were both refreshing and suspicious. Whose touch, brief and seemingly accidental during their last encounter, left an imprint of warmth she still felt.

Was this his operation? Had every interaction been calculated to gather information about the FBI's investigation? Or was this something else, a message, perhaps, a breadcrumb deliberately left for her to find?

"Recognize anything?" Dominic asked, he was far closer

than she expected.

Amanda controlled her expression with practiced ease. "Several pieces that match descriptions of works stolen from European collections over the past decade." She avoided mentioning the Flemish landscape or her connection to it. Something in her gut, the same instinct that kept her alive during undercover operations, told her to keep that recognition private.

***

From his vantage point above the hidden room, Javier watched through a narrow slat in the warehouse's second-level roof, his body still despite the cramp developing in his left leg. Every muscle in his body was taut with tension, his focus unwavering as he catalogued Amanda's movements below.

She moved through the space with a grace that belied her analytical precision, her slender fingers hovering above surfaces, her eyes missing nothing. Her dark hair pulled back in a functional ponytail, exposing the elegant line of her neck. In the practical attire of an FBI agent on a clandestine mission, dark jacket, sensible boots, minimal jewelry, she carried herself with an unconscious dignity that tightened something in his chest.

He saw the exact moment when she recognized the Flemish landscape. The subtle stiffening of her shoulders, the almost imperceptible tilt of her head, the way her fingers curled inward as if physically restraining herself from reaching out to touch it. She was brilliant, connecting dots that others wouldn't see as related. It made her both the perfect ally and the most dangerous liability.

Dominic Hayes moved through his peripheral vision, and Javier's jaw clenched involuntarily. Hayes was playing a role as dangerous as he was, the difference being, Hayes thought no one knew his true allegiance. The way he circled the room with artificial casualness, the strategic placement of his body to monitor Amanda's reactions, the calculated distance he maintained from certain pieces, all of it confirmed what Javier already knew. Dominic Hayes wasn't complicit in the Consortium's operations; he was orchestrating them.

Javier's hand moved unconsciously to the concealed weapon at his side. One clean shot. One moment of truth. It would blow his cover irrevocably, but it would also remove Amanda from immediate danger.

But then what? The Consortium's reach extended beyond Hayes, beyond Los Angeles, beyond American borders. Removing one piece from the board would only accelerate their timeline, only placing Amanda in the crosshairs of enemies she couldn't yet identify.

No, he had to trust she would find the clue. That she would understand its significance. That she was as extraordinary as he believed her to be.

***

Amanda moved deeper into the room, her eyes continuing their methodical sweep while her mind raced several steps ahead. Near a stack of stretched canvases, a wooden crate sat partially open, its contents half-concealed by bubble wrap and acid-free tissue. Something about its positioning deliberate, too casual, too accessible in a room where everything else was meticulously arranged.

She approached it with measured steps, conscious of Dominic's gaze on her back. With a subtle shift of her body, she partially blocked his view as she bent to examine the crate more closely. Her fingers brushed along its edge, feeling the grain of the wood, the slight dampness of newly applied shipping labels.

That's when she saw it, a small slip of paper, folded tight and tucked beneath a rolled canvas protruding from the crate. The placement was too intentional to be accidental, too hidden to be careless. With a movement disguised as adjusting her stance, she extracted the paper and palmed it, then pretended to examine the shipping label more closely.

"Anything interesting?" Dominic asked, his voice carrying that same unsettling casualness.

"Possible origin point," she replied, straightening up. "We'll need to check shipping manifests."

When Dominic turned to examine a nearby painting, Amanda used the moment to unfold the paper in her palm. Her eyes widened at what she found, not shipping information or a name, but a sequence of characters she recognized as the beginning of an FBI case file number. Not any case file, but one from a restricted database only senior agents had access to.

The implications sent a cold ripple down her spine. This wasn't an art forgery operation. This was evidence of internal corruption, someone inside the Bureau feeding information to the Eclipse Consortium, giving them advance warning of investigations, helping them stay perpetually one step ahead.

Could it be Dominic himself? The thought came unbidden, unwelcome yet impossible to dismiss. His behavior tonight, his too-convenient discovery of the hidden door, his unusual lack of excitement at their find, it all suggested foreknowledge, preparation rather than discovery.

She refolded the paper and slipped it into her coat pocket, her fingers lingering against the fabric as if to reassure herself of its presence. Her mind was already cataloging the steps she would need to take: checking the file number through back channels, identifying who accessed it recently, establishing a timeline of information leaks against Bureau operations.

"You recognize any of this?" Dominic asked, gesturing broadly at the room's contents, his expression revealing nothing.

"Some," Amanda replied, the word weighted with deliberate vagueness. "Enough."

Like light snowflakes on skin, Amanda's awareness was electric, her senses heightened by the danger she now recognized. The room transformed from a significant discovery into a possible trap. Every shadow might conceal surveillance, every object might be rigged to record their conversation. She needed to leave, carefully, naturally, without alerting Dominic to her suspicions.

"We should document this and get a full team in here," she said, allowing a controlled enthusiasm to color her voice. "A find like this might break open the whole Consortium case."

Dominic nodded, a gesture that struck her as oddly mechanical. "I'll call it in. This is definitely worth waking up the Assistant Director."

As they prepared to leave, Amanda cast one final glance at the Flemish landscape. In the painting, a solitary figure stood at the edge of a dark forest, looking out over a valley illuminated by a break in storm clouds. The juxtaposition of shadow and light, danger and possibility, struck her with new resonance. She memorized every detail, the brush technique, the frame construction, the specific colors used for the sky's delicate gradation.

If Javier was connected to this, she would find out how.

If he left this breadcrumb trail for her to follow, she would understand why. If he was playing her, manipulating her with careful charm and calculated encounters, she would expose him. And if he was something else, something she hadn't yet allowed herself to consider, then she needed to know that too.

"What do you think this means?" Dominic asked as they approached the exit, his tone studied, casual.

Above them, unseen in the warehouse's shadowed upper level, Javier allowed himself to exhale slowly as they departed. He remained motionless long after the sound of their footsteps faded, after the distant purr of Amanda's car engine dissolved into the night.

She had found the clue. Now everything depended on what she did with it, and whether he could protect her from what came next.

The game was in motion. The players revealed. And somewhere in the darkness between them, the truth waited like a predator, patient and hungry.

Chapter 9

Amanda's apartment glowed blue in the dim light of her laptop screen, her fingers tapping a restless rhythm against the keyboard. The search for Javier Morales became less of an investigation and more of a haunting, his face appeared in her dreams, his voice echoed in empty rooms. Tonight would be different. Tonight, she would find him.

She sat perched on the edge of her couch, one leg tucked beneath her, the other stretched toward her coffee table where an empty mug bore the brown ring of her fourth coffee of the day. Outside, Los Angeles hummed its eternal evening song, car horns, distant sirens, the occasional burst of laughter floating up from the street below. Inside, there was only the sound of her breathing and the soft click of keys as she searched.

"Where are you hiding?" she said to the screen, scrolling through yet another list of high-end art events. The glow painted her features in sharp relief, hollowing her cheeks and darkening her eyes until she looked like something carved from shadow rather than flesh.

Amanda's finger froze mid-scroll. There it was. A private auction in West Hollywood, invitation only, minimal publicity. The catalog listings caught her eye, three paintings matched descriptions of pieces she documented at the warehouse. She clicked through to the guest list, secured through channels that skirted the edges of protocol. Names jumped out at her, connections forming like constellations: two collectors who had little fear purchasing questionable provenance works, a gallery owner suspected of laundering money through art sales, and an expert restorer who specialized in "authentication."

Her pulse quickened. This was it. This had to be it.

She glanced at her watch, enough time to prepare. Amanda closed her laptop with a decisive snap and moved to her bedroom, where the contents of her closet offered little for infiltrating the upper echelons of LA's art scene. "Caramel" she said to herself. She pulled out the designer dress Sarah mentioned, a simple sheath hugging her athletic frame without drawing attention. Not flashy enough to stand out, expensive enough not to stand out for the wrong reasons.

No backup tonight. This wasn't an official operation, it was reconnaissance, she told herself. Information gathering. The lie settled in her chest with a thud, but she ignored it as she slipped her service weapon into a discrete thigh holster and covered it with the dress. Some habits couldn't be broken, even when they weren't necessary.

The auction house occupied the penthouse of a sleek building that screamed old money trying to look new. Amanda arrived moments after sunset, stepping from her rideshare with practiced confidence. The security at the entrance checked her invitation, a digital forgery that would hold up to cursory examination, and waved her through with the indifference of men paid to recognize wealth rather than faces.

The elevator ascended, carrying her toward whatever waited above. Amanda used the moments of solitude to steady her breathing, to shift into the persona she crafted for tonight: Amanda Chen, private art consultant to a handful of selective clients, looking for new acquisitions. Her backstory was solid, her knowledge of art sufficient to maintain the illusion unless someone dug too deep.

The doors slid open to reveal a space transformed from mere real estate into a temple of wealth and prestige. The penthouse had been stripped of anything resembling a home, its walls now displaying lit artwork, its floors cleared for the elegant circulation of people who considered a hundred thousand dollars a reasonable impulse purchase.

She accepted a flute of champagne from a passing server, using it as a prop rather than a pleasure as she began her circuit of the room. Her eyes catalogued faces, postures, conversations, looking for patterns, connections, anomalies. The paintings which drew her here displayed on the far wall, each one lit to accentuate its particular charm, each one bearing a discrete tag with a lot number rather than a price. In this world, if you had to ask, you couldn't afford it..

She turned, following the disturbance to its source, her breath catching for a moment.

Javier Morales entered the room with the easy confidence of a man who understood his own worth. Dark gray suit tailored to accentuate broad shoulders, white shirt open at the collar in calculated dishevelment, hair tousled in a way that suggested fingers rather than product. He looked like he'd stepped out of an advertisement for expensive watches or rare whiskey, the kind of man who made women turn and men reassess their own appearances.

But it wasn't Javier alone who caused the stir. On his arm was a woman whose beauty was as deliberate as a well executed brushstroke. Isabel Serrano moved with fluid grace, her black satin dress catching light and shadow in equal measure. Her deep auburn hair swept up in an elaborate and effortless crown of waves, and her eyes, those eyes moved through the room like scalpels, dissecting, analyzing, cataloguing.

They made a stunning pair, their easy intimacy suggesting a connection deeper than professional acquaintance. Isabel's hand rested in the crook of Javier's elbow with the casual possessiveness of someone who believed they belonged there. They spoke, heads inclined toward each other, sharing observations that made Isabel's lips curve in a private smile.

The twist in Amanda's stomach came unbidden, sharp and unexpected. Professional interest, she told herself. The target and his associate arrived. This was good. This was what she wanted.

The lie was even less convincing than before.

She almost glowered as they worked the room, Javier greeting people with warm handshakes and easier smiles, Isabel offering more reserved acknowledgments but commanding no less attention. They moved like dancers following choreography known only to them, seamlessly navigating the social currents of the room.

They weren't here to buy, Amanda realized. They were here to be seen, to establish presence and position. The question was why.

She shifted her attention to the three paintings. Up close, they were even more impressive, a Caravaggio-inspired still life, a landscape reminiscent of Turner, and a portrait that echoed Sargent's technique without mimicking any specific work. Beautiful pieces, masterfully executed. And if her suspicions were correct, perfect forgeries.

"Exquisite, aren't they?"

The voice beside her belonged to a middle-aged woman dripping in diamonds that caught the light with every movement. Amanda offered a practiced smile. "The brushwork on the portrait is particularly compelling."

"You have a good eye," the woman said, seeming pleased. "Are you bidding tonight?"

"Only observing for now," Amanda replied. "My client prefers I research thoroughly before committing."

The woman nodded. "Wise approach. Though I hear these particular pieces won't be available for long. Private interest, you understand."

Amanda tilted her head. "Pre-arranged sales at an auction? That's unusual."

"Oh, nothing so crass," the woman said. "But there are collectors with... specific tastes, who recognize quality when they see it."

Before Amanda could probe further, the woman's attention drifted over her shoulder, and her expression brightened. "Ah, Javier! I was hoping you'd be here tonight."

His aura enveloped her before she could see him, a shift in the air, a prickle along her spine having nothing to do with threat assessment and everything to do with something she refused to name. She turned, composing her features into polite interest rather than the complicated tangle of emotion that threatened to surface.

"Evelyn," Javier said the older woman with genuine warmth. "Still collecting beautiful things, I see."

Three pairs of eyes turned to Amanda, their attention like physical pressure. This was it, the moment of contact, of calculation, of risk.

She extended her hand, her smile cool and professional. "Amanda Chen. Art consultant."

Javier took her hand, his grip firm but not aggressive. The look when his eyes met hers contained none of the recognition she expected, just polite interest and something else, something that made her stomach tighten with an different kind of tension.

"Javier Morales," he replied, holding her hand a fraction too long. "And this is Isabel Serrano."

Isabel nodded, not offering her hand. "You're new to the circuit," she said, her voice carrying the faint music of a Spanish accent.

"New to Los Angeles," Amanda corrected. "Not to art."

A small smile played at the corners of Isabel's mouth. "Of course."

Evelyn looked between them with the bright interest of someone sensing interesting undercurrents. "Well, I should check on the Sotheby's representative. Lovely to meet you, dear," she said to Amanda before drifting away.

And then it was the three of them, agent, suspect, and the woman whose role Amanda couldn't quite determine. The space between them charged with unspoken questions and invisible calculations.

Amanda felt jealousy curl in her chest like smoke, unwelcome, irrational, dangerous. She had no claim on Javier Morales. He was a suspect, a target, very likely a criminal. And yet the sight of Isabel's hand resting on his arm, the easy intimacy of their postures, struck her with an intensity that had nothing to do with professional interest.

This was why personal involvement compromised judgment. This was what she couldn't afford.

***

Javier's hand settled on Isabel's lower back, reassuring, familiar, before dropping away. The gesture shouldn't have bothered Amanda. It did.

She stepped into their space with confident precision, her voice pitched loud enough to be heard by them alone, sharp enough to leave a mark. "Well, well. I didn't realize art forgery came with a cocktail hour."

The accusation hung in the air between them, bold and dangerous. Around them, the auction's wealthy patrons continued their elegant circling, oblivious to the tension crackling in their midst.

Javier turned to face her full in the face, and his smile, a smile should have been illegal. It transformed his face from handsome to devastating, his eyes held genuine warmth despite everything she knew about him. He looked at her as if she were a pleasant surprise rather than a calculated threat.

"You say that like you're not enjoying the party, Agent Chen."

Amanda's smile didn't falter, though something shifted behind her eyes. "You're not supposed to know that."

"I'm not supposed to know a lot of things," Javier replied, his voice dropping to a register speaking of inexplicably intimacies despite their surroundings. He took a sip of his drink, watching her over the rim with eyes that missed nothing.

Isabel stood beside him, her posture relaxed but her attention razor-sharp. She did not react to the revelation of Amanda's profession, either she already knew, or she was good at hiding surprise. Neither option was comforting.

Amanda glanced at Isabel, then back to Javier. "Friend of yours?"

"Protege," Javier said without flinching, the lie, if it was a lie, sliding from his tongue with practiced ease. "She's got real talent. I expect she'll be in the best galleries soon."

Isabel's lips curved in a small, private smile that could have meant anything from genuine pleasure at the compliment to amusement at whatever game they were playing. Amanda couldn't read her, which was unsettling, reading people was what she did best.

"How fascinating," Amanda replied, every syllable controlled. "And what exactly is your area of expertise, Ms. Serrano? Restoration? Reproduction? Or something more... creative?"

Isabel's eyes narrowed, the only indication the barb landed. "I specialize in bringing beauty back to life, Agent Chen. Some might call it resurrection."

"Isabel is beautiful," she said, smile edged in sarcasm. "But I thought you'd prefer the chic Italian supermodel type. You know, high cheekbones, venom in her voice, likes to sneak into FBI agents' apartments with a knife?"

Javier's mask didn't crack, but his knuckles whitened around the stem of his glass. It was all Amanda needed.

"Isabel, ¿podrías darnos un momento? Parece que la agente Chen tiene algunas preguntas para mí."

Isabel hesitated, her eyes moving between them with undisguised suspicion. She responded in the same language, her voice soft and musical despite the edge underneath. "Ten cuidado, Javi. Esta no es como las otras."

Amanda understood enough Spanish to catch the warning,

Be careful, Javi. This one isn't like the others, a flicker of satisfaction rushed through her. So there had been others. Other agents? Other women? Both, perhaps.

Isabel nodded, but not before giving Amanda a long, calculated look that contained equal parts assessment and warning. She moved away with the fluid grace of a woman accustomed to being watched, the crowd making space for her passage.

"Walk with me," Javier said.

She didn't answer, just followed.

They moved to a quiet corner of the gallery, near an arched doorway leading to a dim hallway. The noise of the auction fell away, replaced by the hum of tension between them.

"You've seen her," Javier said, voice soft.

Amanda turned to face him, crossing her arms. "You mean Supermodel? The woman who handcuffed me in my own apartment and threatened my best friend? Yeah. We're *acquainted*."

Something in his face shifted, concern, carefully buried.

"She's dangerous, Amanda," he said. "More than you know. She's not a collector's pretty bodyguard. She's a paid assassin. Discreet. Ruthless. Expensive."

"And you know that because?" Amanda asked, lifting a brow.

He hesitated. "Because I know the circles she runs in. And I know what she's capable of. Her name is Ginevra Sforza"

"You're not answering the question."

"I'm giving you what I can." His tone was calm, but his jaw was tight. "Don't push this. Not here."

"Why not? Because I might trip over the truth? Or because you're not ready for me to find out who you really are?"

He stepped closer, and for a moment she was aware of nothing but his scent, warm, clean, and the steady intensity in his eyes.

"I don't want you to get hurt."

Amanda faltered for a moment. Her chest tightened, torn between the sharp edge of her training and the way his voice, so muted, so certain, threaded under her skin like heat.

"Why do you care?" she asked, quieter now. "If you're part of this, if you're in bed with the Consortium, why *care* what happens to me?"

Javier didn't answer.

He didn't need to.

His gaze searched her face, and something unspoken passed between them. Not quite trust. Not yet. But something softer, older, and far more dangerous.

"I care," he said , "because I can't seem to stop."

Resolve beginning to crack, her breath catching enough to betray her. Her mind screamed warnings, but her body leaned in, drawn to the gravity between them.

He reached out, slowly, deliberately, and brushed a strand of hair from her cheek.

"I shouldn't," he said.

"But you do," she whispered back.

For one charged second, they stood there, close enough to kiss, close enough to confess, but suspended in a space too delicate to move through.

And then Amanda stepped back.

Not because she wanted to, but because she had to.

"We're not done," she said.

Javier's smile was faint, rueful. "We never are." After a brief pause he said, "What do you believe in?"

"Why would you care?" she asked.

"That's the question, isn't it?" He shifted closer, the

distance between them narrowing to something dangerous. "Why would I care what happens to the FBI agent who's been tracking me for weeks? Why would I risk exposure to warn you about things you haven't spotted? Why would I, "

He stopped, seeming to catch himself on the edge of revealing too much. The silence between them stretched, taut with unspoken words.

"You could have let me walk around blind," Amanda said. "It would have been easier for you."

"Easier isn't always better." His voice roughened, the polished charm giving way to something more raw. "Sometimes the hardest path is the only one worth taking."

The current changing direction, something shifting between them, a balance tipping. The game they'd been playing suddenly less like cat and mouse and more like something neither of them understood or controlled.

"Who are you really, Javier?" she asked, the question emerging more vulnerable than intended.

His smile returned, but different now, tinged with resignation and something that might have been regret. "I'm who you think I am, Amanda. And nothing like it at all."

Before she could press further, his attention shifted beyond her shoulder. His expression changed, hardening into something more guarded. Amanda turned, following his gaze, and spotted Isabel watching them from across the room. The other woman's face was neutral, but her eyes burned with an intensity that made Amanda's skin prickle.

"Your protege seems concerned," Amanda said, unable to keep a hint of sarcasm from her voice.

"Isabel is... protective," Javier replied. "With good reason."

"Of you, or of whatever operation you're running here

tonight?"

He laughed, the sound warming something inside her despite her resistance. "You see plots and schemes everywhere, don't you?"

"In my line of work, they usually exist."

"And in my line of work, perception is everything." He glanced at the paintings nearby, then back to her. "What if I told you that not everything is what it seems? That sometimes, the forgery protects the original rather than replacing it?"

Amanda frowned. "What are you saying?"

Javier leaned closer, his breath warm against her ear, his words so quiet she had to strain to hear them even at this proximity. "I'm saying that sometimes, Agent Chen, the criminal isn't the enemy."

He pulled back as Isabel approached them, her smile practiced but her eyes watchful. "Javi, the collector from Dubai has arrived. He's very eager to speak with you."

Javier nodded, his public persona slipping back into place with seamless ease. The man who whispered those cryptic words vanished behind the charming exterior she'd first encountered.

"Duty calls," he said to Amanda, his tone light but his eyes intent. "It's been a pleasure, Agent Chen. I'm sure we'll meet again."

"Count on it," she replied, the professional mask firm over her features.

As they moved away, Amanda took in the easy confidence of his stride, the respectful distance he now maintained from Isabel despite their earlier closeness. Nothing about him made sense. Nothing about her reaction to him made sense either.

She turned back to the painting of the separated lovers,

studying their frozen yearning with new eyes. What had Javier meant? What game was he playing? And why did she feel, with growing certainty, that they were both caught in something larger than either of them anticipated?

The questions circled in her mind like predators, patient and hungry. But beneath them, deeper and more dangerous, was the undeniable truth that she wanted to see him again, not to solve the puzzle he presented, but because something in her recognized something in him, like a lock finding its key after years of wrong attempts.

That recognition terrified her far more than any criminal ever could.

***

Amanda's apartment felt smaller tonight, the walls closer, the silence louder. She moved through the darkened rooms without turning on lights, her body casting shifting shadows as she passed the windows where moonlight spilled across the hardwood floors. Sleep would not come, not with her mind racing, not with her skin still remembering the phantom touch of his fingers against her cheek.

She lay on her back in bed, one arm flung above her head, the other resting on her stomach, fingers splayed across the thin cotton of her tank top. The ceiling above her became a screen where her mind projected the night's events in vivid detail, Javier entering the auction, Isabel at his side, the moment in the corner when everything shifted.

Moonlight painted her ceiling in soft silver, a gentle interrogation light that exposed her thoughts without mercy. Amanda closed her eyes, but that only made the images sharper, more insistent. The warmth of Javier's jacket around her shoulders. The scent of his cologne that still clung to her hair. The way his eyes darkened when she stepped close to him.

"Damn it," she said to the empty room, her voice swallowed by the silence.

She sat up with a start, sheets pooling around her waist, and reached for her phone on the nightstand. The screen's glow was harsh in the darkness, making her squint as she pulled up her messages. There was a text from Sarah, her colleague at the Bureau, sent hours ago while Amanda was still at the auction.

Any sign of our charming suspect?

Amanda's thumbs hovered over the keyboard. What could she say? Yes, I found him. Yes, I was alone with him. Yes, I almost kissed him on a balcony until our supervisor interrupted. Yes, I'm lying in bed thinking about his hands.

She set the phone down without responding.

The clock on her nightstand read 2:17 AM. Outside, a car passed on the street below, its headlights sweeping across her wall like searchlights, illuminating the organized chaos of her living space, case files stacked on the desk, running shoes by the door, a half-empty coffee mug on the nightstand. The routines and artifacts of a life dedicated to order and justice.

What if Sarah was right? What if your instincts aren't failing you, terrifying you?

The thought surfaced unbidden, a whisper from some corner of her mind she normally kept locked. Sarah had said those words, after Amanda had first mentioned her suspicions about Javier, that something about his involvement in the Eclipse Consortium cases didn't quite add up, that his patterns of appearance and disappearance seemed too calculated, too convenient.

"Sometimes the criminal isn't the enemy," he said on the

balcony, his breath warm against her ear.

Amanda clenched her sheets between her fingers, the fabric bunching in her fists. Her body ached with a want she refused to name, but her mind screamed with warning. This was how assets were compromised, how careers were destroyed, how lives were lost. Professional distance existed for a reason.

She released the sheets and lay back again, forcing her muscles to relax one by one, an exercise from her training days. But the tension coiled deeper than physical tissue, wrapped around thoughts she couldn't control, desires she couldn't dismiss.

***

Across the city, Javier stood at the window of his flat, shirt half-unbuttoned, watching the night gather around buildings that shimmered like mirages in the distance. The ice in his glass had long since melted, diluting the whiskey left untouched. The night air rolled in through open windows, carrying with it the faint scent of the ocean and the persistent hum of a city that never slept.

His apartment was a study in careful contradiction, expensive enough to maintain his cover, spartan enough to facilitate quick departure. The furniture was selected for style rather than comfort, the art on the walls valuable but not irreplaceable. Nothing that showed the man behind the mask, nothing that couldn't be abandoned at a moment's notice. The space of a man who was always prepared to become someone else.

Javier took a sip of his watered-down drink, the liquid warm against his tongue. He shouldn't be thinking about her. Shouldn't be remembering the softness of her hair when he brushed it from her face, the slight widening of her eyes when he stepped closer, the way she leaned toward him almost without thought.

Javier set his glass down on the windowsill and ran a hand through his hair, disheveling it further. He was getting distracted, losing focus. Amanda Chen was supposed to be a complication to manage, not a woman who occupied his thoughts in the quiet hours of the night.

The thought made something twist in Javier's chest, an uncomfortable heat that he recognized as protective instinct wrapped around something deeper, something he didn't dare name.

"You're in too deep," he told himself, the words dissolving in the empty air of his apartment.

But he already knew. And he wasn't sure he wanted to come up for air.

***

Amanda got up from her bed, giving up on sleep that clearly wouldn't come. She moved to the kitchen, her bare feet silent on the hardwood, and filled the kettle with water. The familiar ritual of making tea, something her mother insisted was the cure for all night-time disturbances, gave her hands something to do while her mind continued its relentless analysis.

The facts: Javier Morales appeared at multiple scenes connected to the Eclipse Consortium. He maintained relationships with known or suspected forgers and black market dealers. He possessed knowledge about security systems and art authentication that suggested insider expertise. He warned her about a trap at the warehouse, potentially exposing himself in the process.

The questions: Why warn her? Why engage with her at all

if he was part of the Consortium? What did he mean when he said the criminal wasn't the enemy? And why did Dominic seem almost personally invested in connecting Javier to the Consortium?

The kettle clicked off, steam rising in a thin column that dissipated into the cool air of her apartment. Amanda reached for a mug, then paused, her hand hovering in the cabinet.

What if Javier was undercover? The possibility occurred to her before, but she dismissed it as wishful thinking, as her attraction seeking justification. But what if?

It would explain his pattern of appearances, his knowledge, his warning at the warehouse. It would explain the careful way he navigated conversations, revealing enough to appear cooperative while maintaining plausible deniability. It would explain the sadness in his eyes when he told her he was not who he appeared to be.

But it wouldn't explain Dominic's certainty about Javier's criminal connections. Unless,

Amanda's hand fell to the counter, the mug forgotten. Unless Dominic didn't know. Or unless Dominic knew who Javier was and wanted to ensure Amanda saw him as a criminal.

Her heart raced with the implications. If Javier was undercover and Dominic knew it, why push her to investigate him? If Javier was undercover and Dominic didn't know it, who authorized his operation? And if Javier was part of the Consortium, why did every instinct she possessed tell her to trust him?

She poured steaming water over the tea bag, watching the color bleed from the leaves, staining the water in expanding tendrils. Her reflection wavered on the surface, fractured, distorted, uncertain.

***

Javier responded to Isabel's text with a simple, "We'll discuss in person." Too many eyes could be watching digital communications, too many ears listening. The Consortium's reach extended into places most people never imagined, including law enforcement. Especially law enforcement.

He moved away from the window, unbuttoning his shirt the rest of the way and draping it over a chair. The apartment was warm despite the open windows, the night air heavy with lingering heat from the day. He poured the remains of his drink down the sink, rinsed the glass, and placed it in the rack to dry. Every movement deliberate, controlled, a counterpoint to the chaos in his thoughts.

Amanda Chen complicated everything. Her investigation was getting close to truths that could get her killed. Her presence at the auction tonight had been a calculated risk, she was too smart not to follow the art connection, but her confrontation with him, their moment on the balcony, Dominic's interruption... all of it pushed the operation into dangerous territory.

He should report the complications to his handler. Should request reassignment, or at least a clear directive on how to manage an FBI agent who was getting too close to the Consortium and too close to him.

But reporting Amanda's involvement would put her on more radars than just his own. It would make her a variable to be controlled rather than an ally to be protected. And despite everything, despite the risks and complications, Javier couldn't bring himself to do that to her.

His reflection stared back at him from the bathroom mirror as he prepared for a night of restless sleep, the same face he wore for years, the same eyes that saw too much, the same mouth that told too many necessary lies. Who was he now? Agent? Criminal? Something in between?

He bent to splash water on his face, the coolness a momentary relief from thoughts that offered no resolution. When he straightened, droplets clung to his skin like tears he wouldn't allow himself to shed.

"Compromised," he said to his reflection, using the word Amanda used on the balcony. It was apt in ways she couldn't yet understand, compromised missions, compromised identities, compromised hearts.

Javier dried his face and turned away from the mirror. Tomorrow would bring new complications, new risks, new decisions. But one thing was already decided, had perhaps been decided from the moment he first laid eyes on Amanda Chen examining evidence at a crime scene with those perceptive eyes and determined set to her jaw: he would protect her, even if it meant compromising everything else.

The question was whether he could protect her from himself.

***

Amanda carried her tea back to bed, settling against the headboard with her legs drawn up beneath her. The warm mug cradled in her palms provided comfort her spinning thoughts could not. She sipped, letting the gentle bitterness ground her in the present moment rather than the maze of possibilities her mind constructed.

Facts, she reminded herself. Focus on facts, not feelings.

Fact: Javier had opportunities to harm her and didn't.

Fact: Isabel Serrano was known to have connections to art forgery circles.

Fact: The Eclipse Consortium operated with a level of

sophistication that suggested inside information.

Fact: Dominic had been unusually interested in the Consortium case from the beginning.

Fact: When Javier looked at her, she felt seen in ways that terrified and thrilled her in equal measure.

That last one wasn't a fact, at least, not the kind that would stand up in court or in a case file. But it was true, a truth her body recognized even when her mind resisted.

Amanda set her empty mug on the nightstand and slid down in bed, pulling the sheets up around her. Outside, the first hint of dawn lightened the edge of the sky, not true morning yet, but the promise of it, the certainty that darkness, however complete it seemed, was always temporary.

She closed her eyes, not expecting sleep but needing rest. Tomorrow would bring reports to file, evidence to review, questions from Dominic that would require careful navigation. Tomorrow would bring decisions about Javier Morales and the Eclipse Consortium and her own involvement in both.

But tonight, in these final hours of darkness, Amanda allowed herself to remember the almost-touch of his lips near hers, the warmth of his jacket around her shoulders, the unexpected vulnerability in his eyes when he told her he was compromised too.

Whatever Javier Morales was, criminal, agent, something in between, Amanda understood one thing with absolute certainty: their paths were now irreversibly entangled, their stories written in the same ink. Where that story led, what price it would demand, she couldn't yet see.

But she would follow it to its end, wherever that might be. Some mysteries demanded solutions, not because of professional obligation, but because they became part of who you were, questions you had to answer to understand yourself.

Javier Morales became that kind of mystery to Amanda Chen, not just a case to solve, but a mirror reflecting parts of herself she'd never recognized until his eyes cast them back at her.

Chapter 10

The message glowed on Amanda's screen with an almost radioactive intensity, its white text burning against the dark backdrop of her email. She spent three hours combing through financial reports, tracing shell companies that dissolved like sugar in rain, and now this, five words made her coffee go cold in her hand. "El Fantasma will be there." Her breath caught, not quite a gasp, more like the moment between pulling a trigger and the recoil hitting your hand.

The Los Angeles FBI Field Office hummed with the drowsy energy of a night shift, phones ringing at half the daytime frequency, footsteps echoing through hallways grew wider after dark. Amanda Chen sat alone in her cubicle, surrounded by the glow of monitors and the wreckage of her dinner: a half-eaten container of lo mein from the place downstairs that knew her order by heart. The digital clock on her desk read 10:07 PM, a time when most agents retreated to families or empty apartments or the comfort of a bar stool.

She read the message again, her dark eyes narrowing. "Shipment incoming. Pier 37. Midnight. El Fantasma will be there."

No sender information. No identifying markers. The IP address would be masked, she knew without checking. But something in her gut, something deeper than training or intuition, told her this was real.

El Fantasma. The Ghost.

A shadow that haunted international law enforcement for years. The Eclipse Consortium's most elusive operative, leaving fingerprints so faint they might as well have been myths. Except the bodies were real. The missing artifacts were real. The corrupted officials and the laundered money and the trails that went cold when they were at their hottest, all real.

Amanda's fingers hovered over the keyboard, uncertainty flickering across her face like a passing shadow. Protocol dictated she alert her supervisor immediately. Forward the message. Assemble a team. Yet her hand remained suspended in midair, caught between duty and something else.

Her gaze drifted to the corkboard beside her desk, where photographs and maps formed a constellation of connections. At the center, a question mark where a face should be. Three years she'd been building this case, piecing together fragments while the Bureau shifted resources to more "pressing" concerns. Three years since the operation went sideways, leaving her with a puckered scar on her lower back and a promise to herself, she would find the one responsible.

"Midnight," she said, glancing at her watch. Less than two hours.

If she followed protocol, they'd never make it in time. Forms would need signing, approvals would need granting, and El Fantasma would slip away again like smoke through fingers.

Her coffee went from tepid to cold, the cream forming a skin on its surface. She pushed it aside and stood, decision crystallizing in her mind with the clarity of a diamond cutting glass. Her chair rolled backward, bumping against the partition with a soft thud that punctuated her resolve.

From her desk drawer, she retrieved her service weapon, checking it with practiced efficiency. The weight of it against her palm was reassuring, solid in a world of digital ghosts and whispers. Next came her badge, the metal cool against her fingers as she clipped it to her belt.

Her reflection in the darkened window showed a woman transformed, not by any physical change, but by the quiet intensity that straightened her spine and hardened the set of her jaw. The athletic build which once made her feel inadequate beside her ex-husband's new flame was now perfect for what lay ahead: lean muscle, quick reflexes, nothing to slow her down.

Amanda pulled her hair back into a tight ponytail, her movements economical and precise. No jewelry. Nothing that could catch or reflect light. From her gym bag, she extracted a set of dark clothes, practical, forgettable, perfect for blending into shadows.

The women's bathroom was empty, fluorescent lights humming overhead like restless insects. She changed quickly, the familiar ritual of preparation calming her racing thoughts. Black tactical pants. Fitted dark blue shirt. Lightweight jacket with inside pockets for credentials and extra ammunition. Boots laced tight.

As she washed her hands, Amanda caught her own gaze in the mirror. The woman who stared back had eyes like obsidian, hard, reflective, revealing nothing. A question floated to the surface of her mind, unbidden: What if it's a trap?

She dried her hands, considering. Of course it could be a trap. El Fantasma hadn't evaded capture this long by being careless. But something about the message, its brevity, its directness, the specific mention of Pier 37, suggested authenticity. Intelligence, not enticement.

And if it was a trap... well, she hadn't survived this long by being careless either.

Back at her desk, she packed a small go-bag: flashlight, zip ties, first aid supplies, an extra magazine for her Glock. Her movements controlled, automatic, muscle memory built through years of training and field work. Her mind, raced ahead to Pier 37, mapping approaches and exits, calculating risks.

Amanda shut down her computer and gathered her things. As she moved through the office, she nodded to the few agents still at their desks, her expression neutral, betraying nothing of her intentions. At the security desk near the exit, she paused.

"Heading out, Chen?" asked the night guard, a friendly veteran nearing retirement.

"Just going to grab some real coffee," she replied, gesturing at the empty cup in her hand. "The stuff upstairs must have been filtered through a gym sock."

He laughed, the sound echoing in the marble lobby. "Don't work too hard. Whatever it is, it'll still be there tomorrow."

Amanda smiled, the expression not quite reaching her eyes. "That's what I'm afraid of," she said, stepping into the elevator.

As the doors closed, sealing her in momentary solitude, her pulse quickened. The message might be bogus, the tip false. El Fantasma might be miles away, laughing at the FBI's futile attempts to catch a ghost.

But if there was even a fraction of a chance, even the slimmest possibility of bringing down the phantom who haunted her professional life for so long, she had to take it.

The elevator reached the parking garage, doors sliding open with a soft chime. Amanda stepped out, keys already in hand. Her footsteps echoed against concrete as she moved toward her car, each step precise and deliberate, carrying her closer to the confrontation she'd been preparing for since that bullet tore through her back in Istanbul.

If El Fantasma would be at Pier 37 tonight, then so would she. And this time, one way or another, the ghost would reveal itself.

***

The Port of Los Angeles stretched like a mechanical beast at rest, its metal limbs, cranes and containers, frozen against the night sky. Amanda killed her headlights half a mile before the entrance, letting momentum carry her car to a soundless stop in the shadow of an abandoned warehouse. Midnight passed in the three minutes it took her to scale the fence, her body moving with the fluid precision of someone who had long ago memorized the limitations of muscle and bone. The fog rolled in from the Pacific, thick and spectral, swallowing the security lights until they were nothing more than hazy orbs suspended in a milky void.

Amanda landed on the other side of the fence with almost no sound, her boots absorbing the impact. She drew her weapon, the familiar weight an extension of her arm, and paused to orient herself. Pier 37 lay to the northeast, a quarter mile of rust-streaked containers and shadow-strewn alleyways between her position and her destination. The tang of salt and diesel hung in the air, undercut by the mineral scent of the fog itself, water and pollution suspended in equal measure.

She moved like water finding the path of least resistance, each step calculated to minimize noise. The concrete beneath her feet cracked and weathered, painted with decades of maritime commerce and neglect. Puddles reflected fragmented light, and she skirted them, knowing that even the softest splash could travel in this hollow silence.

Her breath formed small clouds that dissipated into the greater fog. Despite the chill that seeped through her jacket, a thin film of sweat gleamed on her forehead. Not from exertion, but from the electric current of adrenaline that hummed beneath her skin, sharpening her senses until every shadow breathed a life of its own.

Shipping containers loomed on either side, stacked like the building blocks of giants. Red, blue, green, their colors muted by night and mist, their surfaces slick with condensation. Some bore the scars of oceanic crossings, salt corrosion, dents from rough seas, while others appeared newer, their corporate logos still crisp against the metal canvas.

Amanda paused at an intersection, pressing her back against a container as she listened. Water lapped against the pilings somewhere to her right. A seagull called once, then fell silent. Nothing else. She checked her watch: 12:17. If El Fantasma was here, he was punctual. If this was a trap, it was a patient one.

She withdrew a compact flashlight from her jacket, keeping the beam low and narrow as she swept it across the ground. The concrete here was different, cleaner, marked with recent tire tracks that cut through a thin layer of grime. Someone had been here recently.

Following the tracks, Amanda moved deeper into the maze

of metal. The flashlight cast strange shadows that shifted and elongated with each step, transforming simple objects into threatening silhouettes that dissolved upon closer inspection. The fog grew thicker near the water, reducing visibility to less than twenty feet in any direction.

Her training kept her calm, but beneath it, something else stirred, a cocktail of anticipation and dread that she refused to acknowledge. For three years, the specter of El Fantasma haunted her professional life. The architect of operations that spanned continents. The ghost behind the Eclipse Consortium's most audacious successes. The phantom whose existence some in the Bureau began to doubt.

A sound drifted through the fog, the soft scrape of shoe against concrete, barely audible above the ambient noise of the port. Amanda froze, her breath caught in her lungs, her fingers tightening around her weapon. She killed the flashlight with a flick of her thumb, plunging herself into relative darkness.

Twenty yards ahead, a silhouette materialized from the mist. Tall, male, standing with the relaxed posture of someone at ease in their environment. He stood near a stack of crates, his back half-turned to her, head inclined as though listening for something. Even through the fog, she saw the confident set of his shoulders, the way his stance suggested both alertness and control.

El Fantasma. It had to be.

Amanda moved forward, each step a careful negotiation between speed and silence. She kept her weapon at the ready, her eyes never leaving the figure ahead. The distance between them closed, twenty yards, fifteen, ten, her heart keeping time with a rhythm that peaked with every foot of ground she gained.

At five yards, she paused, taking shelter behind the corner of a container. From here, she could make out more details: dark hair, broad shoulders encased in what appeared to be an expensive suit jacket, a hand that may have drifted toward what might be a concealed weapon.

She took a breath, steadying herself for what came next. In her mind, she rehearsed the words, FBI, hands where I can see them, you're under arrest, the ritual language of apprehension that came as natural as breathing.

The figure shifted, turning obliquely, and Amanda tightened her grip on her weapon. This was it. The moment that would define her career, that would justify every late night and obsessive hour spent building this case.

She stepped forward, emerging from cover, weapon raised. "FBI! Don't mo...,"

The words died in her throat as the man turned toward her, his face emerging from shadow into the weak glow of a distant security light.

Javier Morales.

Everything in Amanda froze, mind, body, breath. Her heart slammed against her ribs like a warning. The world narrowed to a pinpoint, then expanded again with dizzying speed.

She had always suspected his connection to the Eclipse Consortium. But this... this was confirmation of her worst suspicions and deepest fears. Javier wasn't just connected to the Consortium. He wasn't simply a facilitator or an associate.

He was El Fantasma.

His eyes locked with hers, filled with equal parts shock and something else. Something raw and complex that she couldn't decode in the split second their gazes met. Recognition. Alarm. And something that looked impossibly like relief.

"Javier...?" she said, disbelief crashing into her like a wave.

His lips parted, forming what might have been her name, but before he could speak,

The crack of gunfire shattered the silence. A bullet ricocheted off the container beside Amanda's head, sending sparks flying into the fog like fireflies. A second shot followed, then a third, the sounds echoing across the water and between the metal canyon walls of the containers.

Amanda dropped into a crouch, pivoting to locate the source of the gunfire. More shots rang out, coming from somewhere to her left, higher up, a sniper on one of the stacked containers. She squinted through the fog but saw nothing except vague shapes and the occasional muzzle flash.

She was exposed. The realization hit her with brutal clarity. She was positioned in a narrow corridor between containers, with only Javier's position ahead offering any cover. The shooter had a clear line of sight, and the next bullet might not miss.

Amanda started to move, to scramble for better position, but the timing was wrong. As she shifted her weight, another shot exploded from the darkness. She could almost feel its trajectory, a line of deadly intent cutting through the fog directly toward her.

Javier was already moving, a blur of purpose and desperation. He lunged forward, covering the distance between them in three long strides, his arms outstretched. Amanda saw it all with strange clarity, the determination in his face, the precise moment his decision crystallized into action.

His arms wrapped around her as another shot rang out. The impact came a fraction of a second later, a jolt that passed from his body to hers as they collided. His momentum carried them both backward, away from the line of fire, behind the shelter of a container.

They hit the ground hard, Javier's weight on top of her driving the air from her lungs. For a moment, everything was confusion, the cold concrete against her back, the pressure of his body, the sound of more bullets striking metal somewhere above their heads.

And then it registered. Warm. Wet. Spreading across her hands where they gripped his torso.

Blood.

Not her blood. His.

"Javier!" she gasped, rolling him onto his side, keeping them both low as the gunfire continued overhead.

His face was pale even in the dim light, his breathing shallow but controlled. A dark stain spread across his shirt, below his left shoulder, black in the darkness but with the unmistakable copper scent of blood.

He took a bullet meant for her. The ghost she'd been hunting, the criminal mastermind responsible for deaths across three continents, threw himself into the path of a bullet to save her life.

Nothing made sense. Nothing aligned with the profile constructed over time, with the evidence gathered, with the narrative she built of who and what El Fantasma was.

Yet here he was, bleeding in her arms, his hazel eyes fixed on her face with an intensity that made her chest constrict. One of his hands reached up, fingers brushing against her cheek in a gesture so gentle it belonged to another time, another place, another version of themselves.

"Amanda," he said, her name almost inaudible above the continued gunfire and the sudden pounding of blood in her ears. There was recognition in the way he said it, intimate knowledge that spoke of more than their brief encounters.

She tightened her grip on him, one arm supporting his upper body while her other hand pressed against the wound, trying to staunch the bleeding. The irony not lost on her, after years of hunting El Fantasma, she was now fighting to keep him alive.

Because whatever the truth was, whatever lay beneath the layers of deception and counter-deception, one thing was clear: the man in her arms saved her life. And that single act rewrote everything she thought she knew.

***

Blood had a way of making time viscous, stretching seconds into miniature eternities. Amanda pressed her palm against the wound in Javier's shoulder, feeling the warm seep between her fingers, watching his face for signs of shock. They were wedged in a narrow space between shipping containers, the metal walls amplifying the sound of his labored breathing. Five feet away, bullets continued to pepper the ground where they'd been standing, each impact a reminder of how narrowly they'd escaped death.

"Keep pressure on it," she said with emphasis, shrugging out of her jacket with one hand while maintaining pressure with the other. The fabric tore as she ripped a strip from the lining, folding it into a makeshift bandage. "This is going to hurt."

"I didn't know if I could trust you then," she replied, pressing the bandage against the wound. "I still don't."

He hissed through his teeth, the sound sharp and sudden, but made no move to stop her. His normally perfect hair was damp with sweat, clinging to his forehead in a way that made him look younger, more vulnerable than the suave figure who showed up in her investigation with suspicious regularity.

"I... I wasn't lying," he stammered, his voice steadier than his complexion suggested it should be. "I never wanted to lie to you."

Amanda's throat tightened, something between disbelief and bitter amusement rising in her chest. "What are you talking about? Your whole existence is a lie. El Fantasma. The ghost. The mastermind behind the Eclipse Consortium. I've spent three years building a case against a shadow, and it turns out you've been right in front of me, flirting over champagne while people die."

Javier's eyes, those damnable hazel eyes, locked onto hers with an intensity that made her pause. "I'm Secret Service. Deep cover. El Fantasma's not me, it's someone else. Higher than anyone realizes."

The words hit Amanda like physical blows, each one reorganizing her understanding of the past three years. Her fingers, sticky with his blood, stilled against the bandage. "Secret Service? Not FBI or CIA?"

"Treasury Department investigation at first," he said, each word measured, as though it cost him something to speak. "Eclipse Consortium has been laundering money through art acquisitions, high-end real estate. But it evolved. We discovered connections to diplomatic security breaches, classified information leaks. My position was... uniquely advantageous."

Another burst of gunfire, closer now, splintered the wood of a crate beyond their hiding place. Both of them ducked lower, Amanda's body half-shielding his despite his larger frame.

"You let me chase you," she said when the shooting paused, her voice tight with emotions she couldn't name. "Suspect you. You let me,"

"I had to," he said, his voice ragged. "It was the only way to protect the operation. To protect you."

Amanda stared at him, emotion threatening to crack her down the middle. What he was saying contradicted three years of meticulous investigation, of evidence carefully assembled, of a profile she constructed with obsessive precision. Yet it aligned with the inexplicable gaps in that same profile, the contradictions she had never quite resolved.

Most of all, it aligned with the man who had now taken a bullet for her.

"Why would you need to protect me?" she asked, the question softer than she intended.

Javier's hand found hers, his fingers wrapping around her wrist with surprising strength for a man who had lost as much blood as the stain on his shirt suggested. "Because people who get too close to the truth about El Fantasma tend to disappear. Istanbul wasn't a coincidence, Amanda. You were getting too close even then."

The scar on her lower back throbbed at the mention of Istanbul, a phantom pain from the bullet that had nearly severed her spine. She had always believed it was a random act of violence during an operation gone wrong, wrong place, wrong time. But if what Javier was saying was true...

"How long have you known who I am?" she asked.

"Since before you knew who I was," he replied, a ghost of his usual charm flickering across his face. "Your reputation precedes you, Special Agent Chen. The Bureau's rising star in transnational criminal investigations. The agent who never quits."

Another round of gunfire erupted, closer this time. They

both flinched. Dust and splinters rained down from above as bullets struck the container sheltering them. Whoever was shooting was sweeping the area in search of targets.

"We can't stay here," Amanda said, calculating angles and escape routes in her head. "We need to get you to a hospital."

"You need to go," he said, struggling to sit upright, his face contorting with the effort. "I can't just let you, "

"You can't just let me drag your bleeding ass to safety after you took a bullet for me?" she said, anger flaring suddenly. "That's what's going to happen."

"You have to," he said, pressing something into her hand. It was small, metallic, warm from being kept close to his body. A flash drive. "Take this. It'll help you find the real leader. I'll find you later... if I can."

Amanda looked down at the object in her palm, then back at Javier. In the dim light filtering through gaps in the containers, his face was all shadows and angles, but his eyes remained clear, urgent.

"What's on this?" she asked.

"Everything I've gathered over two years undercover. Bank accounts. Shell companies. Meeting locations. Most importantly, evidence pointing to the real identity of El Fantasma." He paused, swallowing hard. "It's not complete. There are gaps I still need to fill. But it's enough to keep you moving in the right direction, and enough to get you killed if the wrong people know you have it."

Amanda closed her fingers around the flash drive, its edges pressing into her skin. Her instincts warred with every vulnerable nerve in her body. As an FBI agent, she should arrest him, wounded or not. Take him in, verify his story, process the evidence according to protocol. But if what he was saying was true, if he really was deep cover, if the real El Fantasma was still out there, standard procedure would get them both killed.

"Why give this to me now?" she asked. "Why not take it to your handlers?"

Javier's expression darkened. "Because I don't know who I can trust anymore. The operation's been compromised. Someone on the inside has been feeding information to the Consortium. That's why I came alone tonight."

"And I walked right into it," Amanda said, realization dawning. "The message I received, it was meant to lure you out, wasn't it? Not me."

He nodded. "They're cleaning house. Anyone who gets too close to the truth becomes a liability."

The implications settled over her like a cold shadow. If Javier was telling the truth, she had stumbled into something far more complex than she realized. Not only a criminal organization, but a conspiracy that had tendrils in the very agencies meant to fight it.

"I can protect you," she said, the words emerging before she was able to examine them. "Come with me. We'll figure this out together."

His smile was sad, almost tender. "They'll be watching you now. If I'm with you, I'm a liability. And if I go in officially, I'll have to surrender that drive to people I can't trust." He shook his head. "No, I need to disappear. Regroup. Find another angle."

Another burst of gunfire, this time accompanied by voices, distant but approaching. They were running out of time.

"How do I know this isn't an elaborate setup?" Amanda asked, even as she helped him to his feet, supporting his weight as he swayed. "How do I know I can trust you?"

Javier leaned against her, his breath warm against her hair. "You don't. But you're trusting your instincts right now, and they've gotten you this far."

Their eyes met, and for a moment, the chaos around them receded. There was something in his gaze that reached past her professional defenses, something that spoke to the woman beneath the badge. In another life, in another story, this might have been the moment where they kissed, desperate and passionate, a collision of desire and circumstance.

Instead, Amanda helped him to his feet, watching as he steadied himself against the container wall. "There's a maintenance corridor fifty yards east," she said, gesturing with her chin. "It leads to a service road outside the main gate. No cameras."

He nodded, already shifting his weight away from her, preparing to stand alone. "I'll find you," he promised. "When it's safe."

Amanda stared at him, at the man she'd almost kissed on a balcony at the Getty, who haunted her thoughts during sleepless nights, and who now bled for her on a freezing dock. With trembling hands, she helped him to his feet, their fingers lingering in contact for a heartbeat longer than necessary.

"Don't die," she said, "I have questions that need answers."

The corner of his mouth lifted in a shadow of his usual smile. "I've always liked that about you, Amanda. Your priorities."

Then he was moving, slipping away from her, a figure dissolving into the fog like the ghost he had been named for. He disappeared while her eyes strained to follow, the flash drive clutched in her palm like a talisman, its edges cutting into her skin, a physical reminder that what happened was real, not a product of adrenaline and wishful thinking.

El Fantasma was still out there. But so was Javier Morales. And for the first time in three years, Amanda wasn't sure which ghost she was more determined to find.

***

The chaos ended, leaving behind a stillness that felt artificial, like a held breath. Amanda stood alone on the dock, weapon still drawn but pointing at nothing, the acrid odor of gunpowder hanging in the air like invisible smoke. The shooters vanished, melted back into whatever shadows had birthed them, leaving only scattered bullet casings that winked dully in the security lights. Blood marked the spot where Javier fell, already turning brown at the edges, a Rorschach blot that asked questions she wasn't ready to answer.

In the distance, a siren wailed, port security, perhaps, or police responding to reports of gunfire. Too late to be useful, too soon for her to linger. Amanda holstered her weapon with hands that remained steady despite everything, a professional reflex that persisted even as her mind reeled.

The fog thinned somewhat, revealing the angular silhouettes of cranes against the night sky. She moved silently back through the maze of containers, retracing her steps with the focused attention of someone who knows they're leaving evidence behind with every footfall. Her jacket torn, the makeshift bandage she created now missing, given to a man who might be a hero or a liar or both.

As she scaled the fence back to where she left her car, Amanda felt the weight of the flash drive in her pocket, pressing against her thigh like a secret trying to burn its way out. She slipped behind the wheel, started the engine, and pulled away from the port with her headlights still off, guided only by the ambient glow of the city and the muscle memory of the roads she traveled earlier that night.

Only when she was three miles from the port did she switch on the headlights, the sudden illumination making the world seem too sharp, too real after the dreamy quality of the fog-shrouded docks. Her reflection in the rear view mirror was a stranger's, hair escaping from its ponytail, a smudge of dirt or blood across one cheekbone, eyes that were darker than usual, pupils still dilated from adrenaline.

The drive back to her apartment in downtown LA's Historic Core neighborhood took twenty-three minutes. Amanda counted each one, focusing on the mechanical act of driving to keep her thoughts from spiraling into chaos. Left turn, stop-light, right turn, overpass. The rhythm of routine navigation anchored her to the moment, preventing her from dwelling on either the past or the future.

She locked the door behind her weapon in hand, engaged the deadbolt, and slid the chain into place. Standard proce-dure, but tonight the routine was hollow, inadequate protec-tion against the implications of what transpired at the port, Amanda methodically cleared the apartment, the memory of Ginevra still fresh in her mind. "Clear." she thought.

Without bothering to turn on more than a single lamp, Amanda moved to the bathroom, stripping off her blood-stained clothes and stepping under the shower's scalding spray. As water turned pink, then clear, carrying away the physical evidence of the night's events but doing nothing to wash away the questions that circled her mind like hungry predators.

Afterwards, she sat on the edge of her bed, still wrapped in a towel, hair dripping onto her shoulders. The flash drive lay on her nightstand, innocuous and ordinary except for the brownish smear of blood along one edge. She picked it up, turning it between her fingers, feeling its weight, literal and metaphorical.

If what Javier had told her was true, this small object contained enough information to upend three years of investigation. To rewrite her understanding of the Eclipse Consortium and its elusive leader. To expose corruption within the very agencies tasked with fighting such organizations.

And if he was lying? If this was an elaborate misdirection, a way to throw her off the scent or feed her false information?

Each time, telling herself he was a person of interest, nothing more. Each time, she catalogued his movements, his associations, his apparent connections to the Consortium. And each time, she failed to convince herself that he was what her evidence suggested: a criminal, a facilitator, maybe El Fantasma himself.

Now she understanding why. Her instincts had been trying to tell her what her mind refused to accept, that there was more to Javier Morales than met the eye. That the contradiction she sensed in him was real, not imagined.

Secret Service. Deep cover. A man living a double life so convincing that it fooled not just the Consortium but also the FBI's best analysts. Including her.

Amanda changed into clean clothes, cotton sleep shorts and a faded Berkeley Swimming t-shirt, a uniform of sorts for the few hours of rest she permitted herself between cases. She plugged the flash drive into her personal laptop, not her Bureau-issued one, and waited as it scanned for malware before revealing its contents.

Folders appeared on her screen, labeled with dates and

locations. The most recent titled "Getty Museum - Los Angeles," dated one week ago. She clicked it open, revealing a series of photos: Javier in conversation with a silver-haired man she recognized as the museum's director; the same man meeting later with a tall statuesque woman whose face turned away from the camera; a final image of a painting being packed for transport, its provenance documents clearly visible.

Now that we have met, I have no doubt the woman is Ginevra.

Not conclusive evidence of anything, but suggestive. A thread to pull, a path to follow.

She closed the laptop without exploring further. Better to review everything, in daylight, when her mind was clearer. For now, the existence of the files was enough to suggest Javier had been telling the truth, or at least part of it.

Amanda moved to the window, pulling back the curtain to look out at the city. Los Angeles sprawled beneath her in a glittering tapestry of lights, each one representing lives being lived in parallel to her own. Somewhere out there, Javier was nursing a bullet wound, fighting for his life. Somewhere out there, the real El Fantasma was orchestrating their next move, unaware that their identity might now be compromised.

She let the curtain fall back into place, decision crystallizing in her mind with the clarity of a diamond cutting glass. She would review the evidence on her own first. Verify what could be verified. Build a case that was airtight before bringing it to anyone else. And in the meantime, she would look for Javier, not to arrest him, but to understand. To get answers to questions that had nothing to do with the case and everything to do with the man who had taken a bullet for her.

The scar on her lower back tingling, a phantom echo. She pressed her hand against it, remembering the pain, the fear, the determination that followed. If that attack hadn't been random, if it had been a targeted attempt to eliminate her when she got too close to the truth, then she had been on the right track all along, just following the wrong map.

Amanda moved back to the bed, sitting on its edge, the exhaustion pressing down on her shoulders. Sleep would come, but not yet. First, she needed to plan, to think, to recalibrate her understanding of the past three years in light of what she now knew, or thought she knew.

She lay back, staring at the ceiling, the flash drive clutched in her hand like a talisman. The question that haunted her for weeks now had an answer. Javier wasn't who she thought. But who was he, really? A hero? A manipulator? Something in between?

Outside, the city pulsed in silence, millions of lives intersecting in ways both meaningful and mundane. But for Amanda, there was only one intersection that mattered now, the point where her path crossed with Javier's, changing the trajectory of both.

The chase was far from over. It had only just begun.

11

Chapter 11

Amanda's government-issue sedan melted into the shadows of a leaning palm tree, hidden just enough to avoid curious eyes. The sun hung close to the Pacific horizon, painting the small beach town in deceptive tranquility. She sat motionless behind the wheel, her training telling her to leave, her instincts urging her forward, and somewhere between those warring impulses, a dangerous curiosity bloomed, the kind that derailed careers more promising than hers.

She killed the engine and listened to the tick of cooling metal. Her phone lay face-up on the passenger seat, Javier's message still illuminated: "Meet me. No more lies.-J." Six words that dragged her across three counties against direct orders, a professional suicide note authored by her own hand.

Amanda checked her watch. Fifteen minutes early. Tactically sound. She reached beneath her blazer, confirming the reassuring presence of her Glock. The weight anchored her to reality, a reminder of who she was and why she was here. Special Agent Amanda Chen, not some lovesick rookie falling for pretty words from a suspect.

She stepped from the car, the sea air tangling in her practical ponytail. The dark slacks and white button-down marked her as an outsider in this world of board shorts and sundresses, but blending in had never been her priority. Her badge and ID remained tucked in her pocket, this wasn't an official operation. There would be no backup, no extraction plan.

No witnesses to her career implosion.

The beach stretched to her right, a curved smile of sand separating civilization from the endless blue of the Pacific. Families were packing up their umbrellas and coolers, surrendering the shore to the approaching evening. Amanda scanned each face, each group, each potential threat. The Eclipse Consortium had eyes everywhere, a fact that her supervisor emphasized during their last heated exchange.

"Chen, you're off this case. That's an order." Deputy Director Wallace's voice echoed in her memory. "Your objectivity is compromised."

Her jaw tightened at the recollection. Years of immaculate service, and one suspect, one enigmatic, infuriating suspect, had been enough to question her professionalism.

She hadn't told Wallace about the text. Hadn't told anyone. She had only told them she followed up on a lead at the port which led to the gunshots.

The wind picked up, carrying the scent of salt and fried food from a nearby cafe. Amanda moved with calculated casualness, each step measured, her eyes sweeping the surroundings. Three exits from the main street. Two potential bottlenecks. One police cruiser parked outside the local hardware store, the officer inside laughing with the clerk.

Her mind cataloged it all, even as it replayed fragments of her encounters with Javier Morales. The art gala in Los Angeles where she'd first spotted him, his tailored suit and easy charm making a mockery of his criminal file. The brief, electric moment their hands touched as he passed her a champagne flute. The way his eyes lingered on hers, both of them aware of the cat-and-mouse game unfolding beneath the veneer of polite society.

Subsequent encounters, each one a dance of half-truths and veiled intentions. Each one leaving her more certain that Javier was embedded in the Eclipse Consortium, and certain that something about his involvement didn't add up.

The wind tugged at her hair, loosening strands from her ponytail. Amanda tucked them behind her ear with an irritated gesture. Her ex-husband had always complained about her hair, its tendency to escape whatever style she attempted, its refusal to be tamed. "A reflection of its owner," he said, not unkindly, before leaving her for a colleague whose blonde locks apparently posed fewer challenges.

Amanda pushed the thought away. Ancient history. Irrelevant.

She approached the cafe Javier specified in his text. "The Blue Shell, where the dunes meet the boardwalk." It was a weathered single-story building painted a faded cerulean, with a wooden deck extending toward the beach. Half a dozen tables dotted the deck, most empty now as the day waned. A string of unlit patio lights swayed overhead.

Amanda slowed her pace, every sense heightened. This was the moment any trap would spring, the exposed approach to an unknown territory. Her throat tightened, not with fear but with the uncomfortable recognition that part of her was hoping Javier would be there. That his message had been genuine.

And now he wanted to meet. Alone. "No more lies," he'd

written, as if lies weren't the foundation of everything he was.

Amanda circled the cafe once, noting the rear exit, the kitchen windows, the narrow alley that ran behind it. Standard procedure, though nothing about this meeting was standard. Her exposure was almost complete, not just physically but emotionally, as if Javier could see through the professional armor she spent years perfecting.

The sensation unnerved her more than any threat of physical danger.

A movement caught her eye, a figure standing at the edge of the deck, his back to the water. Even from this distance, she recognized the set of his shoulders, the casual-yet-deliberate way he held himself. Javier wore dark jeans and a light blue button-down with the sleeves rolled to the elbows, sunglasses shielding his eyes. One hand rested in his pocket. He looked like any other vacationer enjoying the view.

Amanda's pulse quickened. For a moment, she allowed herself to acknowledge the attraction that had been simmering beneath her professional veneer since their first meeting. Javier Morales moved through the world with a confidence that bordered on arrogance, but there was something else there too, an intelligence that matched her own, a complexity that her analytically-trained mind couldn't help but want to unravel.

He turned, as if sensing her presence, and removed his sunglasses. Even at this distance, impact of his gaze struck her, direct, intense, with an odd vulnerability.

As the distance between them closed, as Javier's face came into sharper focus, the strong line of his jaw, the hint of stubble, the wariness in his eyes that hadn't been there in their previous encounters, Amanda's equilibrium shifted deep in her core. A dangerous recognition that whatever was about to happen between them would change everything.

He didn't move as she approached, didn't speak, just watched her with an expression that seemed to strip away her defenses. For once, the charming mask he wore was absent, replaced by something raw and unfiltered.

Amanda stopped a few feet away from him, close enough to see the slight rise and fall of his chest, the tension in his shoulders. Close enough to notice the faint scar above his left eyebrow that hadn't been mentioned in any of his files.

"Agent Chen," he said, her title a gentle acknowledgment of the line she crossed by coming here.

"Morales," she replied, her voice steadier than she felt.

The ocean murmured behind him, waves kissing the shore with hypnotic persistence. A seagull cried overhead. And between them stretched a silence filled with unasked questions and unspoken truths.

But as Javier's eyes held hers, as the wind carried his scent, subtle cologne mixed with salt air, to her, Amanda faced an uncomfortable truth: she was here because, against all logic and training, she needed to know who Javier Morales really was.

And that need terrified her far more than any danger he might represent.

***

The space between them hummed with unspoken accusations. Amanda stood her ground, feet planted on the weathered boards of the cafe deck, the ocean a restless witness at Javier's back. His eyes, those perceptive hazel eyes invaded her thoughts for weeks, searched her face with an intensity that made her skin prickle. The charming criminal she'd been tracking had vanished, replaced by something far more dangerous: a man with nothing left to lose.

"I thought you'd bring a team," Javier said, his voice low enough that only she could hear it, intimate in a way that sent an involuntary shiver down her spine.

Amanda kept her expression neutral, professional. "I thought you'd be halfway to Argentina by now."

A ghost of a smile touched his lips, not the practiced charm she saw him deploy at galas and auction houses, but something smaller, more genuine. "You've been tracking my movements."

"It's my job to know where suspects might run."

"Is that all I am to you? A suspect?"

The question hung between them, loaded with implications that Amanda refused to acknowledge. The cafe emptied as evening approached, leaving them alone on the deck. A lone server wiped down tables several yards away, paying them no attention. The ocean breeze carried the scent of salt and cooling sand, a peaceful backdrop to their tense exchange.

"What am I supposed to think, Javier?" She crossed her arms, a defensive posture she immediately regretted. "Every lead in this case traces back to you. Every transaction, every smuggled artifact, every connection to the Eclipse Consortium."

"And yet, no evidence." His eyes never left hers. "Nothing substantial enough for an arrest. Doesn't that strike you as convenient?"

Amanda's training in forensic psychology taught her to read people, to catch the micro-expressions that betrayed deception. But Javier Morales had always been a blank page to her skills, either exceptionally controlled or, more disturbingly, genuinely honest when he claimed innocence.

"You're not easy to pin down," she said.

"I wasn't trying to be." He took a step closer, and she fought the urge to step back. "Until now."

The dying sunlight caught the planes of his face, highlighting the tension in his jaw, the wariness in his eyes that contrasted with his casual stance. He looked exhausted beneath his composure, Amanda realized, the kind of bone-deep fatigue that came from carrying secrets too heavy to share.

He leaned in, his voice dropping even lower. "There's a mole, Amanda. Inside the Bureau. That's why I've been evasive. That's why I've kept you in the dark."

Amanda's stomach clenched. The accusation was outrageous, the kind of diversion she'd expect from someone in his position. And yet... certain inconsistencies in the investigation suddenly aligned in her mind, breadcrumbs leading to a truth she refused to see.

"That's convenient," she said, but her voice lacked conviction. "Blame a mysterious mole for your crimes."

"Not mysterious." His eyes hardened. "Someone close to your investigation. Someone feeding information to the Consortium about every move you make."

A face flashed in Amanda's mind, Deputy Director Wallace's right-hand man, always present for briefings, always watching her with calculating eyes. The one who pushed the hardest to remove her from the case when she started connecting Javier to the Consortium's activities in ways that didn't align with their working theory.

"Dominic," she said, almost to herself.

Javier's expression shifted, a flash of surprise quickly masked. "You've suspected something."

"I didn't say that."

"You didn't have to."

Amanda turned away, needing distance from his scrutiny. The ocean stretched before them, endless and indifferent to human complications. Her mind raced through fragments of evidence, operations that had inexplicably failed, tips that led nowhere, the strange timing of Consortium members always being one step ahead of Bureau raids.

"The artifacts destined for Dubai," she said after a moment, piecing it together. "The intercept failed because they knew we were coming."

"Yes."

"And the banking records we tracked through Monaco, "

"Altered before you could access them," Javier said. "They've been three steps ahead of you from the beginning."

Amanda turned back to him, professional instincts wrestling with a growing sense that he was telling the truth. "Why tell me this now? Why the cloak and dagger meeting?"

"Because you're the only one I trust." The simplicity of his statement hit her like a physical blow. "You're the only agent who's been looking at the evidence rather than the convenient narrative."

"Trust?" She said, a sharp, brittle sound. "You don't even know me."

"I know enough." He stepped closer, close enough that she could see the flecks of gold in his hazel eyes. "I know you joined the Bureau after excelling at forensic psychology at Berkeley. I know you gave up a promising swimming career to pursue justice. I know you live alone in downtown LA and still swim at five AM three times a week to clear your head."

Amanda stiffened. "You've been investigating me?"

"Protecting you," he replied. "The moment you started questioning the official theory about my role in the Consortium, you became a target."

The information should have alarmed her, and it did, but beneath the alarm was a disturbing flutter of something else. No one paid such close attention to her in years, saw the pieces that made up Amanda Chen beyond the badge and the case files.

"I should arrest you," she said, but her voice lacked conviction.

Javier's expression softened. "For what? For trying to keep you alive? For working undercover in the most dangerous criminal organization in the hemisphere?"

"Undercover?" Amanda's mind stuttered over the implication. "You expect me to believe you're, "

"Secret Service." His eyes never left hers, steady and unwavering. "Deep cover assignment for the past 26 months. My handler is the only person who knows my true role, and I'm starting to question even his security."

The deck beneath Amanda's feet seemed to tilt. If he was lying, it was the most elaborate deception she'd ever encountered. If he was telling the truth...

"I never wanted to involve you," Javier said, his voice dropping to nearly a whisper. "I tried to keep you away, for your safety."

Something snapped inside Amanda, a dam breaking against the flood of revelations. "Don't you dare pretend this is noble," she hissed, stepping closer until they were inches apart. "You played me. And I let you."

"I did what was necessary for the mission," he countered, his own composure cracking. "Everything I've done, "

"Save it." Amanda's hands clenched at her sides. "If you're undercover, show me credentials. Give me a contact to verify. Give me something other than pretty words and convenient excuses."

"I can't." Frustration bled through his control. "Any communication through official channels could expose both of us. Why do you think I texted you from a burner phone? Why do you think I chose this godforsaken town for our meeting?"

The rational part of Amanda's mind, the trained investigator, the analyst, knew his explanation made tactical sense. But the part of her that had been hurt before, that protected herself with sarcasm and skepticism, resisted.

"Convenient," she said again, but the word lost its bite.

Javier ran a hand through his hair, the gesture vulnerable. "Amanda, I'm not asking you to trust me blindly. I'm asking you to look at the evidence, to use that brilliant mind of yours to see what's been happening."

The compliment slipped past her defenses, warming places that had been cold for too long. She took a step back, needing distance from the magnetic pull he exerted.

"Even if I believed you," she said hesitantly, "what do you expect me to do? Go rogue? Throw away my career on your word?"

"I expect you to stay alive." The raw emotion in his voice startled her. "The Consortium doesn't leave loose ends, and you've been tugging at threads they'd rather keep hidden. The next time they send Ginevra you won't see her coming."

His words settled over her. If Javier was telling the truth, she was in danger whether she helped him or not. If he was lying... the same conclusion applied.

The server disappeared inside, leaving them alone on the

deck. The sun slipped below the horizon, painting the sky in deepening shades of purple and navy. In the fading light, Javier looked less like the suave criminal she'd been tracking and more like a man carrying an impossible burden.

"Why me?" she asked.

His eyes met hers. "Because you see what others miss. Because you question what others accept. Because from the moment I met you, I knew you were different."

The tension between them shifted, electric and dangerous. Amanda was aware of his proximity, of the heat radiating from his body, of the way his eyes dropped to her lips before returning to meet her gaze.

"I don't trust you," she said, but even to her own ears, the words sounded hollow.

"I know." His hand moved toward hers, not quite touching. "But you will."

Their fingers brushed, an accidental contact that sent a current racing up Amanda's arm. His skin was warm against hers, the touch feather-light yet somehow more intimate than anything she'd experienced in years.

The rational voice in her head screamed warnings, about professional boundaries, about possible deception, about the danger of trusting a man who lived so long in the shadows that he might have forgotten where the truth ended and the lies began.

But a deeper instinct, the same one that made her an excellent investigator, whispered that Javier Morales was showing her his true self for the first time.

The tension coiled tighter between them, a tangible thing she could almost touch. His hand hovered near hers. Her breath shortened. Their anger, their suspicion, their undeniable attraction, it all collided in a rush of motion that neither seemed to initiate yet both surrendered to.

He kissed her. Hard. Desperate. Real.

Amanda's mind went blank, swept clean by the sensation of his lips against hers, his hand cradling the back of her neck with surprising gentleness. She should push him away. She should remember who they were, what they represented.

Instead, she leaned in. Melted against him. Fought the urge to want more than this stolen moment.

The kiss deepened, and with it came a cascade of sensations, his scent enveloping her, the slight stubble on his jaw rough against her skin, the solid warmth of his body pressing against hers. The cafe, the ocean, the case, the danger, it all receded, leaving only this unexpected connection, this moment of truth between lies.

Amanda's hand found its way to his chest, feeling the rapid beat of his heart beneath her palm, proof that he was as affected as she was, that whatever game they'd been playing shifted into something neither could have anticipated. He recoiled from the pain left from his wound.

The shrill ring of a phone shattered the moment.

Javier broke the kiss, breath ragged, his forehead resting against hers for a heartbeat before he pulled away. The loss of contact left Amanda dizzy, off-balance in a way that had nothing to do with physical equilibrium.

He pressed the phone to his ear, his eyes never leaving hers. "Yes?" A pause, his expression darkening. "When?" Another pause. "Understood."

The transformation was immediate, the vulnerable man who kissed her vanishing behind a mask of cold efficiency. He ended the call and looked at her, his eyes now sharp with urgency.

"We have to move. Now."

"What is it?" Amanda's mind shifted back to agent mode, the kiss relegated to a complication she would examine later.

"They know we're here." Javier's voice was tight, controlled. "My cover's blown."

In that moment, staring into his eyes, Amanda made her choice, not based on the kiss or the attraction, but on her instinct as an investigator. She would follow this lead, determine the truth, and face the consequences of her decision later.

She nodded once, a silent agreement, and then they were moving, leaving behind the peaceful cafe where everything changed.

***

The change in the air alerted Amanda before she heard it, a subtle compression, the world holding its breath. Her body reacted before her mind could process: muscles tensing, senses sharpening, time stretching like taffy pulled to its breaking point. The first bullet announced itself with a crack that split the evening calm, followed by the musical shatter of the cafe window exploding inward.

"Down!" Javier's hand was on her shoulder, pushing her toward the wooden deck just as the second shot splintered the railing where she'd been standing.

Amanda rolled with the momentum, years of training taking over. Her hand found her weapon, drawing it in one smooth motion as her eyes tracked the source of the attack. A black SUV rounded the corner onto the beach access road, its tinted windows lowered just enough for the barrels of semi-automatic weapons to emerge.

"Move!" She didn't wait to see if Javier followed, already

scrambling toward the edge of the deck where a three-foot drop separated them from the sandy ground below. The Consortium wasn't here to talk.

Bullets stitched a deadly pattern across the cafe's facade. Glass shattered. Wood splintered. A waitress's scream cut through the chaos as she dove behind the counter. Two elderly patrons who had been lingering over coffee abandoned their table, the man shielding the woman with his body as they stumbled toward the cafe's interior.

Amanda hit the sand in a controlled fall, rolling beneath the deck where support beams offered minimal cover. Javier landed beside her a heartbeat later, his movements hampered by his wound, his body angling to present the smallest possible target.

"Stay low," he said, though she hardly needed the instruction.

The SUV skidded to a stop twenty yards away. Doors flew open. Amanda counted four figures emerging, three men and a woman, all dressed in nondescript dark clothing that wouldn't draw attention but allowed for free movement. Professional. Methodical. The woman's blonde ponytail bounced as she rounded the vehicle, her weapon held with the comfortable grip of someone familiar with its use.

Not local muscle. Specialists.

"They're cutting off the beach exit," Amanda said, her mind already mapping possible escape routes. "The cafe back door?"

"First place they'll check." Javier's breathing was controlled, his eyes constantly moving. "The alley behind the buildings. There's access between the cafe and the surf shop."

She nodded once, trusting his knowledge of the terrain.

Trust, such a fragile thing in this new reality where Javier might be an ally rather than a target. The kiss still lingered on her lips, an absurd detail to remember with death approaching in tactical formation.

They began to crawl through the sand beneath the deck, keeping the wooden structure between them and their attackers. Amanda's white button-down collected grit and dampness, her practical slacks offering little protection against the rough ground. Javier moved beside her, his larger frame somehow just as nimble, his proximity both reassuring and distracting.

A bullet punched through the decking above them, sending splinters raining down. Too close. They needed to move faster.

"On my count," Javier said, his mouth close to her ear. "Three, two, "

Before he reached one, the deck above them erupted in gunfire. Someone circled around, firing down through the wooden slats. Amanda felt a splinter slice across her cheek, a minor injury that leaked warm blood down her face.

Abandoning stealth for speed, they scrambled toward the narrow gap between buildings. Amanda burst from beneath the deck, weapon raised, and fired two precise shots at the figure who had been shooting down at them. Not aiming to kill, her FBI training was too ingrained, but her bullets found their target. The man grunted in pain, stumbling back as one round caught him in the shoulder.

Javier was beside her in an instant, his own weapon drawn, a matte black pistol she didn't recognize. He fired once, twice, providing cover as they sprinted for the alley.

"Who the hell are they?" Amanda said as they pressed their backs against the stucco wall of the cafe, momentarily hidden from view.

"Consortium muscle." Javier's voice was tight, his eyes scanning for movements. "The kind you don't see twice."

"How did they find us so quickly?"

His expression darkened. "Your phone. My phone. The cafe's security cameras. Take your pick."

Tourists scattered across the beach, screaming and running from the gunfire. A siren wailed in the distance, local police responding, but they would be outmatched against these professionals. Amanda wiped blood from her cheek with the back of her hand, leaving a smear that felt sticky and warm against her skin.

"We need to split up," she said, the logical tactical move.

Javier's response was immediate and firm. "No."

"I can draw them off, "

"They're not after you." His eyes met hers, intense and unyielding. "Not yet. But if we separate, they'll take you to get to me."

The implication hung between them, that whoever these people were, they valued Javier's capture enough to use her as leverage. Which meant either he was too valuable to kill outright, or they wanted information from him. Neither scenario fit with Amanda's understanding of how the Consortium operated with threats.

Unless he really was telling the truth about being undercover.

A bullet struck the wall inches from Javier's head, sending chunks of stucco flying. No time for debate.

"The alley leads to a parking lot," he blurted. "Three buildings down is a narrow passage that cuts through to the next street. Your car?"

"Two blocks east, under a palm tree."

He nodded, and in that brief exchange, a plan formed without words. They would run together, using the maze of alleyways and side streets to reach her vehicle. Standard evasion tactics, but effective only if they moved fast enough.

Javier checked around the corner, then pulled back as another burst of gunfire peppered the wall. "Four seconds between volleys. They're being careful, avoiding civilian casualties."

"Small mercies," Amanda said, but the observation registered. Professional killers who were exercising restraint, unusual for the always ruthless Consortium.

"On my mark." Javier held up three fingers, then two, then one.

They burst from cover together, sprinting down the narrow alley behind the row of beachfront businesses. Amanda ran half a step behind Javier, her weapon ready. The pavement was uneven, littered with delivery pallets and overflowing dumpsters that provided momentary cover but also potential obstacles.

Footsteps pounded behind them, their pursuers spotted their escape route. A bullet ricocheted off a metal dumpster with a high-pitched whine. Another struck a pipe overhead, sending a spray of water cascading down.

"Left!" Javier called, veering sharply into a narrow passage between buildings.

Amanda followed, her lungs burning, adrenaline pushing her forward. The passage was just wide enough for them to run single-file, a claustrophobic tunnel of concrete walls rising on either side. No room to maneuver if their pursuers caught up. No place to take cover if bullets found them here.

They emerged onto a quiet residential street lined with small bungalows. An elderly woman watering plants on her porch froze at the sight of them, disheveled, armed, and clearly fleeing something dangerous. Amanda flashed her badge as they passed, not slowing her pace.

"FBI! Get inside and lock your door!"

The woman's eyes widened, but she had the good sense to follow instructions, retreating into her house as Amanda and Javier continued their desperate run.

Two more blocks. Each step was muscle memory now, her body operating on training and instinct while her mind processed their situation. If Javier was telling the truth, they were running from Consortium assassins who had somehow discovered his undercover status. If he was lying... she was helping a dangerous criminal escape justice.

Javier's step stuttered for just a moment, long enough for Amanda to register. She grabbed his elbow, steadying him without breaking stride.

"Stay with me," she said, and he heard the double meaning in his words.

They rounded another corner and Amanda spotted her sedan, still parked beneath the leaning palm where she left it. Twenty yards of exposed street stretched between them and escape.

Behind them, an engine roared, the SUV had circled around, cutting off their retreat. Ahead, another dark vehicle turned onto the street, moving with deliberate slowness.

"Dumpster," Amanda directed, pulling Javier toward a large metal container positioned against a building's wall. They ducked behind it just as bullets struck the pavement where they'd been standing.

Crouched in the narrow space between dumpster and wall, breathing hard, they assessed their diminishing options.

Amanda's sedan was tantalizingly close yet impossibly far with gunmen closing in from both directions.

"Which means your mole theory might be right," Amanda conceded, the pieces falling into place despite her resistance.

He met her eyes, something like grim satisfaction crossing his features. "Trust me now?"

"Let's survive this first," she countered, but the hostility drained from her voice. Whatever game they'd been playing before, they were now united by the very immediate threat of death.

A bullet struck the dumpster, the metal reverberating with the impact. Another followed, then another, systematic fire designed to keep them pinned until the shooters could advance to a killing position.

Amanda checked her weapon, full magazine, one in the chamber. Standard Bureau issue, reliable but outmatched against the firepower directed their way. Javier's pistol looked to have similar capacity. Not enough to fight their way out against trained killers with semi-automatic weapons.

"Your car," Javier said with urgency. "Do you have the key fob?"

She nodded, pulling it from her pocket.

"Range?"

"Twenty-five yards, give or take."

His eyes lit with a dangerous plan. "Hit the panic button. Three seconds after the alarm starts, we run, not for the car, but for the house behind it. White fence, red door."

Amanda didn't waste time questioning his strategy. In their current situation, any plan was better than slow execution behind a dumpster. She positioned her thumb over the button on the key fob, meeting Javier's eyes.

They shared a look, her eyes blazing with fire, his tight with fear and resolve. In that moment, whatever barriers existed between them, agent and suspect, hunter and hunted, dissolved into something simpler and more primal: two people determined to survive.

"On three," she said. "One... two... three."

The sedan's alarm split the evening air, lights flashing in a strobing pattern designed to draw attention. As predicted, gunfire redirected toward the vehicle, bullets punching through metal and glass.

Three seconds later, they sprinted from cover, not toward the car, but perpendicular to it, using the vehicle as a distraction rather than a destination. Amanda's legs burned with effort, her lungs straining as she pushed herself to maximum speed.

The white fence appeared ahead, the red door beyond it like a target in a shooting gallery. Javier reached it first, vaulting the fence in a single fluid motion. Amanda followed, her own athletic background allowing her to clear the obstacle with similar grace.

They hit the door together, Javier's shoulder leading in a practiced breach technique. The wood splintered around the lock, either weaker than it appeared or yielding to Javier's desperation. They tumbled inside, rolling away from the doorway as bullets splintered the frame behind them.

The house was empty, a vacation rental between occupants, judging by the generic furnishings and absence of personal items. Javier slammed the broken door shut, dragging a heavy sideboard across to barricade it while Amanda checked the rear of the house for alternate exits.

"Back door leads to another street," she called. "Clear for

now, but they'll circle around soon."

Javier joined her, his breathing controlled despite their exertion. Blood seeped from a small cut on his forehead, a splinter or bullet fragment grazed him during their run.

"We need to keep moving," he said, heading for the back door. "They'll have the streets covered in minutes."

As they slipped out the rear of the house into a small, neat garden, Amanda realized that they crossed a threshold in their relationship. They were now in this together, running from the same enemy, fighting for the same survival.

It was more than survival now. They were in this together.

***

Amanda and Javier moved like shadows through the beach town's hidden arteries, service alleys choked with delivery crates, narrow passages between buildings, backyards connected by broken fences. Her FBI training prepared her for pursuit scenarios, but this was different. This was primal, a hunt where they were both predator and prey, their bodies synchronized in a desperate dance of survival. The sun surrendered to darkness now, streetlights casting elongated shadows that provided both concealment and danger.

They paused behind a restaurant's delivery entrance, breathing hard, listening for pursuers. The alley reeked of old grease and rotting produce, the stench almost a physical presence in the humid evening air. Amanda's once-crisp white shirt clung to her skin, darkened with sweat and dirt. A thin line of blood caked her cheek where the splinter cut her. Beside her, Javier looked disheveled, his hair wild from running, a smudge of grime across one cheekbone, his eyes constantly scanning for threats.

"We need to circle back to my car," Amanda said, calculating routes and risks.

Javier shook his head. "Too obvious. They'll have someone watching it."

"We can't stay here." She peered around the corner, seeing only empty sidewalk. "And we can't outrun them on foot forever."

"The marina," he said. "Half a mile east. Boats, multiple escape routes."

It was a solid tactical suggestion, but Amanda hesitated. The marina meant civilian-dense areas, potential hostages if their pursuers were ruthless enough. More immediately, it meant putting their lives in Javier's hands, a test of trust she wasn't entirely ready to make.

He read her hesitation, his expression softening despite the urgency of their situation. "I know a guy with a boat. No questions asked. But if you have a better plan..."

Amanda weighed their options. Her training emphasized containment, calling for backup, following protocols that no longer applied in this upside-down scenario where she was running alongside a man she'd been hunting.

"My car is our best option," she said. "But we approach from the east, use the buildings for cover."

Something like respect flickered in Javier's eyes, acknowl-edgment that she wasn't blindly following his lead. "If we can get to it without being seen, maybe. But we'll need a distraction."

Amanda's gaze fell on a row of motorcycles parked behind the restaurant, likely belonging to kitchen staff. "How are your hotwiring skills?"

A smile touched his lips, unexpected in their dire circum-stances. "Better than my cooking."

Five minutes later, they crept toward the edge of the alley, a hotwired Kawasaki rumbling quietly beside them. The plan was simple but risky: Javier would create a diversion with the motorcycle, drawing attention away from Amanda's sedan long enough for her to reach it. Then she would circle back to pick him up two blocks away.

"If I'm not there in three minutes, don't wait," Javier said, his hand resting on the motorcycle's throttle.

"That's not how this works." Amanda checked her weapon one last time. "Three minutes. Then I come looking for you."

Their eyes met, an unspoken current passing between them. The kiss they shared at the cafe felt like it happened in another lifetime, yet the echo of it lingered in the way they looked at each other now, partners in this moment of crisis, whatever they might have been before.

"Ready?" he asked.

"Go."

Javier gunned the motorcycle, its engine roaring to life as he tore out of the alley and down the main street in the opposite direction from Amanda's car. As predicted, the black SUV that had been idling halfway down the block pulled away in pursuit, tires squealing against asphalt.

Amanda waited ten seconds, then began moving through the shadows toward her sedan. The streets were eerily empty now, the earlier gunfire sent tourists and locals alike scurrying for safety. In the distance, police sirens wailed, but they seemed to be concentrated near the cafe where the shooting started. No help would arrive in time to matter.

She approached her car from behind, using parked vehicles as cover. The driver's side window had been shot out, glass glittering on the pavement like scattered diamonds. The body riddled with bullet holes, the metal punctured and dented. But it was the tires that concerned her most, if they'd been shot out, the plan was finished before it began.

Amanda crouched, inspecting each tire in turn. Some how, all four were intact. The Consortium team had been focused on finding them, not on disabling potential escape routes. A tactical error she intended to exploit.

Staying low, she slipped into the driver's seat, glass crunching beneath her as she settled behind the wheel. The key fob survived their mad dash through town, and the engine started on the first try, another small miracle in a day that had seen too few of them.

She pulled away from the curb, driving without headlights for the first block before turning them on as she approached the rendezvous point. Two minutes passed since Javier's diversion. She would give him exactly one more before going after him.

Thirty seconds later, she spotted him sprinting between buildings, the motorcycle nowhere in sight. Amanda pulled alongside him, the passenger door already open. Javier dove in, and she accelerated before the door had even closed, tires squealing as they left the beach town behind.

"The motorcycle?" she asked, eyes flicking between the road ahead and the rear view mirror.

"Ditched it in the ocean," Javier replied, his breathing ragged. "Led them on a chase through the marina first. Should buy us some time."

Amanda pressed harder on the accelerator, the sedan's engine protesting but responding. The coastal highway stretched before them, a ribbon of asphalt winding along cliffsides. Behind them, the town receded, its lights growing smaller in the rear view mirror.

"They'll shoot the tires," Javier muttered, twisting in his seat to watch for pursuers.

"Then we drive fast," Amanda replied, pushing the sedan to speeds well beyond legal limits.

The car hugged the curves of the coastal road, ocean to their right, steep hillsides to their left. The perfect place for an ambush, the tactical part of Amanda's mind noted. Limited escape routes, predictable trajectory. If the Consortium team had a helicopter or called ahead to position shooters...

"Take the next turnoff," Javier directed suddenly. "Unmarked road, looks like a driveway."

Amanda spotted it, a narrow gravel path cutting up into the hillside, barely visible in the gathering darkness. She slowed just enough to make the turn without rolling the car, then accelerated again up the steep incline.

"Where does this lead?"

"Old fire road. Connects to the highway five miles north. Used it once before."

She didn't ask when or why he needed to know escape routes in this area. That conversation could wait for when they weren't fleeing armed killers.

The sedan bounced and jolted over the uneven terrain, its suspension groaning in protest. Amanda gripped the wheel, keeping the vehicle centered on the narrow path. Branches scraped against the windows, undergrowth whipping past in a dark blur.

After fifteen minutes of punishing driving, they emerged onto a wider dirt road that connected with the highway, just as Javier promised. Amanda checked the mirrors, but no headlights followed them, no dark SUVs materialized in pursuit.

"Think we lost them?" she asked, easing off the accelerator as they rejoined paved road.

"For now." Javier's voice was tight with tension. "But they'll be monitoring police reports, traffic cameras, airports, train stations."

"So we're still running." It wasn't a question.

"Until we can figure out who compromised my cover and why."

Amanda drove in silence for several miles, processing everything that happened since she received his text that morning. Her world turned inside out in the space of a few hours, the suspect she'd been tracking now sitting beside her, claiming to be undercover, with enough evidence of a Bureau mole to make her question everything about the investigation.

Minutes stretched into a half hour with no signs of pursuit. The adrenaline that carried them through their escape began to ebb, leaving exhaustion and a growing awareness of minor injuries in its wake. The cut on Amanda's cheek stung. A bruise was forming on her hip where she landed hard during one of their many falls. Beside her, Javier held himself with the careful stillness of someone managing pain, a pulled muscle or bruised rib, perhaps.

Amanda eased the car into cruise control, her white-knuckle grip on the steering wheel relaxing fractionally. The highway stretched empty before them, a path to nowhere and anywhere. She glanced at Javier, finding him watching her with an expression she couldn't quite read.

"You shouldn't have come," he said, his voice rough with fatigue.

Amanda's laugh was sharp, brittle. "You shouldn't have

texted."

The absurdity of their situation evident, two professionals trained in different aspects of law enforcement, now fugitives together based on a hunch and a text message. The sedan's air conditioning struggled against the night heat, the vents blowing tepid air across their skin.

Javier shifted in his seat to face her head on. "I mean it, Amanda. I wanted to warn you about the mole, but I never intended for you to be dragged into this."

"Too late now." She kept her eyes on the road, afraid of what he might see if she looked at him, the confusion, the lingering suspicion, the uncomfortable awareness that despite everything, she was drawn to him in ways that defied professional boundaries.

His hand moved across the console, resting gently over hers on the steering wheel. The simple contact sent an electric current up her arm, a ridiculous reaction given everything they'd just survived. She should pull away. She should maintain whatever professional distance remained between them.

She didn't move.

"I can't promise this will end well," Javier said, his thumb tracing a small circle on the back of her hand. "The Consortium has resources most federal agencies can only dream of. And if there really is a mole in the Bureau..."

"Then we trust no one but each other," Amanda said, glancing at him. The intensity in his eyes made her breath catch. "And that's an issue, because I'm still not sure I trust you completely."

A smile touched his lips, tired but genuine. "Smart woman. I'd be disappointed if you did."

They lapsed into silence again, but his hand remained on hers, a point of warmth in the uncertain night. The highway curved along the coastline, the ocean a vast darkness to their right, visible when the moon emerged from behind clouds.

Amanda eased the car into a turnout overlooking the water, killing the engine but leaving the key in the ignition, ready for a quick departure if needed. They sat in the thick, hot quiet, the only sound the soft tick of the cooling engine and their own breathing.

"What now?" she asked.

"We need somewhere to regroup. Somewhere safe." Javier ran a hand through his hair, exhaustion evident in every line of his body. "I have a contact in San Diego. Someone outside both agencies, someone the Consortium doesn't know about."

Amanda nodded, accepting the plan without questioning it, a measure of the trust that had been forged in gunfire and desperate flight. Whatever happened next, they were in this together now. Her career, her reputation, her life, all now tied to the man beside her, for better or worse.

Javier's hand found hers again in the darkness of the car, his touch gentle despite the strength she knew he possessed. "You shouldn't have come," he repeated, but this time the words held a different meaning, concern rather than regret.

"You shouldn't have texted," she replied, softer now, her fingers intertwining with his almost of their own accord.

They sat in wordless communion, bodies tense, lips still swollen from the kiss that changed everything back at the cafe. Their decision filling air between them, the choice to trust each other, to run together, to face whatever came next as allies rather than adversaries.

The road stretched ahead of them, endless and uncertain in

the gathering darkness. But they would face it together, the FBI agent and the undercover operative, bound by danger and something deeper that neither was ready to name.

Amanda started the car again, pulling back onto the empty highway. Whatever waited for them in San Diego, whatever truth lurked behind Javier's revelations about the mole, they would confront it side by side.

The night enveloped them, a cloak of darkness that offered both danger and possibility. And for the first time since receiving Javier's text, something close to certainty settled in her chest, not about the outcome, which remained shrouded in doubt, but about the rightness of her choice to trust this man who upended her world with seven simple words:

"Meet me. No more lies. -J."

Chapter 12

The fire whispered in the stone hearth, spitting glowing embers that mirrored the glint in Amanda's exhausted eyes. She sat cross-legged on the worn cabin floor, shoulders hunched beneath a thin wool blanket, fingers tracing the edge of a document that might connect all the pieces. Outside, darkness swallowed the mountainside, but inside, shadows danced across the walls in rhythm with the flames, watching as two people who had been strangers just days ago sifted through secrets that could get them both killed.

The shiver Amanda suppressed had nothing to do with the mountain chill. The smell of the cabin a mix of pine and wood smoke, with undertones of dust and someone else's memories. They found it through one of Javier's connections, no questions asked, no names recorded. Just cash and a set of keys that opened a door to temporary sanctuary.

The floor around her was a constellation of evidence: USB drives like fallen stars, printouts arranged in careful patterns, handwritten notes connected invisible threads between money trails and dead bodies. Three days of sleepless work left her eyes burning, but her mind remained sharp, cutting through deception with the precision of a surgeon's blade.

"I know this handwriting," she said, holding a page closer to the lamp's warm glow. The loops of the penmanship curled with familiar arrogance, each stroke deliberate, controlled. Like its owner.

Javier looked up from his position across from her, his posture relaxed, knees bent, forearms resting casually. But Amanda learned to read the vigilance in the set of his shoulders, the perpetual readiness in his hands, hands accustomed to pulling triggers and other things, yet had somehow been gentle when they brushed dried blood from her face two nights ago.

"You recognize it?" he asked, voice low like distant thunder.

Amanda nodded, a strand of dark hair falling across her face. "This timestamp, it lines up with the San Diego drop. Michael said he wasn't there, but this proves he was." Her voice cracked on the final word, betraying the personal wound beneath her professional armor. She exhaled, forcing steadiness into her trembling fingers.

Don't lose it now, she commanded herself. Not with him watching.

But Javier was watching, his eyes moving from the document to her face with an acuity that made her feel transparent. He had a way of looking at her as though he was reading more than just her expressions, as if he could see the fault lines beneath her well constructed facade.

"Amanda," he said, feint enough that it might shatter, "you're doing everything right. But you look like you're carrying more than the case."

She glanced up, defensive barriers rising, but something

in his expression, an echo of familiar pain, perhaps, made them falter. The mask she wore at the Bureau, in interrogation rooms, even with her own team, suddenly became heavier than she could bear.

"It's Dominic," she said, surprised by the admission as it left her lips.

The confession hung in the air between them, and Amanda found herself continuing, words spilling out like water from a cracked vessel. "I thought I knew him. Trusted him with everything, case files, confidential informants. My back."

She looked up, meeting Javier's eyes with sudden defiance. "So yeah, I've got issues with trust. Mostly with men who keep secrets."

The last part aimed at him, and they both knew it. Javier hadn't been forthcoming about his own involvement with the Eclipse Consortium. Their partnership, if that's what this was, began with her suspecting him of being part of the organization they were now trying to bring down. His explanation of being deep undercover still carried loose ends and shadows she couldn't quite penetrate.

Javier nodded, accepting the implicit accusation without defense. His eyes never left hers, steady as a harbor light. "I get it," he said after a moment, his voice carrying the weight of something personal. "My first op, deep cover in Argentina. I trusted a local contact. She gave me intel and it got two agents killed."

He reached for his coffee mug, wrapping his hands around it though the liquid lost its warmth hours ago. "I found out later she was Consortium. Had been from the start." His knuckles whitened. "And the worst part is, I still don't know if she cared."

The air in the cabin thickened with their shared confessions.

"I cared," he said, with such naked honesty that something inside her chest cracked open.

She recognized the cost of his admission, how he guarded his vulnerabilities, how little he allowed genuine emotion to surface through his calculated demeanor. It was a gift, this small truth. An offering.

Amanda's shoulders eased, her expression softening. For the first time, she looked at him not as a suspect or an ally, but as something more complex. More human. A man with scars mirroring her own.

"I didn't want to care," she said, surprising herself again. "About any of this. It was meant to be straightforward, track the money, find the suspect, build the case." She gestured at the evidence surrounding them. "Not... whatever this became."

The firelight caught the angles of Javier's face, illuminating one side while casting the other in shadow. A perfect visual metaphor for the man himself, part revealed, part hidden. The silence between them was different now, charged with something neither dared to acknowledge aloud.

Amanda shifted, her knee brushing against his as she reached for another document. The contact sent an electric current racing up her leg, a sensation so disproportionate to the touch it almost made her laugh. She was not some inexperienced rookie, flustered by proximity to an attractive man. She was FBI Special Agent Amanda Chen, no stranger to staring down cartel hitmen without blinking.

Yet here she was, pulse quickening because her knee touched his.

Their eyes met over the spread of documents, and she saw

the same awareness reflected in his gaze, a recognition of this unexpected current between them. His hand moved, of its own accord, fingers brushing against hers where they rested on the worn rug.

The touch was tentative, questioning, so unlike the confident man who navigated the criminal underworld for years. He was asking permission, she realized. Giving her the choice to pull away.

Amanda didn't move. Her fingers remained steady beneath his, her breath held captive in her lungs. The moment stretched between them, delicate and dangerous, neither willing to break it with words or movement.

His hand was warm against her cooler skin, the calluses on his fingertips telling stories of weapons handled and battles fought. She wondered, with startling intensity, what those hands would feel like against other parts of her body.

The thought made heat bloom across her cheeks, and Javier's eyes darkened in response, as if he could read her mind. His fingers curled tighter around hers, crossing another threshold.

And then, a ping.

The sound from Javier's phone was jarring, an intrusion from the world outside their fragile bubble. His expression shifted, vulnerability replaced by alertness. He pulled his hand away, reaching for the device sitting on the edge of the low wooden table.

Amanda felt cold in the absence of his touch, despite the fire and the blanket around her shoulders. Javier read the message, his face transforming before her eyes, warmth draining away, leaving behind a mask of professional detachment that still couldn't quite hide the flash of fear in his eyes.

"What is it?" she asked, her own voice returning to the crisp tones of an agent.

Without speaking, he turned the phone screen toward her. The message was brief, clinical in its delivery of a death sentence:

Ginevra Sforza officially activated. Contract on both targets. Lethal. Immediate.

Amanda inhaled, her heart slamming against her ribcage. The moment between them shattered like glass, falling away to reveal the deadly reality of their situation.

Ginevra Sforza. The name alone now sent ice through her veins. The woman born to Italian nobility transformed herself into one of Europe's most efficient killers. No survivors. No failed contracts. A ghost who left nothing but cooling bodies in her wake.

"She's coming," Javier said, moving to check the windows, his body language transformed into coiled readiness. "And she doesn't miss."

Amanda was on her feet in an instant, sliding from vulnerable woman to trained agent with practiced ease. She reached for her weapon, the weight of it familiar and grounding.

"How much time do we have?" she asked, efficiency replacing emotion.

"Hours, not days," Javier replied, closing blinds and checking locks. "My contact can get us transportation at first light, but until then, "

"We're trapped," Amanda finished for him.

Their eyes met across the room, and in a moment of shared danger, the connection between them seemed to deepen rather than diminish. The vulnerability remained, but now it layered with something else, a partnership forged in fire, a trust born of necessity.

"Not trapped," Javier said, a gleam of determination replacing the fear in his eyes. "Prepared."

Amanda nodded, her own resolve strengthen. Whatever sparked between them minutes ago would have to wait. Right now, they needed to focus on surviving the night.

But as they moved through the cabin, transitioning from exposed targets to hunters preparing for prey, the fundamental shift between them obvious to Amanda, something the threat of death couldn't erase.

***

The weapons laid out on the kitchen counter looked like surgical instruments under the harsh overhead light, precise, purposeful, lethal. Amanda's SIG Sauer sat beside Javier's Glock, different in make but identical in intention. They stood shoulder to shoulder, their movements a silent choreography as they loaded magazines, checked sights, and tested the weight of each piece in their palms. An outsider might have mistaken them for long-time partners, the way they anticipated each other's needs without speaking, a box of ammunition sliding across the counter just as a hand reached for it, a cleaning rod passed without asking. But the electricity that crackled between them whenever their fingers brushed revealed a different truth: this was no comfortable partnership worn smooth by years. This was something raw and new, dangerous as a live wire in floodwater.

"She'll come at night," Amanda said, her voice steady despite the knot of tension coiled at the base of her spine. She slid a magazine into her Glock with a satisfying click. "Silenced rounds. Close quarters. Probably thermal optics."

Javier nodded, his face cast in harsh shadows by the kitchen light. The wound on his shoulder, a reminder from their narrow escape at the dock two days earlier, reacted as he reached for a box of hollow points. He didn't wince, but Amanda saw the slight tightening around his eyes, the fractional hesitation before extending his arm.

"We control the entrances," he replied, his voice pitched down as if Ginevra might already be listening from the darkness beyond the windows. "I'll disable the power line. Force her into flashlight range."

Amanda checked the sight on her backup piece, a compact .38 that once belonged to her father. "She'll expect that. Professionals always have contingencies."

"So do we." Javier's eyes met hers, a hint of grim humor glinting beneath the determination. "I've dealt with her type before. They rely on precision. Control. We introduce variables."

"Chaos theory for assassins?" The corner of Amanda's mouth twitched upward.

"Something like that." Javier laid out three flash-bangs in a neat row. "Sensory overload. Disrupt her rhythm. We don't have to be better, just more unpredictable."

Their conversation flowed with the efficiency of water finding its path downhill, rapid-fire, seamless, each thought connecting to the next without hesitation. They moved around the small kitchen with unconscious grace, bodies navigating the tight space as if they had been doing this dance for years instead of days.

Amanda reached for a roll of duct tape at the same moment Javier did. Their fingers collided, lingered, withdrew. A small moment that sparked like flint against steel.

"Sorry," they said in unison, then exchanged glances that acknowledged the absurdity, apologizing for a touch when they might be fighting side by side for their lives in hours.

A strange intimacy developed between them, one born of shared danger and forced proximity. Three days ago, she'd been ready to arrest him as a suspect in her investigation. Two days ago, they ran through gunfire together. Yesterday, he'd cleaned a cut above her eyebrow with surprising gentleness. And tonight, they had almost,

Amanda cut off the thought, refocusing on the tactical map they'd drawn of the cabin and surrounding woods. Romance had no place in survival planning. Yet she couldn't ignore how they moved like lovers in waiting, their minds aligned, their bodies aware, their chemistry undeniable.

She pulled her hair back into a low knot at the nape of her neck, securing it with an elastic band from her wrist. The blue glow from her laptop, still running decryption algorithms on the files they recovered, cast her face in an otherworldly light. For a moment, she caught her own reflection in the darkened window, hollow eyes, tension etched into the set of her jaw, the faint shadow of a bruise still visible on her cheekbone.

What looked back at her was unrecognizable. Not the polished FBI agent who started this case. Not the focused profiler who kept emotional distance from her subjects. This woman in the glass looked haunted, hunted, and strangely alive, danger having stripped away everything but her essential self.

You've come this far, she reminded herself, taking a long, deliberate breath. There's no room for fear now.

Behind her, Javier approached, his presence announced by the subtle shift in the air rather than sound. For a man of his size, he moved with remarkable quiet, a skill that had likely saved his life countless times undercover.

"We'll make it through this," he said, his voice a deep rumble that she felt as much as heard.

Amanda turned to face him, not bothering to hide the doubt in her expression. "You don't know that."

"No," he conceded, standing close enough for faint traces of gunpowder and sandalwood which clung to his skin to reach her nostrils. "But I know I'll die trying before I let her touch you."

The words landed with physical weight in Amanda's chest, squeezing something tight beneath her ribs. Not fear, she cataloged that emotion long ago, understood its contours and how to manage it. This was different: a glow spread despite the danger surrounding them, despite the professional boundaries she maintained throughout her career.

Javier wasn't offering protection as one agent to another. This wasn't about professional duty or tactical necessity. The fierce promise in his eyes spoke of something deeper, something personal creeping between them when neither was looking.

Amanda reached for him, her hand lifting toward his face, then stopped herself. The motion hung incomplete between them, vibrating with possibilities. This wasn't the time. They were preparing for a battle that might leave one or both of them dead. Emotions complicated things. Created vulnerabilities. Made people hesitate when hesitation meant death.

She let her hand fall back to her side. "We should get some rest. Take shifts. Four hours on, four off until dawn."

"I'll take first watch," Javier said, scanning the windows, calculating sight lines.

"No," Amanda countered. "Your shoulder needs time. I'll go first."

He opened his mouth to argue, then thought better of it.

"Two hours," he compromised. "Then we switch. Neither of us can afford to be foggy."

Amanda nodded, appreciating that he didn't insist on some misguided chivalry. They were partners in this, equals despite their different backgrounds and agencies.

"You should take the bed," she said, nodding toward the single bedroom door. "Get some real rest while you can."

"I'll take the couch," Javier said, his tone making it clear this wasn't negotiable.

Amanda blinked, surprised by his vehemence. "You're bleeding from your shoulder and planning to fight a trained assassin, maybe you should take the bed."

The wound reopened earlier during their hasty fortification of the cabin. She redressed it herself, fingers careful against his skin, trying to ignore the landscape of scars that told stories of his dangerous past. The injury wasn't severe, but coupled with exhaustion, it could slow his reactions. In their current situation, milliseconds mattered.

Javier's mouth curved into a small, tired smile that softened the hard planes of his face. "I wouldn't sleep if you weren't safe."

The simple statement carried weight far beyond its words. It settled in her chest, next to an unfamiliar warmth that grew despite her best efforts to contain it.

A silence settled between them, rich with things unspoken. Possibilities hovered just out of reach. Questions without simple answers. In another life, without Ginevra Sforza hunting them or the Eclipse Consortium's shadow looming over their futures, perhaps those possibilities might have room to breathe, to develop on their own. But here, now, they existed in a compressed timeline where tomorrow is not a guarantee.

Amanda nodded her acceptance of his arrangement, then gathered her laptop and a few essential items. She moved toward the bedroom, strangely reluctant to put a door between them. Their partnership, whatever it was becoming, had been forged in constant contact, in shared space and shared danger. Separation, even by a few feet of wood and plaster, struck her as wrong somehow.

At the threshold, she paused, one hand on the doorframe. Javier had already pulled a worn blanket from the back of the couch and was arranging it with military precision, his movements economical despite his fatigue.

"Javier?" His name left her lips unbidden.

He looked up, dark eyes finding hers across the dimming room, a question in their depths.

"I'm glad it was you," she said, the words barely audible above the growing wind outside. "The kiss. The trust. Even the lies."

She didn't know why she needed to say it now, with possible death hours away. Perhaps because there might not be another chance. Perhaps because facing mortality had a way of distilling truth to its essence.

Javier's eyes softened, the vigilance in them replaced by something warmer, more vulnerable. "It still is," he said.

Three words acknowledged everything, what existed between them wasn't past tense. Despite the circumstances, despite the danger, despite the professional complications, this connection remained present, continued to grow.

The corner of her mouth lifted in a small, private smile. Then she stepped into the bedroom and closed the door behind her, leaving just enough space for sound to travel between them.

Outside, the wind picked up, rattling the windows with

ghostly fingers. Branches scraped against the cabin roof, mimicking footsteps that made both agents tense until they recognized the source. Clouds scudded across the moon, illuminating and obscuring the clearing around their temporary sanctuary.

Inside, despite the physical separation, Amanda and Javier remained connected by the knowledge of what awaited them, both the approaching danger and the unresolved current that hummed between them. Two storms: one external, one internal. Both gathering force, both inevitable.

Amanda lay on the bed, clothed, weapon within reach, ears attuned to every sound. On the other side of the door, she knew Javier sat in similar readiness, his body oriented toward the bedroom, placing himself between her and any threat that might come.

They waited, separate yet together, for whatever dawn would bring.

13

Chapter 13

Amanda paced the length of the cabin, creating a hollow rhythm against the wooden planks. Outside, the rain battered the windows with relentless fury, each drop a tiny accusation. Dominic Hayes, mentor, superior, friend, was part of the Eclipse Consortium. The revelation sat in her stomach like a block of ice, refusing to melt away no matter how many times her mind circled back to the evidence they'd uncovered.

She paused at the window, watching rivulets chase each other down the glass. In the dim morning light, the forest surrounding their hideaway was a blur of grays and greens, trees bending beneath the storm's assault. Three years working under Dominic's supervision, trusting his guidance, following his orders. Three years of lies.

The cabin creaked around her, weathering the storm as she was weathering hers. A modest safe house tucked away in the mountains, it offered little in the way of comfort, a kitchenette with chipped countertops, a bathroom with temperamental plumbing, and a main room that served as both living space and command center. The fireplace in the corner offered the only real luxury, its flames creating dancing shadows that mocked her restlessness.

"Maybe she can't find us, maybe that's why she hasn't struck yet." Amanda nearly blurted, the tension reaching a boiling point.

Javier sat at the small wooden table across the room, his attention fixed on a map spread before him. Red circles marked known Consortium locations, a constellation of criminal activity spanning across continents. His dark hair fell across his forehead as he leaned forward, the golden glow of the firelight catching the angles of his face. Even in concentration, he carried himself with the easy confidence that had first drawn her eye, and her suspicion, when they'd crossed paths months ago. The memory flooded back unbidden. Istanbul, Ginevra, Death...

The lights of Istanbul sprawled before him like fallen stars, glittering against the inky canvas of night. Javier Morales swirled the liquid in his glass, watching as it caught the soft glow from the rooftop bar's lanterns. The scotch burned pleasantly against his tongue but did nothing to ease the knot of tension coiled tight between his shoulder blades. Two buyers were missing, one encrypted drive vanished, the evening had slipped from his grasp like sand through fingers, and in his line of work, failure rarely came without blood.

The Bosphorus stretched below him, a dark ribbon splitting continents, its surface dappled with the reflected lights of ships passing silently through the night. From this height, the muezzin calls to prayer were distant echoes, haunting reminders of ancient faith in a city where gods and devils did business over drinks.

He loosened his tie, a subtle concession to the warm Turkish night, though the gesture did little to alleviate the weight of the day's events. The Eclipse Consortium didn't tolerate loose ends. Missing buyers meant questions, and questions meant scrutiny he couldn't afford. Not now, not when he'd carved his way so deeply into their operation that sometimes he woke up forgetting which life was the lie.

"Enjoying the view?" The voice was silk running over steel.

Ginevra Sforza settled into the chair beside him without invitation, her movements fluid and precise as mercury. Her blouse was white silk, impossibly fine against olive skin, paired with black pants embracing every dangerous curve. Her dark hair was swept up, revealing the vulnerable line of her neck, though there was nothing vulnerable about the woman herself.

Javier didn't answer immediately. Instead, he studied her reflection in the glass balustrade, noting the perfect composure, the calculating eyes that missed nothing. Her lipstick was red. Always red. Like a warning sign painted in blood.

"You were supposed to wait for my signal," he finally said, keeping his voice low and measured despite the anger simmering beneath the surface. In the six months he'd worked with her, he'd never seen her follow protocol. It made her unpredictable, deadly in their world.

She shrugged one elegant shoulder and reached for his glass, her fingers brushing his deliberately. She took a sip, leaving a perfect crescent of red on the rim.

"They were stalling," she said, setting the glass down. "I hate stalling."

The statement hung between them, deceptively simple. In their line of work, stalling often meant a double-cross brewing or a target preparing to flee. But it could also mean innocent hesitation, fear, or simple business caution.

"Now they're missing," he said, not a question but an accusation.

Her lips drew into a smile while her eyes remained flinty. "I know," she replied, leaning back in her chair with the languid confidence of a predator at rest. "It's cleaner this way."

She reached into her clutch, a small thing of black leather Javier knew contained at least one ceramic blade able to pass through any metal detector and withdrew a flash drive. With delicate fingers, she slid it across the table toward him.

Javier picked it up, turning it over in his hands. The drive was clean, wiped of fingerprints, and repackaged as though it had never been opened. The kind of meticulous work leaving no trace, no evidence. Just the way the Consortium liked things handled.

"You killed them?" he asked, his voice carefully neutral, though his stomach clenched. His cover demanded complicity, but each death added weight to his conscience, a weight he carried alone in the silent hours before dawn.

Ginevra leaned in, close enough that the warmth of her breath against his ear caused the hair on his arms to stand on end. Her scent enveloped him, dizzying in its intensity, a deliberate distraction technique he recognized but couldn't quite resist.

"I never said that," she whispered, her voice low and sultry, the Italian lilt more pronounced in these intimate moments.

In the dim light of the rooftop bar, her golden eyes seemed almost to glow, predatory and hypnotic. Her fingers brushed his jaw, a touch so light it might have been imagination, but the spark it sent through him was undeniable. For a moment, the air between them shifted, hot, dangerous, magnetic, charged with something beyond professional partnership. Something that threatened to blur the lines Javier had so carefully drawn.

She pressed something cool and metal into his palm, a room key, he realized. From one of the floors below them in the luxury hotel. An invitation. A test. A trap, perhaps.

"Don't be long," she murmured, her lips close enough to his ear that he felt rather than heard the words. "I'm not a patient woman."

She was standing, smoothing her silk blouse with the same hands that had likely ended lives hours earlier. She walked away, her stride unhurried and feline, drawing the eyes of every man and several women in the bar.

Javier watched her go, feeling the key grow warm in his palm. He knew better than to trust her, Ginevra Sforza was as loyal to the Consortium as a mercenary could be, and as deadly as a viper. Her elegance and beauty were weapons as finely honed as the knives she favored.

He tucked the flash drive into his inner pocket and slowly finished his drink, the scotch no longer burning but flat on his tongue. The condensation from the glass had dampened his fingers, leaving them cold and slightly numb, but he felt a warmth in his chest, an uncomfortable heat that he recognized as something between desire and dread.

The key in his hand bore the number 1217. Twelfth floor. A quiet floor, less traffic, more privacy. The perfect place for a clandestine meeting, or an assassination.

Ginevra was a ghost in silk, leaving death in her wake. And Javier was about to willingly walk into her lair. The smart move would be to leave now, contact his handler, find another way to salvage the operation. But smart wasn't always possible in this world of shadows and half-truths.

Sometimes, the only way forward was through the jaws of the beast.

It was a good mask. He hoped it would be enough tonight.

The elevator began its descent, carrying him down to whatever waited in room 1217. Down to Ginevra, with her red lips and honey-hued eyes and hands that dealt death with elegant precision.

Down into the heart of darkness, where duty and desire collided like continents, creating something new and terrible in the impact.

***

He entered silently, closing the door behind him with practiced care. The soft snick of the lock engaging sealed him into a different world, one painted in shades of crimson from a single lamp draped with a red scarf. The heavy curtains were drawn, blocking any hint of Istanbul's glittering nightscape, creating a chamber divorced from time and place.

The copper and fear hit him first, the unmistakable scent of a man who knew his life hung by the thinnest of threads. Then his eyes adjusted to the dim light, picking out details in the bloody chiaroscuro: the plush hotel suite transformed into an interrogation room, the furniture pushed aside, and the man.

He sat slumped in one of the room's armchairs, wrists bound behind him with what looked like a silk necktie. His head lolled forward, revealing salt-and-pepper hair matted with sweat. A line of dark blood trailed from a precise cut along his jaw, dripping onto the collar of his expensive shirt. His mouth was sealed with tape.

He wasn't dead yet. His chest rose and fell in shallow, irregular breaths. His eyes, when they flickered open, were glassy with pain and glazed with fear.

Ginevra stood over him, one stiletto heel pressed into the man's thigh with enough pressure to keep him conscious through pain. Her posture was relaxed, almost bored, as though she were waiting for a delayed train rather than conducting an interrogation.

"You're late," she said without looking up, her voice cool and detached.

Javier moved deeper into the room, careful to stay out of any potential blood spatter radius, a professional courtesy he'd learned early in his undercover work.

The prisoner was middle-aged, with the soft hands and manicured nails of someone who worked behind a desk. The cut of his suit, visible despite the blood and rumpling, suggested European tailoring. A businessman, perhaps, or a banker. Someone with access to information valuable enough to warrant this private performance.

"I thought this was an interrogation," Javier said, eyes scanning the room for signs of what information Ginevra might have already extracted.

She finally looked up, her eyes catching the red light making them appear almost feral. The knife in her hand, small, elegant, with a mother-of-pearl handle that matched her perfectly manicured nails.

"It is," she replied, her lips curving into the ghost of a smile. "He just didn't know it."

The man made a sound behind his gag, a desperate, garbled plea in what Javier recognized as Russian. His eyes, widened with renewed terror at Javier's arrival, darted between them with the frantic energy of prey, sensing its final moments.

Ginevra leaned down, her back a perfect arc, and spoke in flawless, unbroken Russian. Her voice was different in the language, colder, more precise, stripped of the warmth that occasionally colored her Italian-accented English. She spoke with the clipped efficiency of someone who had learned the language not for pleasure but for utility.

The prisoner's response was muffled by the gag, but his violent head shake was universal in its meaning: denial, or perhaps refusal.

Ginevra straightened, twirling the small knife between her fingers with the casual dexterity of someone who had held such tools since childhood.

"Do you know what's fascinating about pain, Javier?" she asked, switching back to English as though they were discussing wine pairings over dinner. "It's not the sensation itself, but the anticipation. The human mind is remarkably adept at imagining worst-case scenarios."

To demonstrate, she lowered the knife until it hovered a millimeter above the man's eye. She didn't touch him, didn't move, holding it there with perfect steadiness as beads of sweat formed on his forehead and ran down his temples.

"See? I haven't even touched him, and his pulse has doubled." She smiled, a cold expression unnerving. "The body betrays what the mind tries to conceal."

Javier kept his face carefully blank, though his stomach twisted. He'd witnessed interrogations before, had even conducted a few himself to maintain his cover, but Ginevra's clinical detachment was something different. Something in it spoke of years of refined technique, of an artist's approach to suffering.

"He's been playing both sides, or at least has profited from it" Ginevra said, withdrawing the knife from its position near the man's eye. "Selling information about shipping routes to competitors, selling information about those competitors back to us." She circled the chair like a shark, her movements fluid and unhurried. "Very entrepreneurial. Very stupid."

She leaned down and whispered something in the man's ear, something too low for Javier to catch, all color drained from the prisoner's face.

When she straightened, her smile was faint but present, like the Mona Lisa's if the Mona Lisa had ever executed anyone.

"He gave up the middle man that has been providing info to Interpol," she announced, sliding the knife into its sheath inside her calf-high Italian leather boots. The movement was practiced, sensual in its efficiency.

Javier took a sip of vodka, using the burn to center himself. "You could've gotten that without torture," he said, the words slipping out before he could censor them. A dangerous lapse, revealing more of his true self than was safe in this blood-red room.

Ginevra's head tilted slightly, her dark hair falling in a perfect curtain across one shoulder. She studied him with renewed interest.

"Would you have trusted it then?" she asked, stepping closer to him. Close enough there was no mistaking her perfume mingled with the metallic scent of blood. Close enough that the perfect steadiness of her hands, uncalloused by hesitation or remorse was visible.

And she didn't wait for an answer. Why would she? In their world, hesitation was weakness, and Ginevra Sforza had eliminated weakness from her life with the same precision she applied to her targets.

She walked behind the man, her movements graceful despite the stiletto heels. From the bathroom, she retrieved a plush white towel, embroidered with the hotel's gold insignia. The contrast between the luxury item and its intended purpose created a cognitive dissonance that felt deliberately staged, as though she were putting on a performance for Javier.

"You might want to look away," she said, though her tone suggested she knew he wouldn't. Couldn't. His role demanded he witness this.

With practiced efficiency, she wrapped the towel around the man's throat. No drama, no hesitation, just the clinical application of force. The man's bound hands scrabbled uselessly against the chair back, his legs kicked once, twice, then stilled as his oxygen depleted.

Javier's face a mask of professional indifference that belied the churning in his gut. This was what his mission required, bearing witness, gathering evidence, earning trust. But in moments like these, the line between who he was and who he pretended to be blurred until he was unable to distinguish them.

Ginevra maintained pressure for thirty seconds after the man went limp, ensuring completion. She unwrapped the towel, folded it neatly as though it were fresh laundry, and placed it on the bathroom counter.

She brushed past Javier on her way to the door, close enough their shoulders touched, a deliberate contact that sent an unwelcome jolt of electricity through him despite the horror he'd witnessed.

"Have housekeeping come at noon tomorrow," she said, her voice back to its normal timber, as though they'd concluded a business meeting rather than an execution. "Tip generously."

She was gone, leaving behind only the lingering scent of blood and her perfume, trailing behind her like a signature.

***

His phone buzzed, breaking the quiet. Amanda watching as he checked the screen, his expression hardening.

"Ginevra's looking for Isabel," he said without looking up, his voice steady and measured. "Hoping she can provide information about where we might be hiding."

Amanda's muscles tensed. "Isabel wouldn't give you up, would she?"

"Not willingly." Javier's eyes met hers, and something unspoken passed between them. Isabel Serrano, brilliant forger, occasional informant, and the closest thing to a friend Javier had in this world of shadows. "But Ginevra has methods."

The implication hung in the air between them, another weight added to the burden they already carried. Amanda resumed her pacing, memories of her failed marriage surfacing like debris after a flood. Michael had made promises too, had seemed solid and trustworthy until he wasn't. The pattern was becoming painfully familiar, trust, betrayal, isolation.

"Do you ever forget?" she asked, the question escaping before she could reconsider.

Javier looked up, one eyebrow raised in question.

"Who you really are," she clarified, stopping her pacing to face him. "After so long undercover, do you ever forget which version of yourself is real?"

His fingers stilled on the map, and something flickered across his face, surprise, perhaps, at the personal nature of her question, or maybe recognition of a truth he little acknowledged.

239

"Sometimes," he admitted, leaning back in his chair. The wood creaked beneath his weight. "There are moments when the lines blur. When Javier Morales, trusted member of the Eclipse Consortium, feels more natural than Special Agent Javier Morales of the Secret Service." His gaze drifted toward the window, where lightning illuminated the sky. "It's the silence that gets to you. Years of carrying secrets with no one to share them with, crafting a self that fit the role but hollows you out bit by bit."

Amanda moved closer, drawn by the rare vulnerability in his voice. She'd spent weeks investigating him, convinced he was a criminal, before learning the truth of his undercover assignment. Now they were reluctant allies, thrown together by circumstance and a common enemy.

"How do you do it?" she asked, perching on the edge of the table. "Stay sane when you're living a lie?"

Javier's eyes returned to hers, dark and contemplative. "You find anchors, small truths you can hold onto when everything else is performance. My love for my mother's arroz con gandules. My hatred of the Yankees." His lips curved into a slight smile. "The satisfaction of knowing someday, it ends. Someday, the truth comes out."

The cabin grew smaller as he spoke, the space between them charged with something Amanda didn't dare name. She'd spent her career analyzing people, reading the micro-expressions that betrayed their thoughts, but Javier remained partially enigmatic, a puzzle with pieces missing.

"And what about now?" she pressed. "With Dominic revealed, the operation compromised... is this still part of the plan?"

Javier stood abruptly, walking to a worn bookshelf that

held nothing but dusty paperbacks and a half-empty bottle of whiskey. "No playbook for this scenario." He poured two fingers into a glass and offered it to her. "My handler's gone dark. Your superior is completely compromised by the organization we're trying to bring down. We're improvising now."

Amanda accepted the glass, their fingers brushing in a moment of contact that sent warmth spreading up her arm. She took a sip, welcoming the burn. "Improvisation isn't FBI protocol."

"And you prefer improvisation." Amanda crossed her arms, but there was no real defensiveness in the gesture. "It's worked out so well for us so far."

The familiar rhythm of their banter eased some of the tension. Javier stepped closer, not touching her but near enough that she would have to acknowledge his presence, his reality.

"And when this is over?" she asked. "When Dominic is in custody and the Consortium dismantled? What then, Javier?"

It was the question he'd been asking himself through the sleepless hours of the night. There were no guarantees in their line of work, no promises that were made with certainty. Their agencies operated in different jurisdictions, their assignments taking them to opposite corners of the world.

"Then we figure it out," he stated. "One day at a time."

The first direct ray of sunlight broke through the trees, streaming through the window to cast golden patterns across the wooden floor. Amanda's hair caught the light, black strands transformed to amber where the sun touched them. For a moment, they stood in silence, the dawn casting everything in new perspective.

"Isabel," Amanda said, turning from the window with renewed purpose. "We need to find her before Ginevra does."

Javier recognized the shift, not rejection, but a return to the work that had brought them together. He followed her lead, moving to the map still spread across the table.

Amanda reached for her phone, scrolling through contacts. "My source at Interpol might have recent intelligence on Ginevra's movements. If we can predict where she's heading, we can intercept."

"Or set a trap," Javier suggested, the tactical part of his mind engaging. "Use her pursuit of Isabel to draw her out, trace her communications back to the Consortium."

Amanda's eyes lit with the challenge, her analytical mind clearly working through possibilities. "Risky. Ginevra's not any assassin, she's meticulous, cautious."

"And yet, she has one weakness." Javier leaned against the table, watching Amanda's quick movements as she gathered her laptop. "Pride. She considers herself an artist. Artists can be provoked into impulsivity if their craft is questioned."

A smile spread across Amanda's face, not the guarded, professional smile she offered colleagues, but something genuine, appreciative. "That's... actually brilliant. We could use Isabel as bait, or rather, the suggestion of Isabel."

"A forgery of the forger," Javier agreed, energy building between them as the plan took shape.

For the next hour, they worked in seamless coordination, Amanda reaching out to contacts while Javier plotted potential locations. The awkwardness of the morning melted away, replaced by the familiar rhythm of partnership. Occasional touches, a hand on a shoulder, fingers brushing as they exchanged notes, carried new meaning but didn't distract from their purpose.

As the sun climbed higher, casting the cabin in full daylight, Amanda paused in her rapid typing. "This could work," she said, looking up at Javier with cautious optimism. "But we'll need to move quickly. My contact says Ginevra was spotted in Venice yesterday."

Javier nodded, already mentally cataloging what they would need. "Makes sense, it has a thriving art scene, lots of young people, exactly where Isabel would feel comfortable. I'll arrange transportation. We can be in Venice by early afternoon if we leave within the hour."

Amanda closed her laptop with decisive movement. "I'll pack what we need." She rose, hesitated, something unspoken in her expression.

"What is it?" Javier asked.

She debated internally before answering. "I want to be clear, about us, about this. Whatever's happening between us doesn't change who I am. I won't compromise the mission, and I won't be less than I am for anyone. Not again."

Javier recognized the declaration for what it was, not a rejection, but a boundary, an assertion of self-worth learned through painful experience. He stepped closer, respecting her space but wanting her to see the truth in his eyes.

"I would never ask you to be less," he said. "It's who you are, the dedication, the intelligence, the fierce commitment to what's right, that..." He paused, choosing his next words carefully. "That matters to me."

Something softened in her expression, a slight lowering of defenses. She nodded once, accepting his words without need for further reassurance.

"Venice, then," she said, turning toward the small bedroom

to collect their sparse belongings. "Let's finish this."

As she left he was struck by the certainty that whatever lay ahead, danger, deception, the complex web of the Consortium, they would face it together. The path forward remained uncertain, fraught with professional and personal challenges.

But as he began dismantling their temporary command center, erasing traces of their presence in the cabin, Javier noted something he hadn't experienced in years of undercover work: hope. Not for the mission's success, but for what might come after, a possibility that would have been unimaginable before Amanda Chen had stormed into his well-defined world, demanding truth and offering, despite her own reluctance, connection.

Outside, the storm had cleared completely, leaving behind a sky washed clean, brilliant blue stretching endlessly toward the horizon. A new day, with all its promise and peril, awaited them. Whatever came next, they would meet it not as individuals but as partners, in purpose, in pursuit of justice, and perhaps, in something deeper that neither was quite ready to name but both had begun to acknowledge.

With resolve setting his jaw and determination quickening his movements, Javier prepared to leave the safety of their temporary haven. Venice beckoned, and with it, the next chapter in their dangerous pursuit of truth, a pursuit that had unexpectedly led them not just toward justice, but toward each other.

Chapter 14

The afternoon light slanted through the high windows of the communal studio, catching dust motes that drifted like microscopic galaxies above half-finished canvases. Javier's fingers hovered over a digital photo pinned to the corkboard, a recent gallery newsletter featuring a painting with swooping brushstrokes that spoke to him in a language few would understand. His eyes narrowed, recognition settling into the corners of his mouth like an old friend.

"It's hers," he said, his voice a whisper. "She never could resist her signature fade from cobalt to indigo. Too proud of the technique."

Amanda stepped closer, the floorboards creaking beneath her practical boots. She studied the image, then Javier's face, cataloging the micro-expressions that flickered across his features, familiarity, admiration, and something more complicated. Three weeks ago, she would have cataloged these reactions as evidence against him. Now, she found herself leaning toward him, seeking his perspective.

"You know where she is," Amanda said. Not a question.

He nodded, still examining the swirls of deep blue, the delicate transitions of light. "She always painted near natural light. Her work depends on it. There's only a few lofts near the Arts District with that kind of exposure."

Amanda didn't question it. She trusted him now. More than she should. More than was safe for an FBI agent investigating the Eclipse Consortium's art smuggling operation. But Javier earned that trust, one rescue, one confession, one shared danger at a time, even as the full truth of his identity remained a shadow between them.

"Let's go," she said, turning toward the door. She caught a glimpse of her reflection in a cracked mirror leaning against the wall, her dark hair pulled back in its customary low pony-tail, her face bare of makeup, eyes alert and wary. The woman staring back looked nothing like someone who belonged in an art studio, among creative souls who painted emotion onto canvas. She looked like exactly what she was: a hunter.

They found the address with ease. Hidden in plain sight, a converted warehouse with a rusted metal door tucked away in a quiet alley. No sign, no indication of what lay within. Javier approached it with the confidence of someone retracing familiar steps, though he'd never mentioned knowing Isabel Serrano so intimately before.

"Ready?" he asked, his hand on the door.

Amanda nodded, brushing her fingers against the holster hidden beneath her jacket, a gesture of reassurance that became ritual over her years with the Bureau.

When they entered, the scent hit them first, linseed oil, turpentine, raw canvas. The air was thick with it, intimate and heady. Amanda's lungs filled with the chemical bouquet, and for a moment, she felt as though she stepped into a world where different rules applied, a world of creation rather than investigation, of expression rather than evidence.

The studio stretched before them, a testament to controlled chaos. Unfinished portraits stacked against walls, their faces half-formed and accusatory. Palettes crusted with paint in shadowy hues sat on tables like abandoned shields. Paint knives gleamed in the late afternoon light, tools that could create or destroy with equal efficiency.

Amanda's eyes swept the space with practiced precision. Every brushstroke on the scattered canvases spoke of tension, of beauty born under pressure. And in the center of it all, Isabel.

She stood before a massive canvas, brush in hand, her body poised like one of her own figures in oil. She didn't startle when they entered, as though she had been expecting them, or someone, to interrupt her solitude. She turned, with the deliberate grace of a dancer changing positions.

"Javier," she said, his name emerging with a hint of nostalgia beneath the edge in her voice. Her gaze shifted to Amanda, assessing. "You must be Special Agent Chen."

Isabel's hair was tied back in a messy knot, streaks of blue paint smudged across her forearm like bruises. Her face carried the intense focus of someone who had been lost in her work for hours, perhaps days. She looked both exhausted and electrified, the contradiction giving her features a strange luminosity.

Amanda crossed her arms, voice clipped. "We're not here to admire your technique."

"No?" Isabel set down her brush with precise care, wiping her hands on a rag that had once been white but now resembled a battlefield of color. "That's disappointing. It's quite good."

Javier stepped forward, moving between them like a translator navigating two incompatible languages. "Isabel," he said, his tone calm. "We know Ginevra is looking for you. She's looking for us as well. We both know her well enough to know she isn't going to stop."

Isabel's smile faltered, a crack appearing in her composed exterior. She glanced toward the door, then back at them, calculation playing across her features.

"Why would she be looking for me? She works for you doesn't she?" She gestured toward a sitting area in the corner of the studio, two paint-splattered armchairs and a low table covered in art magazines and coffee rings.

"I'm, not who you think I am Isabel." Javier almost whispered, as if hesitant to drop his alter ego once and for all. I'm actually ..."

"A cop." Isabel said matter of matter-of-factly. "Or at least some kind of law enforcement."

"Yes but how did you know?" Javier asked

"You played the role well don't get me wrong," Isabel said shaking her head "but you have always had flashes of kindness that just didn't fit with your persona." She scrunched her nose in thought. "With me for example, you cared about my craft, encouraged me to become better so my own painting would improve and give me the tools to open my own gallery.. Those human interactions just never fit with the cold mask you wore."

Isabel returned her eyes to Javier's, "I assume you're here because you want something from me."

Amanda remained standing, her posture rigid. "We want information about the Consortium's operation. Specifically, their plans for the upcoming transfers."

Isabel sank into one of the chairs, now looking smaller, more fragile. The defiance drained from her posture like water through sand. "You don't understand what you're asking. These people, they don't forgive mistakes. They don't allow betrayal."

"You want out," Javier said, not a question but a statement of fact. His eyes caught hers, holding her gaze with an intensity that suggested shared history. "This is your moment."

Isabel's shoulders sagged. The heft of secrets pressed upon her, bending her spine beneath invisible pressure. "It wasn't supposed to be like this," she said, almost in tears. "I just wanted to create. To understand the masters by becoming them, even for a moment."

"But now you forge masterpieces that fund weapons and drugs," Amanda said, unmoved by the artistic justification.

"I didn't know. Not at first." Isabel looked up, her eyes searching Amanda's for understanding. "By the time I realized what they were using my work for, I was already in too deep."

"What changed?" Javier asked, his voice softening. "Why now?"

Isabel stood, moving to a canvas covered by a paint-stained sheet. She pulled it away to reveal a half-completed painting, a dark scene of figures in shadow, faces twisted in expressions of pain and terror.

"Dominic's setting up something bigger. Offshore accounts, encrypted buyers, weapons laundering under the guise of private art transport." Her fingers traced the outline of one shadowy figure, her touch almost reverent despite the darkness of the subject. "I want no part of it anymore."

Amanda's heart pounded as puzzle pieces fell into place. Dominic Hayes wasn't just involved in the Consortium, he was orchestrating the next phase. The art smuggling wasn't the end goal; it was the beginning, the foundation for something much larger and more devastating.

"We'll need names," Amanda said, stepping closer. "Dates. Locations. Everything you have."

Isabel nodded, moving toward a desk in the corner. "I've kept records. Not openly, of course, but encoded in my inventory lists. The paintings themselves contain clues, specific color combinations, background elements that correspond to,"

***

The door exploded inward with a deafening boom, the metal frame warping as the deadbolt tore clean from the wall. A cloud of plaster dust billowed through the studio, illuminated by another flash of lightning. In that strobing moment, a silhouette appeared in the doorway, a woman, tall and elegant, the curves of her body encased in black leather, her posture suggesting the calm before violence.

As the dust settled, Ginevra Sforza stepped through the threshold, her movements liquid and precise. Water dripped from her dark hair, trailing down her face like tears, though her expression held nothing resembling sorrow. In one hand she held a matte-black pistol, the other rested on her thigh, inches from the curved dagger strapped there. Her lips curved into a smile.

"Three targets," she said, her Italian accent lending a musical quality to her words. Her voice carried over the rain's downpour, cool and crisp as winter air. "One blade. Let's see who's still breathing in five minutes."

Amanda's gun was in her hand before she registered reaching for it, muscle memory cutting through shock. She slid to the side, positioning herself between Ginevra and Isabel, who screamed and ducked behind a paint-splattered storage cabinet.

Javier dove behind a concrete support column, his movement drawing Ginevra's attention just long enough for Amanda to adjust her stance. The FBI agent's mind raced through tactical calculations, distance to cover, angle of fire, civilian position.

Ginevra fired first, three rounds in rapid succession. The bullets tore through canvases stacked against the wall, sending splinters of wood frame and shreds of painted linen into the air. Amanda returned fire, two measured shots that forced Ginevra to abandon her position in the doorway, rolling behind a stack of wooden crates.

"Get down!" Amanda shouted to Isabel, who was frozen in place, her eyes wide with terror. The artist dropped to the floor, crawling beneath the heavy workbench as gunfire continued to echo through the studio.

Javier moved along the periphery, using the shadows and stacks of art materials as cover, trying to flank Ginevra's position. His jaw clenched tight, eyes narrowed in concentration. Amanda caught his movement and understood his intention without words, they fell into the rhythms of partners despite having never trained together.

"So far she's alone!" Amanda called out, firing another round to keep Ginevra pinned down.

But Ginevra emerged from behind the crates like water finding its path, fluid and unstoppable. She fired twice at Amanda, forcing the agent to duck behind an industrial shelving unit. The bullets punched through metal, sending art supplies cascading to the floor in a crash of glass and plastic.

Javier lunged forward, attempting to disarm Ginevra, but she anticipated the move. She ducked beneath his swing, twisted at the waist, and slammed the butt of her pistol into his jaw with brutal accuracy. The impact sent him staggering backward, blood welling at the corner of his mouth.

Ginevra spun in a half-circle, her hand dropping to her thigh holster and coming up with a throwing knife. The blade whistled through the air, missing Amanda's shoulder by inches as she dove to the side. The knife embedded itself in the plaster wall with a solid thunk, precisely where Isabel had been crouching seconds before.

Amanda charged forward, abandoning cover for speed, going low to catch Ginevra off-balance. They collided with the force of a car crash, bodies tangling as they crashed through an empty canvas frame. They landed hard on the concrete floor, Amanda on top, pinning Ginevra with her weight.

Ginevra looked up at her, blood smeared at her temple, and smiled with predatory delight. "Still too slow," she breathed, before driving her forehead up into Amanda's face.

Stars exploded across Amanda's vision as pain radiated from her nose. Her gun skittering away under the assault. Ginevra used the momentary advantage to twist beneath her, rolling them both and coming up in one elegant, practiced motion. She drew the curved blade from her thigh, the metal catching the next lightning flash like a sliver of captured electricity.

Amanda scrambled to her feet, tasting copper as blood trickled from her nose down to her upper lip. Her gun, lost somewhere in the chaos of spilled paint and broken frames. She backed up, eyes locked on the blade in Ginevra's hand.

Javier tackled Ginevra from behind, his arms wrapping around her waist as they both went down. They grappled on the floor, the knife slicing through the air inches from his neck as he struggled to control her wrist. He managed to slam her knife hand against a nearby support beam, but she responded by driving her knee into his ribs with enough force to make him gasp.

She twisted free of his grasp, rolling away and coming up in a defensive crouch, blade still in hand, eyes darting between Amanda and Javier as they both circled her. Blood from a cut on her forehead began to trail down her face, giving her the appearance of a Renaissance painting depicting beautiful violence.

Amanda wiped at her own bloodied lip with the back of her hand. "Javier, turn her!" she called out, their impromptu partnership finding its voice in the heat of combat.

He nodded once, understanding her intent without further explanation. He moved in with quick, aggressive strikes, each one just off-center, designed not to land but to draw Ginevra's focus and attention. She parried and countered, her knife creating dangerous arcs in the air between them.

Amanda circled behind, her heart pounding so hard she felt it in her throat. Sweat and blood clouded her vision, but she blinked it away, focused on finding her opening. Javier maintained the distraction, his movements becoming more elaborate, forcing Ginevra to turn further away from Amanda's approach.

But Ginevra hadn't survived this long by missing subtleties. She recognized the feint for what it was, dropping into a low sweep that took Javier's legs out from under him. As he fell, Amanda was already committed to her move, lunging forward with all her strength.

She caught Ginevra with her shoulder, driving the taller woman backward into the edge of the metal workbench. They crashed into it with bone-jarring force, sending tools and paint tubes crashing to the floor. Amanda grabbed Ginevra's knife wrist and slammed it down against the table's edge once, twice, a third time until the dagger clattered to the floor.

Javier scrambled up and seized Ginevra's other arm, twisting it behind her back as Amanda maintained her hold. Together, they forced the assassin down to her knees, though she fought them every inch of the way, thrashing and bucking against their combined strength with the fury of a cornered predator.

"You think arresting me ends this?" Ginevra snarled, her accent thickening with rage. The blood from the opening on her head painted half her face crimson, her eyes burning with feral intensity. "The Consortium is deeper than either of you can imagine."

Amanda tightened her grip, her palm slick with blood, both hers and Ginevra's. Her voice came out cold, flint-edged. "We'll burn every root."

With considerable effort, they secured handcuffs around Ginevra's wrists, forcing her face-down onto the floor as she continued to struggle. Javier's breathing came in ragged gasps, his shoulder trembling from the exertion and pain of the fight. A deep bruise was already forming along his jaw where Ginevra struck him.

Isabel emerged from her hiding place behind a tall shelf of dried canvases, her eyes wide with shock, her hands shaking. She stared at the blood-smeared assassin now restrained on her studio floor.

"Is... is she dead?" Isabel asked, her voice almost drowned out by the continuing storm.

"No," Javier replied grimly, one hand pressed against his ribs where Ginevra had kneed him. "But she's going away."

Ginevra looked up from the floor, smiling despite the blood between her teeth. "You're not ready for what comes next," she said, her voice carrying an unsettling certainty.

Amanda kept her expression neutral, though a chill ran through her at the words. "Neither were you," she replied, maintaining the calm facade that got her through countless previous confrontations.

She turned to Javier, noticing for the first time a shallow cut along his cheekbone that wept a thin line of blood. Their eyes met, and something unspoken passed between them, relief, recognition, perhaps something more complicated that neither was ready to name.

"Your backup better arrive soon," Isabel said, wrapping her arms around herself as she surveyed the destruction of her studio. Canvas slashed, paintings destroyed, blood splattered across the concrete floor, the scene resembled something from one of her darker works. "She won't be the last they send."

Amanda nodded, knowing Isabel was right. The Consortium wouldn't stop with one failed attempt. "We'll move you somewhere safe as soon as the roads clear."

"Safe," Isabel repeated, the word hollow in her mouth. "I don't think that place exists anymore."

Javier retrieved his phone from where it fell during the fight, checking for damage before dialing. "Extraction team ETA fifteen minutes," he reported after a brief conversation. "Weather's clearing enough for vehicle access."

Amanda knelt beside Ginevra, checking the handcuffs to ensure they were secure. The assassin stared up at her with unnerving intensity, as though memorizing every detail of her face.

Amanda nodded once, sharp and professional, though the

tremor in her hands betrayed her. "I will be when she's in a secure facility and Isabel's safe in protective custody."

Outside, the storm began to abate, the rain softening from vengeful downpour to steady rhythm. Through the shattered doorway, Amanda could see puddles reflecting the night sky, city lights smeared across their surfaces like impressionist paintings. The parallel not lost on her as she looked back at Isabel, who stood among the ruins of her forgeries, pale and resolute.

"It's going to get worse before it gets better," Amanda told her honestly.

Isabel nodded, a weary acceptance in her eyes. "It always does," she said, bending to retrieve a fallen painting that had somehow survived intact. "But at least I'll be on the right side of history this time."

Behind them, Ginevra laughed softly, the sound like silk against steel. "There are no right sides," she said. "Only survivors and those who wish they chose differently."

Amanda turned away from her, meeting Javier's gaze instead. In his eyes she saw the same determination that fueled her own actions, a commitment to justice that transcended their complicated beginning. Whatever came next, they would face it together, this strange partnership forged in danger and uncertainty.

Outside, sirens wailed in the distance, drawing closer with each passing second. The storm broke, but Amanda knew from experience that the true tempest was only beginning.

Chapter 15

The safe house crouched between abandoned warehouses like a secret held between cupped palms. Its windows were dark-eyed sentinels, watching the empty street where Amanda's sedan rolled to a stop. She killed the engine and sat for a moment, the silence humming in her ears like a warning. Beside her, Javier's profile was sharp against the shadows, his eyes fixed on the building where everything would change, or end.

"Ready?" she asked, her voice soft in the confined space.

Javier turned, the streetlight catching the golden flecks in his hazel eyes. "As I'll ever be."

They exited the car in synchronized movements, their footsteps crunching on broken asphalt. The night air carried the distant hum of the city, a reminder of the world that continued to spin, oblivious to the web of deception they were about to unravel. Amanda sensed Javier's presence at her back as she approached the building, a warmth that became familiar, almost necessary, in ways she failed to anticipate.

The door opened before she could knock. The man on the

threshold, Javier's handler, had the weathered face of someone who's seen too much of the world's underbelly. His silver-streaked hair cropped close to his skull, and his eyes moved between them with clinical precision.

"You're late," he said, stepping aside.

Amanda entered first, her shoulder brushing against Javier's as they crossed the threshold. The contact sent a current through her skin, a reminder of boundaries blurred and lines crossed. A few scattered lamps bathed the safe house interior in golden yellow light, throwing elongated shadows across concrete floors and sparse furniture. A folding table dominated the center of the room, its surface cluttered with maps, manila folders, and an assortment of gear.

Isabel stood by the window, her slender frame outlined against the night. Her fingers drummed against her crossed arms in a silent rhythm of anxiety. When she turned, Amanda recognized the look of someone who waded too far into dangerous waters to turn back.

"Agent Chen," Isabel said with a slight nod, her accent lilting the words.

Across the room, Sarah looked up from a laptop, the blue screen reflecting on her glasses. A half-smile pulled at her mouth, relief tempered by the gravity of their situation.

"Took you long enough," Sarah said, but the familiar tease lacked its usual spark. "I was beginning to think you decided to take a vacation instead."

"And miss all this?" Amanda gestured around the stark room. "Never. Thank you for coming, I know this isn't your normal day to day anymore, but I don't know who I can trust."

Sarah, waved her hand in a motion that stated, it's nothing. The charged air hummed with unspoken concerns and calculated risks. No one reached for an embrace; there were no warm welcomes, just the quiet acknowledgment that they stood on a precipice together.

Amanda approached the table and unrolled a map of the city, weighed down corners with nearby objects. Her finger traced along the contours of Los Angeles until it landed on a specific location.

"Skirball Cultural Center," the handler said, his finger tapping against the paper. "The shipping access is here, on the east side. According to our intelligence, Dominic plans to move the next batch of laundered artifacts before dawn." He looked up, meeting the eyes of everyone in the room. "We need to cut him off before he connects with the buyer."

Javier pulled a chair closer to the table, the metal legs scraping against concrete. "The window is narrow," he said, his voice carrying the quiet authority that came from years of undercover work. "Dominic's careful. He'll have security, but he'll keep it minimal to avoid drawing attention."

Isabel moved away from the window, her steps measured and deliberate. She placed a thick file beside the map, her hand lingering on its surface as if reluctant to let go of her last lifeline.

"This is everything I have," she said, her voice steady despite the fear flickering in her eyes. "Transaction records dating back three years. GPS tracking data from shipments. Codes linking Dominic directly to accounts controlled by the Consortium." She paused, swallowing. "And forgery verification on pieces that passed through my hands."

Amanda studied Isabel with newfound respect. The art restorer had been manipulated by the Consortium, her exceptional skills exploited for their gain. When she discovered the truth about who she was really working for, she wanted out, willing to risk everything to do so.

"It's enough," Amanda said, recognizing the vulnerability beneath Isabel's composed exterior. "You're the linchpin in all of this. What you've provided is what brings it all down."

Isabel's shoulders relaxed by a fraction, though her eyes remained vigilant. "They'll kill me if they find out."

"They won't," Javier said with such conviction that even Amanda almost believed it was a guarantee rather than a hope.

Sarah closed her laptop with a decisive snap. "I've got the surveillance feed loops ready to deploy. We'll have a fifteen-minute blind spot to work with." She pushed her glasses up her nose. "After that, we're visible."

Javier's handler stepped forward. "Secret Service has been tracking the Consortium's international connections for months. The moment he's in custody, we move on three continents. This is bigger than Los Angeles."

Amanda felt the weight of their collective efforts pressing down on her chest. Across the table, her eyes met Javier's. His gaze was intense, grounding, a silent affirmation that regardless of what awaited them, they would face it together. It was a connection forged in danger and deception, yet somehow more honest than anything she knew before.

The tension in the room threatened to suffocate them until Sarah cleared her throat.

"Okay, is it bad that I miss boring field reports and coffee that doesn't taste like motor oil?" she asked, breaking the heavy moment.

A soft ripple of laughter moved through the room, brief, genuine, and startlingly human against the backdrop of their dangerous reality. For a moment, they weren't agents and assets; they were people united by a common cause, finding fellowship in the eye of the storm.

"The coffee here isn't that bad," Javier's handler said, but the corner of his mouth twitched upward.

As they continued finalizing details, Amanda found herself studying Javier when he wasn't looking. The man who infiltrated the Eclipse Consortium, who walked the knife's edge between darkness and light for so long that she wondered if he remembered which side he belonged to. She distrusted him fiercely at first, believing him to be another criminal. Learning his true identity, a deep-cover Secret Service agent, shifted her world on its axis.

Later, as Sarah and Isabel checked equipment and Javier's handler made calls from the corner, Amanda found herself alone with Javier in the small back room that served as a makeshift armory. The space was tight, forcing them to move around each other in a dance of careful proximity. His cologne, subtle and warm, as he reached past her for extra magazines, gave her comfort.

"What happens after this?" she asked, her voice low enough that it wouldn't carry beyond the doorway.

He paused, turning to face her. The single overhead bulb cast shadows across the planes of his face, making his eyes appear darker, deeper. "You mean if we survive?"

She nodded, refusing to flinch from the reality of their situation.

"I stop running," he said after a moment. "No more covers, no more lies." His gaze held hers steadily. "If you'll let me... I'd like to stop with you."

Amanda's heart hammered against her ribs. They circled each other for months, first as adversaries, then as reluctant allies, and now as something neither of them dared to name. She took a step toward him, crossing the invisible boundary they maintained.

"I never thought I'd find something real in all this," she said, the words feeling foreign on her tongue. Trust didn't come easily to her, not since her ex-husband left her shattered confidence in his wake. But Javier saw her, truly saw her, when she was at her most guarded.

"You didn't find it alone," he said, his hand rising to brush a strand of hair from her face.

The air between them vibrated with possibility. Amanda leaned in, drawn by a gravity she couldn't resist. Javier's breath warmed her lips, the kiss was warm and comforting, like a blanket you wrap around you on a cold winter's night.

A sound from the outer room pulled them back to reality. The moment slipped away, incomplete but not forgotten. There was still too much at stake, too many dangers to navigate before they could claim any future for themselves.

They returned to find the others gathered around the table, their faces set with determination. Amanda straightened her shoulders and outlined her role in the confrontation with Dominic. Her voice remained steady as old betrayals churned in her stomach. Dominic had been her colleague, her mentor at the Bureau. His duplicity cut deeper than any knife.

Throughout the briefing, Javier remained uncharacteristically quiet, his thoughts seemingly far away. When the plan had been dissected from every angle, when every contingency had been addressed, he spoke.

"I'm going to tell Dominic who I am," he announced.

The room stilled. His handler's head snapped up, eyes narrowing.

"You're sure? As of now he thinks you betrayed the Consortium to protect Amanda. Once he is apprehended you could continue your work." the older man asked, but it wasn't a question.

Javier nodded. "Dominic needs to know who brought him down. No more shadows."

Sarah looked impressed, her usual skepticism momentarily replaced with respect. Isabel's face now pale, the implications of Javier's decision clearly disturbing her. But Amanda... a surge of pride so fierce it caught her by surprise welled up inside of Amanda.

"It's time, we can fight them in the light now, no more shadows." she agreed, and when Javier's eyes found hers, she saw the gratitude there.

The next hour passed in methodical preparation. Weapons were checked, communications tested, positions confirmed. No one spoke of failure, though the possibility haunted the edges of their movements. Amanda strapped her holster to her thigh, the weight of her service weapon familiar and reassuring. Across the room, Javier slipped a knife into his boot, a backup for when everything else failed.

When they emerged from the safe house, the night deepened. Stars fought through the haze of city lights, distant witnesses to the drama unfolding below. Their vehicles were parked in formation, dark, anonymous, ready for quick escape if necessary.

Amanda paused before getting into her car, her gaze sweeping over her team one last time. Sarah with her tech bag slung over her shoulder. Isabel, pale but resolute. Javier's handler, his face impassive but his eyes alert. And Javier himself, standing apart from the others, watching her with an intensity that made her breath catch.

No one voiced the anxiety that coiled in their stomachs. No one mentioned that by this time tomorrow, they would either have dismantled one of the most sophisticated smuggling operations in the world, or they would be dead.

Instead, they moved like shadows into the night, car doors closing with soft thuds, engines purring to life. The convoy pulled away from the safe house, each vehicle taking a different route to their destination. In her rear view mirror, The building receded, a nondescript structure that housed their hopes and fears.

Ahead lay the Skirball Cultural Center, and Dominic, and an end to years of deception. Amanda tightened her grip on the steering wheel and drove into the darkness, ready to face whatever waited at dawn.

***

A ghostly veil of fog rolled across the loading bays, its tendrils curling around the shipping containers like spectral fingers. The pre-dawn light painted everything in washed-out blues and grays, transforming the Skirball Cultural Center's utilitarian back lot into something otherworldly. Amanda pressed her back against the cold metal of a container, her breath forming small clouds that dissipated into the mist. The weight of her service weapon was reassuring against her palm, cold, certain, final.

The shipping containers loomed around her like ancient monoliths, their corrugated sides slick with condensation. From her position at the northeast corner of the lot, she had a clear view of the warehouse entrance while remaining hidden in shadow. Overhead, the sky was beginning to lighten, a gradual shift from black to navy that would soon give way to dawn. They had less than an hour before the regular staff would arrive.

Amanda's heart hammered against her ribs, a steady rhythm that matched the ticking seconds. The familiar stillness before action, electric, alive with possibility and danger. It was a intimate sensation, but tonight it was sharpened by personal betrayal. Memories flickered through her mind: Dominic showing her around the FBI field office on her first day; Dominic congratulating her after her first successful raid; Dominic raising a glass at the Bureau Christmas party, his eyes crinkling with what she thought was genuine warmth.

You trained with him. Trusted him.

Her earpiece crackled softly. "Exit door secure," Sarah's voice came through. "Cameras looped. We're invisible."

"Copy," Amanda replied, her words a mere breath against the microphone clipped to her collar. "Any movement on the south side?"

"Negative," Javier's handler replied. Despite his initial reluctance to let Isabel participate in the operation, he recognized her value, not just for the evidence she provided, but for her ability to identify forgeries if they discovered artifacts during the arrest.

Amanda's gaze swept across the loading bay to the service stairwell where Javier positioned himself. In the gloom, she could just make out his silhouette, a darker shadow against the gray concrete. He was unnaturally still, his body poised with the patience of a predator. Even from a distance, she could feel the intensity of his focus as his eyes tracked every angle of approach, every potential threat.

The rooftops. The bay doors. Amanda.

She recognized it over the past weeks, the way his attention always found her in a room, the way he positioned himself to shield her in moments of danger. It annoyed her at first, this unsolicited protection. But now, understanding who he was and why he did it, she found herself grateful for his vigilance.

Keep her alive, Javier repeated to himself like a mantra. *No matter what.*

The mission was critical, the take down of Dominic essential, but in the quiet center of his mind, Amanda's safety became his true north. Too many nights had been spent imagining all the ways this could go wrong, all the ways he could lose her just when he found something worth holding onto.

The sound of tires crunching on gravel broke the silence. A sleek black SUV appeared at the entrance to the loading area, its headlights cutting through the fog like twin searchlights. It rolled to a stop precisely where they anticipated, the engine purring for a moment before falling silent.

Amanda tightened her grip on her weapon, counting her breaths to steady her pulse.

The driver's door opened, and Dominic Hayes stepped out into the misty half-light. He wore a charcoal suit that looked freshly pressed, his sandy blonde hair perfectly styled despite the early hour. His movements were unhurried, confident, a man who believed himself untouchable. He adjusted his cuffs with the casual precision of someone who had long ago mastered the art of appearing ordinary while orchestrating extraordinary crimes.

He surveyed the loading bay, his gaze passing over Amanda's hiding spot without a flicker of recognition. His posture betrayed nothing but relaxed anticipation as he checked his watch and then walked toward the nearest shipping container.

This was the moment they planned for. Amanda stepped out

from the shadows, her weapon lowered but ready.

"Hello, Dominic."

His head snapped toward her, surprise flickering across his face before being replaced with a practiced smile. Recognition dawned in his eyes, followed by something else, amusement.

"I was wondering when you'd stop dancing around me," he said, his voice carrying easily across the quiet loading bay. "But coming alone? Bold." His eyes narrowed. "Or stupid."

Amanda moved forward, each step deliberate. "We've worked together for years, Dominic. You tell me."

"What I can tell you," he replied, his tone conversational, "is that you're making a mistake. Whatever you think you know, "

"I know everything," she cut him off. "The Eclipse Consortium. The forgeries. The smuggling network spanning three continents." She kept her voice calm, controlled. "I know you've been running it all from inside the Bureau."

A flicker of irritation crossed his features, quickly masked. "Impressive theory. Shame about the lack of evidence."

"Oh, I have evidence." Amanda took another step closer. "You taught me to be thorough. I learned well."

Dominic studied her face, his blue eyes calculating. "I trusted you once. You remember what happened last time I made that mistake? With that smuggling ring in San Diego?" His voice dropped lower, infused with false sympathy. "You couldn't pull the trigger. You hesitated. And people died."

The memory stung, a rookie error that had nearly cost Amanda her career. But she was not that same agent anymore.

"You're wrong," she said, her voice steady. "About a lot of things."

Something shifted in Dominic's expression, a realization

that perhaps he miscalculated. His hand drifted casually toward his side.

"I wouldn't," Amanda said, raising her weapon. "Not unless you want this to end badly."

Dominic's smile returned, sharp as a blade. "It's already going to end badly, for you." His gaze flicked past her. "Your backup is two minutes out. I have five men in position. You really think I wouldn't plan for this?"

"Actually," came a voice from behind him, "she planned for you. She even got the Secret Service to help her"

Dominic spun to find Javier emerging from the shadows, his weapon trained with unwavering precision, while his other hand held his credentials. The recognition that flashed across Dominic's face was almost satisfying, the moment when the predator realizes he's become the prey.

"Secret Service," Dominic said, his confidence cracking. "Well played."

The tension between them cracked open like thunder in the pre-dawn stillness. Javier's voice, when he spoke, carried the weight of years spent in the shadows.

"You've run long enough," he said.

Dominic's gaze darted between them, assessing options that were rapidly dwindling. "So the rumors were true." He gave a short, humorless laugh. "I never believed it. A deep-cover agent inside the Consortium? Too good to be true. I guess you are the real El Fantasma. Shame I was beginning to like the moniker"

"Yet here we are," Javier replied, his expression unreadable.

Amanda raised her weapon, her aim unwavering. "It's over, Dominic. The evidence is already secured. Your accounts are being frozen as we speak."

Silence stretched between them, taut as a wire. Then, with a movement so fluid it was almost beautiful, Dominic reached for his concealed weapon.

He never completed the draw.

From multiple positions around the loading bay, agents moved in synchronized precision. Javier's handler emerged from a security door, flanked by two additional agents. The trap had been meticulously planned and flawlessly executed.

Dominic found himself surrounded, his options reduced to a single choice: surrender.

For a heartbeat, Amanda thought he might resist, might force them to make a choice that would end with blood on the concrete. But Dominic had always been a pragmatist. He slowly raised his hands, his face a mask of cold fury.

One of the agents moved forward, securing his weapon and cuffing him with practiced efficiency. "Dominic Hayes, you are under arrest for racketeering, conspiracy, fraud, and trafficking of stolen artifacts."

Amanda stood over him as he was forced to his knees, her breath coming in controlled, even measures. The fog began to lift, the first pale orange streaks of dawn breaking across the eastern sky.

"You trained me to follow my instincts," she said, looking down at the man who had once been her mentor. "I followed them straight to you."

Dominic's eyes were chips of ice. "Congratulations on your promotion, Chen. This will certainly earn you one." His gaze shifted to Javier. "And what about you, ghost? What do you get for your years of service? A medal they'll never let you wear in public?"

Javier didn't respond. He didn't need to. His silent presence beside Amanda spoke volumes, no more hiding, no more pretending.

As other agents arrived to secure the scene and transport Dominic, Amanda felt a strange hollowness where satisfaction should have been. Justice had been served, but it tasted bittersweet. The corruption ran deeper than anyone suspected, reaching into the heart of the Bureau itself.

"Agent Chen," Isabel called from near the SUV. "You're going to want to see this."

The vehicle's hidden compartment yielded what they expected, a collection of expertly forged antiquities prepared for transport. Isabel moved among them with the careful precision of an expert, confirming what they already knew: the forgeries were masterful, almost impossible to detect without specialized knowledge.

"These would have passed any standard authentication," she said, examining a small oil on canvas with reverent fingers. "The craftsmanship is... exceptional."

"Which is why they recruited you," Amanda said. "They needed the best."

Isabel nodded, a mix of pride and shame coloring her features. "And now?"

"Now you help us find the rest," Javier said, joining them. "Your testimony is going to be crucial."

As the evidence was cataloged and secured, as Dominic was led away to a waiting transport vehicle, Amanda found herself standing apart from the activity, watching the sunrise paint the world in new colors. The fog dissipated entirely, leaving behind a symbolic clarity.

Javier moved to her side, his shoulder almost touching hers. They didn't speak , content to share the moment of hard-won peace.

"Your handler mentioned there would be simultaneous raids across three continents," Amanda said.

"Already underway," Javier replied. "Paris, Dubai, Buenos Aires. By noon, the entire network will be exposed."

She nodded, digesting this. "And you?"

"Debriefing. Probably for weeks." His gaze remained on the horizon. "After that... I meant what I said last night."

Amanda turned to face him, studying the lines of his profile against the morning light. The man who lived so many lives, worn so many masks, now stood beside her without pretense. It was terrifying and exhilarating all at once.

"I'm not easy to be around," she said, her voice soft.

"I've noticed," he replied, the corner of his mouth lifting in a half-smile as he rubbed at the wound in his shoulder.

"I work too much. I'm stubborn. I don't know how to let people in."

"Also noted."

She shook her head, fighting the smile that threatened to break through her serious expression. "You're not making this easy."

"Easy is overrated," Javier said, turning to meet her gaze. "I've had enough easy lies to last a lifetime. I'll take complicated truth any day."

Around them, the operation continued, agents securing evidence, processing the scene, preparing reports that would dominate headlines for weeks to come. But in that moment, there was only the quiet satisfaction of justice... and the beginning of something real.

Amanda reached out, her fingers finding his in the new morning light. Not a declaration, not a promise, just a connection. For now, it was enough.

Chapter 16

The heavy glass door of the FBI field office closed behind Amanda with a soft hiss, sealing away the fluorescent glare of debriefing rooms and evidence boards. Dawn spread across Los Angeles like a watercolor wash, painting the concrete towers in hesitant gold and rose. She stood motionless for a moment, her body anchored to the steps by a weariness that settled into her bones hours ago, while her mind raced ahead, electric with adrenaline that refused to fade.

The air carried the scent of night-cooled asphalt warming in the first light. Amanda inhaled, letting the clean morning replace the stale coffee and nervous sweat of the interrogation room where she spent the last six hours. Her reflection ghosted across the mirrored windows of the building opposite, dark circles beneath her eyes, hair pulled back in a tight ponytail that had once been neat, now frayed at the edges like her nerves.

She began walking, each step a deliberate act. Her heels clicked against the pavement, a metronome counting time in a city on the brink of waking up. Twenty-seven hours since she'd last slept. Forty-two since everything changed.

The streets held a peculiar emptiness which exists only in the liminal space between night workers heading home and day workers not yet arrived. A street cleaner hummed in the distance. The occasional car glided past, headlights still on against the strengthening daylight. Amanda was suspended between worlds, the one where she was Special Agent Chen, who helped bring down part of the Eclipse Consortium's Los Angeles operation, and the one where she was only Amanda, a woman walking home at dawn with too many thoughts and not enough sleep.

Images flickered through her mind like slides from a carousel projector. Dominic's face when they arrested him, shock melting into a strange, resigned smile. Ginevra's perfect composure cracking only once, when they mentioned Interpol's interest in her activities in Milan. Isabel's hands, artist's hands, trembling as she signed her statement, ink bleeding where a tear fell on the page.

And Javier.

Amanda's pace faltered at the thought of him. She rubbed her temple, trying to ease the pressure building there. Her training in forensic psychology taught her to read people, to catalog micro-expressions and linguistic patterns, to build profiles from fragments. But Javier defied every category, every assumption.

The sky lightened further, cobalt giving way to cerulean. A flock of pigeons scattered from a nearby awning, wings catching the early light. Amanda saw them wheel away, envying their simple escape.

Her body moved on autopilot while her mind replayed the moment in the Getty Museum's lower gallery, Javier's body crashing into her, pulling her to the ground seconds before Ginevra's bullet violated his body right where Amanda had been standing. The warmth of his breath against her ear as he moaned, "I'm Secret Service."

A barista unlocked the door of a corner cafe, the scent of brewing coffee drifting out to the sidewalk. Amanda almost stopped, caffeine was a medical necessity at this point, but the need for solitude pulled stronger. Three more blocks to her apartment. Three more blocks until she can shed her professional skin and fall apart in private.

A jogger approached on the opposite sidewalk, earbuds in, eyes forward, breathing measured. He passed without glancing at her, without any recognition the woman he ran past had ended someone's life hours earlier. He disappear around a corner, marveling at the strange disconnect. How many people had she passed on city streets, never knowing what they carried inside them? How many had been like her, composure maintained by sheer will, while underneath, everything trembled?

Amanda tugged her blazer tighter around her body. The temperature was climbing as morning established itself, but the chill she from within was persistent. Her limbs were leaden, her eyelids heavy, yet her thoughts refused to slow their frantic pace.

What had they recovered? Smuggled antiquities, forged artworks, a ledger of clients that would keep the team busy for months. Success by any measure. Assistant Director Winters had actually smiled, a rare event, when Amanda finished her preliminary report.

A delivery truck backed into an alley, its reverse alarm beeping in rhythmic warning. A street vendor arranged fruits in precise rows, their colors vibrant against the gray concrete surrounding them. The city awoke, indifferent to her exhaustion, to the weight she carried.

Javier's face filled her mind again. The way light and shadow played across his features as they huddled in the service corridor, the sounds of pursuit fading. How he smiled, that particular smile transformed his face from handsome to devastating, when she confronted him about his real identity.

"You knew," she accused, the pieces clicking into place.

"I hoped you would figure it out," he replied, and there had been relief in his voice, as if carrying the lie had been painful.

Amanda turned onto her street, recognizing the familiar row of buildings, the deli on the corner, the bookstore with its hand-painted sign. Home was close now, her small apartment on the ninth floor with its view of the city and its blessed silence.

She thought of Isabel's final words to her, spoken in the quiet of the observation room while technicians photographed the forged Monet that had been the bait in their operation. "He watched you, you know. When you weren't looking. Not like the others watch women. Like you were a puzzle he was trying to solve without touching the pieces, like a priceless piece of art in need of protection."

Amanda's hand drifted to her neck, fingertips finding the small, hard knot of tension where her shoulder met her trapezius. The muscles there coiled tight as springs. Her feet ached in her sensible heels. Her eyes burned from lack of sleep and the aftermath of adrenaline.

A small groan escaped her as she realized she'd have to return for further debriefing in a few hours. The case would require weeks of paperwork, testimony, evidence processing.

The machinery of justice ground slowly, methodically, with no regard for human frailty.

As she approached her building, Amanda found herself scanning the street, the doorways, the parked cars. The habit ingrained now, heightened by recent events. Nothing appeared out of place, but the prickle at the back of her neck remained. Was it paranoia, or instinct? After the past forty-eight hours, she wasn't sure she could tell the difference.

The doorman nodded as she entered the lobby, his expression neutral despite her disheveled appearance. The elevator arrived with a soft chime, empty at this hour. Amanda stepped inside and pressed the button for the ninth floor, watching the doors slide closed on the lobby, on the world.

Javier's voice echoed in her memory: "We're not so different, you and I. Both of us living in the spaces between truth and lies."

The elevator stopped. The doors opened. Amanda stepped into the hallway, moving toward her apartment door like a compass needle finding north. Home. Safety. Solitude.

She fumbled with her keys, the metal cool against her fingertips. The lock turned. The door opened.

And Amanda stepped forward, ready to shed her badge, her weapon, her armor, ready to be herself in the quiet sanctuary of her own space, where no one saw her fall apart and put herself back together again.

***

The key slid into the lock with a familiar click. Amanda pushed her apartment door open, her body already anticipating the relief of solitude. The hinges whispered as the door swung inward, revealing her small living room bathed in morning light, and the silhouette of a man rising from her

277

armchair by the window. Her hand moved to her holster, but her brain, despite its exhaustion, processed the identity before her fingers could grasp her weapon. Javier. In her apartment. The sharp intake of her breath echoed in the quiet room.

He stood still, hands visible at his sides, a deliberate choice not lost on Amanda. His silhouette was backlit by the morning sun streaming through her blinds, casting golden slats across his figure. In this light, with the city spread out behind him nine stories below, he looked almost otherworldly.

"I should've knocked," Javier said, his voice deliberate and modulated. "I just... needed to see you. Not as a suspect, not as an agent, and not as your source. Me."

Amanda remained frozen in the doorway, one hand still gripping the knob, the other hovering near her weapon. Her mind, foggy with exhaustion moments before, was now painfully alert. A dozen questions competed for priority: How did he get in? How did he know where she lived?

Yet beneath these practical concerns lurked a more troubling question: Why did his presence in her most private space feel like an intrusion and a homecoming all at once?

"Breaking and entering is still a crime, even for undercover agents," she said, her voice steadier than she felt.

A ghost of a smile touched his lips. "Former lockpick. Old habits." He gestured at her lock. "You should upgrade your security."

Amanda released the doorknob and stepped inside, closing the door behind her. The click of the latch soft but strangely definitive. They were alone now, sealed together in her apartment, away from handlers and agencies and the complex web of lies that defined their interactions until yesterday.

"You look like hell," she said, allowing her eyes to assess

him. It wasn't hyperbole. The immaculate Javier Morales she'd first encountered at the Getty benefit, with his tailored suit and perfect smile, had been replaced by this haggard version. His hair was disheveled, dark stubble shadowed his jaw, and beneath his eyes lay smudges of fatigue matching her own. His shirt was wrinkled, as if he'd been wearing it for days. Yet something in the way he carried himself remained undiminished, a core of strength that adversity couldn't erode.

"I've slept worse," he said, a crooked smile tugging at his lips again. The smile had first caught her attention across a crowded gallery, before she knew who he was, before she suspected him of being part of the Eclipse Consortium rather than a fellow agent working undercover.

The morning light infiltrated her apartment, dust motes dancing in the golden beams falling across her simple furniture. Everything looked different with him in it, her threadbare couch, the bookshelf cluttered with forensic psychology textbooks, the single orchid struggling on her windowsill. Her space contracted both smaller and more significant.

"You shouldn't be here," Amanda said, but made no move to ask him to leave. Instead, she shrugged off her blazer and draped it over the back of a chair, a domestic gesture that felt strange in his presence.

"Probably not," Javier said, watching her movements with an intensity that made her skin warm despite her exhaustion. "But there are a lot of things I shouldn't have done in the past forty-eight hours."

He took a careful step toward her, and Amanda noted the slight stiffness in his movement. A stiffness brought on by injuries he got protecting her.

"Are you hurt?" she asked, professional concern overriding

personal confusion.

"Nothing serious. Might have a few interesting scars to add to the collection." He made a dismissive gesture, then winced, betraying his words.

Amanda's gaze tracked the movement, understanding there were wounds beneath the surface as painful as his physical ones. She knew what going deep undercover could do to an agent's psyche, the compartmentalization required, the constant vigilance, the blurring of boundaries. She studied it, written papers on it. But seeing it embodied in the man before her was different from academic understanding.

"I'm not running anymore," he said, voice low and deliberate. "And I don't want to be someone you have to chase or doubt."

The words hung in the air between them, weighted with meaning beyond their simple syllables. Amanda studied him, taking in the earnestness in his gaze, the tension in his shoulders, the way his hands opened at his sides, a gesture of surrender, of vulnerability.

She moved to the kitchen, her body on autopilot, seeking the comfort of routine. "You want coffee?" she asked, not waiting for his answer before filling the kettle. The mundane action gave her hands something to do while her mind processed his presence, his words.

"Black. Thanks." He didn't follow her, maintaining a respectful distance she both appreciated and found herself oddly disappointed by.

The kitchen was separated from the living room by a counter, allowing Amanda to watch him as she prepared the coffee. He moved to the window, looking out at the city that had been the stage for their dangerous dance these past weeks. His profile against the light reminded her of the moment on the pier when he pushed her out of the line of fire, his body shielding hers without hesitation.

"How much of it was real?" she asked without thinking, the question escaping before she could contain it. Her fingers stilled on the coffee canister.

Javier turned to face her, understanding immediately what she was asking. "More than was safe. Less than I wanted." He paused, considering his next words. "My cover was real. My assignment was real. The danger was real." Another pause. "What happened between us... wasn't in any operation plan."

Amanda measured coffee into the French press, focusing on the simple task. "The Bureau will have questions."

"The Secret Service has already started their debrief. I've been answering questions for eighteen hours." He ran a hand through his hair, leaving it more disheveled than before. "They're satisfied my cover wasn't compromised, and the operation achieved its primary objectives."

The kettle clicked off. Amanda poured steaming water over the coffee grounds, watching them bloom and rise. The rich aroma filled the small kitchen, a comforting counterpoint to the tension that vibrated between them.

"Why are you really here, Javier?" she asked, her voice softer now, almost lost beneath the hiss of settling coffee grounds.

He moved closer, stopping at the edge of the kitchen. The counter remained between them, a physical barrier that seemed to represent all the others, agency jurisdictions, professional ethics, the lies told and truths withheld.

"Because when the dust settled and the reports filed, the only clear thought in my head was... I needed to see you," he said. "Not to explain or justify or continue the operation. Just to see you, Amanda. Just to be seen by you, without pretense."

Something in his voice, a raw honesty impossible to feign, made her look up and meet his gaze full force. What she saw there caused her breath to catch: exhaustion, yes, and the hyper vigilance common to deep-cover operatives, but also something warm and unguarded that made her chest tighten.

She pushed the filled French press across the counter toward him, a peace offering of sorts. Their fingers brushed as he accepted it, and a jolt hit them, not static from the dry air, but something more elemental, a current that had been building since their first encounter.

Javier's eyes never left hers as he poured two mugs of coffee. He added a splash of cream to one, hers, without asking, having noticed her preference during their surveillance operations. The small, domestic gesture struck Amanda with unexpected force. This man had been watching her, learning her, even while maintaining his cover.

She accepted the mug, their fingers brushing again. This time, neither pulled away.

"I've spent three years living as someone else," Javier said. "Saying things I didn't believe, befriending people I was investigating, betraying confidences to serve a greater good. I've lied so convincingly that sometimes I forgot what was true." He looked down at their hands, still connected by the ceramic mug between them. "But I never lied about how I felt about you. I couldn't. Even when I should have."

The last remnant of Amanda's professional detachment crumbled. Her shoulders dropped, tension bleeding out of them as something inside her cracked open. The walls she built, walls of training, of past betrayals, of self-protection, couldn't withstand the simple honesty in his gaze.

"I believe you," she said, the words falling from her lips like stones into still water, creating ripples that would reach farther than she could see.

Javier's expression shifted, surprise giving way to something that looked like hope. He set his coffee down untouched and moved around the counter, entering her space with careful deliberation, giving her every opportunity to step back or stop him.

She didn't.

He stood before her now, close enough she felt the warmth radiating from his body, see the flecks of gold in his hazel eyes, smell the faint scent of his cologne beneath the remnants of a long, hard day. In this light, she saw every detail of his face, the small scar above his left eyebrow, the day's growth of beard, the fine lines at the corners of his eyes deepened when he smiled.

"What happens now?" she asked, her voice barely above a whisper.

"I don't know," he said, his honesty continuing to disarm her. "I only know I couldn't walk away without seeing you. Without telling you that whatever comes next, debriefings, reassignments, the continuing investigation, I want to face it knowing where we stand."

Amanda set her own mug down and looked up at him, really looked at him, not as an agent assessing a subject, not as a woman appreciating an attractive man, but as one person seeing another in all their complexity.

"We stand together," she said, the words perfect as they left her lips.

His hand rose to her face, hovering shy of touching her cheek, asking permission with the gesture. Amanda leaned into his palm, granting it. His touch was gentle, reverent almost, his calloused thumb brushing across her cheekbone as if she were something precious and fragile.

They stood for a long moment, coffee cooling forgotten on the counter, morning light streaming around them, the city waking up beyond her windows. In this quiet kitchen, in this suspended moment, they weren't Agent Chen and Agent Morales, weren't FBI and Secret Service, weren't hunter and prey. They were Amanda and Javier, two people who found something unexpected in the chaos of deception and danger.

"Together," he repeated, the word a promise, a question, and an answer all at once.

***

The distance between them vanished like morning mist under sunlight. Amanda's hand rose to Javier's chest, her palm detecting the steady rhythm beneath muscle and bone. The heartbeat of a man, not an agent or an asset or a suspect, a man who walked through fire to stand before her. Javier's fingers traced the edge of her jaw with an appreciation that made her breath catch, as if he were memorizing her by touch. When their lips finally met, the contact wasn't explosive or desperate. It was inevitable, the quiet resolution of a question that had hung between them since the first charged glance across the Getty's marble hall.

Their bodies moved together with a slow gravity, drawn by forces more ancient than the artworks they used as cover for their first conversations. Amanda's fingers curled into the fabric of his shirt, anchoring herself as the kitchen tilted around her. Javier's hand slid from her jaw to the nape of her neck, cradling her head with careful strength. The gentle pressure of his fingers against her scalp released a sigh from her lips that he caught with his own.

Time stretched and compressed. The morning light painted golden stripes across their entwined figures. Outside, the city continued its relentless rhythm, but inside this small apartment, they created their own time signature, measured in heartbeats and shared breaths.

Amanda drew back, her dark eyes studying Javier's face. What she saw there, raw honesty stripped of pretense, made her decision easy. Her hand found his, fingers interlacing with deliberate purpose. Without words, she led him from the kitchen, through the small living room, and toward the bedroom at the back of the apartment.

The bedroom was a facet of Amanda that Javier had never seen, not during surveillance, not in briefings, not in the file the Bureau maintained. Here were the private dimensions of her existence: books stacked on the nightstand, a collection of smooth stones arranged on the windowsill, a Berkeley swimming team photo in a simple frame. The bed was made, military corners on the dark blue comforter suggesting habits formed long before the Bureau's influence.

They paused in the doorway, the significance of the threshold not lost on either of them. Crossing into this space meant leaving behind the final boundaries between their professional and personal lives. Javier's thumb traced small circles on the back of Amanda's hand, a silent question. Her answer came in the gentle tug that brought him into the room, into her most private sanctuary.

The morning sun filtered through half-drawn blinds, casting alternating bands of light and shadow across the bed. Amanda turned to face Javier, her eyes never leaving his as her fingers found the buttons of his shirt. Each one released with deliberate care, as if she were defusing a bomb or unlocking a safe, methodical movements revealed not just skin but vulnerability beneath.

Javier stood still under her ministrations, allowing her this control, this exploration. Only when the last button yielded did he reach for her, his hands finding the hem of her blouse with equal reverence. The silk whispered as it rose, exposing the smooth plane of her stomach, the delicate arch of her ribs, the small puckered scar on her lower left back that saw in her file but never seen. His fingers paused there, tracing its outline with a tender curiosity.

His lips replaced his fingers, pressing softly against the scar, an act of recognition, not pity. Amanda's breath caught at the contact, her hand finding his hair, fingers threading through the dark strands.

Their clothes fell away piece by piece, each layer a barrier removed, a truth revealed. Javier's shirt slid from his shoulders, exposing the bruises blooming across his shoulder where Ginevra's bullet found its mark. Amanda's blouse joined it on the floor, then her practical black bra, her sensible slacks. His belt, his trousers. Each item discarded like the pretenses they maintained.

They undressed one another like it mattered, like each revealed inch of skin was a confession, a secret handed over in trust. When they stood before each other, stripped of all concealment, the vulnerability was mutual and complete.

Javier's gaze traveled over Amanda with unhurried appreciation, seeing beyond the physical to the woman herself, the strength in her swimmer's shoulders, the determination in her straight spine, the subtle signs of exhaustion in the set of her mouth. His hands followed his eyes, skimming along her collarbone, down the elegant line of her arm, across the subtle curve of her waist.

"You're beautiful," he said, voice rough with emotion. The words were simple but held a magnitude of sincerity Amanda felt in her chest, a warmth spread outward to her fingertips.

Her response was to close the final distance between them, skin meeting skin in a contact drawing soft sounds from both their throats. The press of her body against his made phrases like "interagency cooperation" seem absurdly inadequate for what flowed between them now.

The sheets welcomed them as they sank onto the bed, cool cotton warming quickly against heated skin. Javier hovered above her, supporting his weight on forearms braced on either side of her head, careful of his injured ribs. Morning light gilded the planes of his face, caught in the depths of his hazel eyes as they searched hers for any hesitation, any doubt.

Amanda reached up to trace the small scar above his eyebrow, a mark she first saw during their initial meeting but never asked about. "Bogota," he supplied without prompting. "Glass from an explosion. Could have been worse."

Her thumb smoothed over, a wordless acknowledgment of the risks they both lived with daily. Then her hand slid to the back of his neck, drawing him down to her. The kiss deepened, mouths opening, tongues meeting in a slow exploration that spoke of patience despite desire.

Javier's hands mapped her slowly, as if memorizing her through touch alone. His palm curved around the modest swell of her breast, thumb brushing across sensitive skin with a delicacy that made her arch beneath him. His mouth followed, replacing fingers with lips, with gentle teeth, with the warmth of his breath.

Amanda's hands weren't idle, traveling across the landscape of his back, feeling the shift of muscle beneath warm skin, discovery of places made his breath catch or his rhythm falter. They learned each other with the same attention to detail they brought to their professional lives, observing responses, adjusting approaches, filing away discoveries for future reference.

But this was no interrogation or surveillance operation. This was a conversation conducted in sighs and touches, in the press of lips against pulse points, in the whisper of skin against skin. Their bodies spoke a language more honest than any they shared before, translating desire and tenderness into physical dialogue.

When Javier's hand slid between her thighs, Amanda's eyes fluttered closed, her head pressing back into the pillow. He stared at her face with reverent attention, learning which touches drew sharp intakes of breath, which movements caused her brow to furrow in concentration. His own breathing grew uneven as her hand wrapped around him, establishing a rhythm that spoke of both urgency and restraint.

"Amanda," he breathed, her name on his lips a confession and a prayer. Her eyes opened, finding his, holding his gaze as their bodies continued their intimate conversation.

The moment stretched between them, a bubble of suspended time where past and future receded, leaving only this bed, this light, these two bodies learning to speak as one.

When she guided him to her, the joining was slow, deliberate, eyes locked in silent communication. Amanda's fingers threaded into his hair, holding him as if she might lose herself if she didn't. Javier's hands framed her face, thumbs brushing her cheekbones with tender care.

They moved together, in both passion and understanding. Each thrust and response calibrated to the other's rhythm, building a synchronicity that transcended the physical. The intensity built between them, coiling tighter with each shared breath, each murmured encouragement, each revelatory touch.

Release came not as conquest but as mutual surrender. Amanda's body tensed beneath him, her eyes widening in surprise at the intensity before closing on a soft gasp. Javier followed moments later, his forehead pressed to hers, their breath mingling in the narrow space between their lips.

Afterward, they lay entwined, skin cooling in the air-conditioned room, hearts slowing to normal rhythm. Javier's arm curved protectively around Amanda's shoulders, her head nestled in the hollow beneath his collarbone. Their legs remained tangled, neither willing to separate from the other.

Silence wrapped around them, not the tense silence of surveillance or the wary silence of interrogation, but the comfortable quiet of two people who had said what needed saying without words.

The sun shifted, the stripes of light across the bed now angled differently. Outside, the sounds of midday traffic drifted up from the street below, a reminder of the world continuing without them. Inside this room, time had its own quality, elastic and gentle.

Amanda let out a breath, eyes fluttering open. "This... wasn't the plan," she said, voice husky.

Javier smiled against her temple, his lips brushing the spot where her hair met her forehead. "Maybe the plan needed rewriting."

A soft huff of laughter escaped her, vibrating against his

chest. "You intelligence types always think you can improvise."

"And you Bureau people always want everything by the book." His fingers traced lazy patterns on her bare shoulder, raising goosebumps in their wake.

They lay in companionable silence, bodies cooling, breathing synchronized. The city waited beyond the window, with its debriefings and reports, its continuing investigations and unfinished operations. El Fantasma was still out there. The Eclipse Consortium would regroup. There would be more cases, more danger, more difficult choices.

But for now, they had this, this bed, this light, this unexpected connection forged in the crucible of deception and danger.

Amanda shifted, propping herself up on one elbow to look down at Javier. Her dark hair fell in a curtain around her face, tips brushing his chest. In this light, with her defenses lowered, she looked younger, softer, still the formidable agent he came to respect, but also the woman he saw beneath the professional exterior.

"We're in this together," she said, the words simple but weighted with meaning. Not just this moment, not just this bed, but whatever came next, the complications and consequences, the professional fallout, the continuing investigation.

Javier reached up, tucking a strand of hair behind her ear, his fingers lingering against her cheek. His eyes, those expressive hazel eyes that could shift from charming to calculating in an instant, held nothing but truth as they met hers.

He kissed her, slow, deep, lingering. A kiss that spoke of mornings yet to come, of conversations not yet had, of truths still to be shared. Not a kiss of passion, though that element remained, but a kiss of promise. Not of easy days, their lives and work ensured those would be rare, but of presence. Of standing side by side, whatever storms approached.

When they separated, Amanda settled back against him, her head finding its place on his shoulder as if designed to fit there. Javier's arm curved around her, hand resting on the warm skin of her waist, thumb tracing the edge of her scar. Outside, a siren wailed once before fading into the distance, a reminder of the world they would have to rejoin soon.

But not yet. For now, they created this sanctuary of truth between them, this small space where masks could be set aside and armor removed. Whatever came next, and both knew there would be complications, explanations, perhaps even separations, they would face it with the knowledge of this truth between them.

"Together," Javier said, the word both acknowledgment and vow.

Amanda's fingers found his, intertwining on his chest above his beating heart. "Together," she echoed, sealing the promise.

17

Chapter 17

The morning light spilled across the pale travertine like liquid gold, casting long shadows behind Amanda and Javier as they ascended the steps of the Getty Museum. Neither spoke, but the silence between them wasn't empty, it was laden with memories, with echoes of gunfire and whispered confessions, with the weight of identities shed and newfound truths. Each step reverberated through her body, a physical reminder of the last time they stood here, when everything had been different.

Six months ago, she arrived in an emerald green gown with a Sig Sauer strapped to her thigh. Six months ago, Javier had been an enigma, a dangerous figure in the Eclipse Consortium's hierarchy, or so she thought. Six months ago, before she knew the truth.

"It's different in daylight," Javier said beside her, his voice a rumble that vibrated in the space between them.

Amanda tucked a strand of black hair behind her ear, the breeze carrying the scent of jacaranda and distant ocean. "Less champagne, more clarity," she replied, her tone dry but softened by the slight curve of her lips.

They reached the top of the stairs where the sprawling complex opened before them, all clean lines and open space. The city of Los Angeles stretched below, a vast expanse of urban landscape blending into the horizon. Amanda paused, taking a moment to adjust her blazer, a professional defense mechanism so different from the evening wear she donned for the gala.

"I keep thinking about that night," she said, her eyes fixed on the entrance, not focusing on anything. "How convinced I was that I had you figured out."

Javier's laugh was quiet, edged with something like regret. "You had parts of me figured out. Just not the most important ones."

His shoulder brushed against hers as they walked toward the entrance, the contact brief but deliberate. The familiar flutter in her chest, the sensation she fought against for months during their cat-and-mouse game across Los Angeles. Back then, she attributed it to adrenaline, to the thrill of closing in on a target. Now, she knew better.

Inside, the galleries were hushed, bathed in filtered natural light transforming the space into something almost sacred. Their footsteps echoed against the polished floors as they moved past rooms filled with Renaissance paintings and ancient sculptures. A few early visitors nodded in passing, unaware the well-dressed couple walking among them had once orchestrated one of the most complex undercover operations in recent history.

Amanda slowed as they approached the west pavilion, her attention caught by a familiar canvas, a Dutch landscape, all stormy skies and windswept trees. She stopped before it, her reflection ghosting across the protective glass.

"Van Ruisdael," Javier said, coming to stand beside her. "This was part of their route."

"The fourth shipment," she said. "Hidden beneath a forgery so perfect the museum's experts couldn't tell the difference without specialized equipment." She tilted her head, studying the turbulent clouds captured in oil and time. "The Eclipse Consortium was nothing if not thorough."

"We were," Javier said, his hazel eyes meeting hers in the reflection. "That's the hardest part of coming back, isn't it? Remembering which memories are real and which were part of the deception."

Amanda's fingers twitched at her side, a gesture so slight most people would miss it. Javier wasn't most people. He reached out, his hand hovering near hers without quite touching. An invitation, not a demand.

"So much has changed," she said, her voice soft against the ambient quiet of the gallery.

"You've changed," Javier said, turning to face her. The morning light caught in his dark hair. "I've seen you become exactly who you're meant to be."

Amanda tilted her head, studying him. There was none of the performative charm he employed in his undercover persona, just Javier, open and honest in a way that still sometimes caught her off guard. "Head of the task force. Full authority. It's... satisfying."

"And terrifying?" he prompted, one eyebrow raised in a way that had once infuriated her during interrogations.

"Only sometimes." She paused, then said, "The nights. When I wake up and for a moment I think we're still in the middle of it all. That you're still, "

"The bad guy?" His smile held no bitterness, only understanding.

"The unknown variable," she replied. "The piece that never quite fit the profile."

They continued walking, passing from one gallery to another in comfortable silence. A beam of sunlight track across the floor, Amanda was content, remembering how different this place looked under evening lights, filled with the glittering elite of Los Angeles's art world, the perfect cover for the Consortium's exchange.

"The director still sends a Christmas card," she said suddenly. "To thank the Bureau for recovering the stolen pieces without a public scandal. As if we did it for her reputation rather than because it was our job."

Javier snorted. "People see what they want to see. You taught me that."

"Did I?"

"Mmm." He nodded toward a bench positioned before a large canvas, and they sat, their shoulders not quite touching. "You saw the criminal in me because that's what you were looking for. Just like the director sees only what serves her narrative."

Amanda considered this, her dark eyes thoughtful. "But I saw other things too. Eventually."

"You did," he said. "When you started looking for them."

They sat in contemplative silence, watching a docent lead a small group through the adjacent gallery. Amanda's phone buzzed once in her pocket, probably Thompson with an update on the new case, but she ignored it. This moment, this conversation, was more important than whatever bureaucratic detail awaited her attention.

"Have you decided?" she asked after a while. "About what

comes next?"

Javier's expression shifted, becoming more measured. "I've been offered a consulting role. Private security. It's legitimate. Clean. Still useful, but..." he exhaled, "not undercover."

"You're tired of pretending?" she asked, knowing the answer but needing to for him say it.

"I'm ready to live without looking over my shoulder." His gaze was steady, holding hers with an intensity that made her breath catch. "I'm ready to be just one person, not three different versions depending on who's watching."

Amanda nodded, understanding his need for some normalcy. The weight of maintaining covers, of compartmentalizing truths and lies until they blurred together, it wore on the soul. She witnessed it happen to other agents, how they lost themselves in the labyrinth of fabricated identities. Javier survived three years embedded in one of the most dangerous criminal organizations in the world, but not without cost.

"The Bureau would take you," she said. "With your experience, your language skills, "

"No." His response was gentle but firm. "I need distance from all of it. From badges and jurisdictions and the constant pressure to sacrifice everything personal for the greater good." He paused, his expression softening. "But not distance from everything."

The implication hung between them, unspoken but undeniable. Amanda reached out, brushing her fingers across his sleeve in a gesture that might appear casual to anyone watching but carried months of carefully maintained professional boundaries, ready to fall.

"So am I," she said. "Ready to live without looking over my shoulder."

Javier's smile reached his eyes, crinkling the corners in a way that made him look younger, unburdened. "Does that mean we can continue our dinners together? Without insisting we discuss case files over dessert?"

Amanda laughed, the sound bright and unexpected in the hushed gallery. "I make no promises about the case files. But dinner... dinner we can do."

They rose from the bench in unspoken agreement, continuing their circuit of the museum. As they moved toward the garden entrance, something shift inside her, a loosening of the vigilance that defined her for so long, a cautious surrender to possibility.

The sun climbed higher now, burning away the morning mist wrapped around the hills. Ahead, the Central Garden beckoned with its winding paths and verdant tranquility. Behind them, the galleries stood as silent witnesses to their shared past, to mistaken identities and dangerous games, to truths revealed in moments of crisis.

Amanda glanced at Javier, at the profile she'd once memorized as a target and now cherished as something different. His hand found hers as they stepped into the sunlight, and for once, she didn't pull away.

***

The Central Garden unfolded before them like a secret slowly revealed, a cascade of colors and textures designed to both surprise and soothe. The air hung heavy with jasmine and citrus, carrying the subtle perfume of a thousand blooming things. Amanda breathed it in, feeling something inside her unfurl in response. Water trickled through the garden's artful channels, a constant gentle music that seemed to soften the edges of her thoughts. Beside her, Javier walked with measured steps, his presence solid yet undemanding, leaving space for the silence that surrounded between them.

Sunlight dappled the path through a canopy of pruned trees, painting shifting patterns across Javier's shoulders and catching in Amanda's hair. Their shadows stretched and contracted across the ground, two silhouettes moving in perfect synchronicity. There was something comforting in that harmony, something she hadn't expected to find with anyone, let alone with him.

A breeze rustled through the leaves, carrying with it the distant laughter of other visitors. Amanda's fingertips trailed over a deep purple blossom as they passed, its velvet texture a momentary anchor to the physical world while her thoughts drifted elsewhere.

"I've been thinking a lot," she said, her voice soft enough that Javier had to lean closer to hear. The words were inadequate for the tangle of emotions she was trying to express, but they were a beginning.

Javier said nothing, only inclined his head in acknowledgment. This was what surprised her most about him, once she peeled back the undercover persona, his capacity for patience, for listening without rushing to fill the silence.

They rounded a bend in the path, descending deeper into the garden where the plants grew more lush, more wild. A small fountain bubbled nearby, the water catching light and fragmenting it into diamond-bright reflections.

"I'm good at control," she said after a moment. "At order. My whole life has been about discipline, competitive swimming, forensic psychology, the Bureau." She gestured with one hand. "I know how to set parameters. How to stay within lines."

She paused, watching a monarch butterfly alight on a nearby flower, its wings opening and closing in unhurried rhythm.

"But relationships don't operate like task forces," she said, her voice carrying a note of uncertainty that she always feared others could hear.

Javier glanced at her, his hazel eyes warm with understanding. "No," he replied. "But they thrive on honesty."

Amanda looked forward, following the winding path with her eyes. "When my ex left..." she halted, then shook her head. "It wasn't just the betrayal. It was the realization that I'd been reading everything wrong. All my training in behavioral analysis, and I couldn't see what was happening in my own marriage."

"We're all blind to certain things," Javier said. "Especially the things closest to us."

They walked in silence for several steps, the garden path curving beneath a trellis heavy with climbing roses. A memory surfaced, Amanda at twenty-two, slicing through pool water at dawn, counting breaths and strokes, controlling every variable possible. Then, she'd been constructing walls, creating systems, finding safety in predictability.

"Sometimes I wonder if I can be..." she searched for the right word, "soft. Vulnerable. Without losing control."

Javier stopped walking, turning to face her. His expression was thoughtful, his eyes studying her face with careful attention. "You've already let your walls down more than you know."

Amanda raised an eyebrow, skeptical. "Have I?"

"You let me in," he said laughing. "Even when it was the worst idea in the world."

His words triggered a cascade of memories, Amanda discovering his true identity as an undercover operative, the gut-wrenching moment of realization, followed by tentative trust built in dangerous half-moments between official operations. The risk she took, believing in him when every protocol dictated otherwise.

"That was different," she protested weakly. "It was part of the job."

"Was it?" His question hung between them, gentle but pointed.

Amanda looked away, unable to maintain eye contact under the weight of his perception. The truth was more complicated, and they both understood it. Her decision to trust him had never been about protocols or professional judgment. It had been raw, emotional, the very qualities she spent a lifetime disciplining out of herself.

"You knew what you were risking," Javier continued. "Your career, your reputation. But you did it anyway."

A memory surfaced, Amanda standing in her superior's office, arguing Javier's case with a conviction that surprised the cynic in her. The skepticism in Thompson's eyes, the veiled accusations of compromised judgment. She stood her ground then, certainty burning through her doubts.

"I trusted my instincts," she said.

"Exactly." Javier's smile was small but genuine. "That's what relationships are. Trusting your instincts about someone, even when logic suggests caution."

Amanda laughed a light laugh, the sound mingling with the garden's gentle symphony of water and wind. "You make it sound so simple."

"It isn't," he stated. "But neither is infiltrating an international smuggling ring, and we managed that."

His comparison startled a more genuine laugh from her. "Fair point."

They resumed walking, the path sloping downward. Amanda's chest released, a tension unnoticed until it began to dissolve. Ahead, the garden's central waterfall came into view, water cascading in an artful arrangement that appeared both natural and well designed.

"You realize there's another barrier to this whole normal relationship idea," Javier said, his tone lighter.

Amanda glanced at him, curious. "Which is?"

"You drink enough coffee to be a security threat." His eyes crinkled at the corners, amusement softening his features.

She rolled her eyes, the gesture more playful than annoyed. "You love it."

"I tolerate it," he replied, "out of respect for your addiction."

"It's not an addiction," she protested. "It's a... professional necessity."

"Four cups before noon is not a necessity, it's a cry for help."

"Says the man who once memorized four different aliases, complete with backstories and accents."

"That was for survival."

"So is my coffee."

Javier laughed, the sound rich and unguarded, so different from the calculated charm he employed in his undercover role. Amanda nudged him with her shoulder, a casual physical contact that would have been unthinkable six months ago. He swayed with the impact, then settled back into stride beside her.

They approached the waterfall, where the garden path curved around a small pool that caught the falling water. The afternoon sun transformed the cascade into a curtain of liquid light, droplets catching fire as they fell. Amanda paused, watching the play of light and water with unexpected fascination.

"It's beautiful," she said, almost to herself.

Javier nodded, his gaze fixed not on the water but on her profile. "It is."

Something in his tone made her turn, meeting his eyes. The intensity there caught her off-guard, not the manufactured heat he'd once used as part of his cover, but something quieter and far more genuine. Her breath caught, a flutter of nerves awakening in her stomach. This was the moment where she would normally retreat, where the vulnerability would become too acute and she'd pull back into safer territory.

Instead, she held his gaze, allowing herself to exist in the discomfort of the moment. The garden continued its gentle symphony around them, water falling, leaves rustling, distant voices murmuring. Time slowed down, stretching around this silent exchange.

Javier reached for her hand, no pressure, just presence. His fingers hovered near hers, an invitation rather than a demand. In that suspended moment, Amanda saw the choice before her with perfect clarity: she could retreat to the safety of emotional distance, or she could step forward into uncertainty.

She let him take her hand.

After a moment, Javier's fingers tightened around hers, a silent question. Amanda responded with the slightest pressure of her own, an answer. They turned away from the waterfall by unspoken agreement, continuing down the garden path with their hands still linked, venturing deeper into this new territory they were creating step by step.

***

Los Angeles stretched beneath them like a kingdom of light and shadow, buildings catching the last golden rays of sunset and transforming them into something almost magical. From the Getty's western overlook, the city was both vast and intimate, a sprawling entity breathing with millions of lives intersecting in patterns too complex to comprehend. Amanda leaned against the stone balustrade, her dark eyes reflecting the soft glow that painted everything in warm, forgiving tones. Beside her, Javier stood close enough that she could feel the heat radiating from his body, a counterpoint to the cooling evening air that swept up from the canyon below.

The day was dying with remarkable grace, the sky bleeding from gold to pink to deepening blue. Far in the distance, where city met ocean, the horizon shimmered with the last remnants of daylight. A plane making its slow descent toward LAX caught her eye, its lights throbbing against the darkening canvas of sky. Six months ago, she might have been on that plane, tracking a suspect or pursuing a lead. The thought struck her as distant now, as though it belonged to another lifetime.

The breeze picked up, teasing the edges of her blouse and the collar of Javier's jacket. Her hair, unlike her practical ponytail during work hours, was loose now, dark strands dancing across her face. She tucked them behind her ear with an absent gesture, her thoughts elsewhere.

"Do you still think about it?" she asked, her voice having trouble carrying over the ambient sounds of distant traffic and rustling foliage.

Javier turned toward her, his profile outlined in fading gold. "What?"

"If we hadn't met at the gala." Her fingers traced an idle

pattern on the stone beneath her hands. "If it had been someone else. Another case. Another night."

The question hung between them, weighted with possibilities. Amanda didn't plan to ask it, had never really allowed herself to consider these alternatives even in private moments. But here, with the day surrendering to night and the city transforming beneath them, the boundaries between spoken and unspoken thoughts more permeable.

Javier was quiet for a long moment, his expression thoughtful. When he spoke, his voice carried a resonance that echoed in the narrow space between them.

"Then I'd still be running," he said. "And you'd still be alone, pretending you didn't need anyone."

His words struck with the peculiar sting of truth recognized and always ignored. The ripple in her chest, not pain, but a sharp recognition. She spent years constructing a life that required no one else, that functioned with the precision and self-containment of the mechanical watches her father collected. Relationships were variables, unpredictable and therefore dangerous.

She smiled, but her voice caught momentarily. "I don't want to be alone anymore."

The admission cost her something, pride, perhaps, or the barriers she held for so long. But as the words left her lips, she felt lighter somehow, as though she set down the burden, carried for years without recognizing its weight.

"You're not," Javier said, his voice low and certain. He turned toward her now, his face half in shadow as the sunset deepened behind him. "You haven't been for a while."

Amanda's chest rose with a deep breath, her exhale shaky and unsure. "I still have trust issues," she said, her mouth curving into a self-deprecating smile.

"And I still have scars from hiding who I am," Javier replied, matching her honesty with his own. There was no artifice in his expression now. This was Javier stripped to essentials, a man who had lived too long in shadows, navigating the treacherous space between identities.

Amanda studied his face, noticing details she cataloged a hundred times before but now appreciated with new eyes, the small scar above his left eyebrow from a childhood accident, the faint lines that formed at the corners of his eyes when he smiled, the way his jaw tensed when he spoke of his past. She'd once memorized these features as part of her investigation, filing them away as data points. Now they were simply facets of someone she,

She stopped herself before completing the thought, still cautious in the privacy of her own mind.

"But somehow, with you..." Javier said, his eyes meeting hers with an intensity that made her breath catch, "I feel seen."

The simple statement resonated somewhere deep inside her. Isn't that what everyone ultimately wanted? To be seen, not just surveilled or analyzed or categorized, but recognized on some fundamental level? In her line of work, Amanda was trained to see beyond surfaces, to read the stories written in body language and verbal patterns. But to be on the receiving end of such perception, to be understood, and still accepted, that was rarer and far more precious.

The sky deepened to indigo now, the first stars appearing like distant beacons. Below them, the city was transforming, street lights and building illuminations creating constellations of man-made stars to mirror those emerging above. Far to the west, the last streak of sunset lingered, a final brushstroke of amber against the darkening canvas.

"Whatever comes next..." Amanda said, then hesitated, uncertain of her words. Accustomed to briefing rooms and formal reports, to the precise language of investigation and evidence. This territory, the vocabulary of personal futures and shared possibilities, felt foreign to her tongue.

"We face it together," Javier said, his voice carrying quiet conviction.

Javier nodded, his free hand moving to brush a strand of hair from her face. The gesture was tentative, almost reverent, his fingertips grazing her cheek. Amanda felt her pulse quicken, a response she once would have controlled and analyzed but now allowed without thought.

"I spent three years becoming whoever the Service needed me to be, the Consortium needed me to be," he said. "Changing my opinions, my preferences, my reactions, until sometimes I wasn't sure what was real and what was fabricated. But with you..." He paused, his hand settling against the curve of her jaw. "With you, I never had to question what I felt. Even when it was inconvenient. Even when it was dangerous."

Amanda's breath caught in her throat, her usual verbal agility deserting her. Instead, she leaned into his touch, the simple movement communicating what words could not.

He kissed her, slow, meaningful, full of everything unspoken. His lips were warm against hers, the contact both familiar and new. They kissed before, in moments of heightened emotion or tactical necessity, but never like this, never with the full truth between them, never with the promise of tomorrow undisturbed by deception.

Amanda's hands found his shoulders, then slid upward to trace the line of his jaw. She felt his arms encircle her waist, drawing her closer until the space between them disappeared. The kiss deepened, years of controlled tension finding release in this honest connection at last.

When they pulled apart, the last rays of sun slipped beyond the horizon. The city was illuminated now, a glittering tapestry of light against the darkness. Overhead, a single star blinked into the deepening night sky, then another, and another, the ancient patterns emerging as they had for countless generations before.

Amanda looked up at Javier, at the face she had once memorized as part of her investigation and now recognized through an different kind of attention. His expression held a certainty that echoed something unfurling within her own chest, a willingness to step forward into unknown territory, not alone but together.

The past was behind them. The mission was over. But life? That was just beginning.

With her hand still in his, Amanda turned back toward the museum, ready to descend from this elevated perspective and enter the more complicated landscape of everyday existence. Whatever came next, bureaucratic obstacles, public scrutiny, the inevitable adjustments of two strong individuals learning to build a shared life, they would navigate it as they had navigated the treacherous waters of their professional entanglement: with courage, with honesty, and with the hard-won knowledge that some risks were worth taking.

Beneath the emerging stars, two former enemies, lovers, and now partners stood ready for the next page of their story, one they would write together, without covers or codes, in the clearest language of all.

Epilogue

Rain sliced through the night air, transforming the asphalt into a mirror that reflected fragmented blue and red emergency lights. Detective Kelly hunched his shoulders against the downpour, the collar of his coat already sodden as he approached the wreckage. The car lay on its side like a wounded animal, smoke twisting upward despite the rain. The familiar hollowness in his gut was there, not sadness, not anymore, but a peculiar emptiness came with witnessing the aftermath of violence that made less sense the more you looked at it.

The crash drew half a precinct, uniforms huddled in small groups, their faces washed out beneath the unforgiving pulse of squad car lights. Shattered glass crunched beneath Kelly' shoes as he ducked under the yellow tape, nodding to the officer who recognized him with a grim acknowledgment. Water pooled in the depressions of the street, carrying thin ribbons of crimson away from the scene.

"Jesus," Kelly said, taking in the full scope of the destruction.

The car's windshield was a spider web of fractures, the driver's side door peeled back like the lid of a tin can. Behind the wheel, Kelly saw a fit middle aged man, sat slumped against his seat belt, his face slack and colorless beneath the streaks of blood. In the passenger seat, Another man who could have been the first's twin based on his build, lay with her head at an angle that made Kelly' stomach clench.

A technician in a clear poncho knelt beside the vehicle, photographing something Kelly couldn't see. The flash illuminated raindrops, turning them into brief, falling stars that vanished as quickly as they appeared.

"What do we know?" Kelly asked, pulling his collar tighter against the wind determined to find the gaps in his clothing with cold, probing fingers.

Officer Chandler turned from the wreckage, water streaming from the brim of his cap. "Two secret service agents, no Ids. Both DOA."

"Time of death?" Kelly asked, his eyes scanning the wreckage with a professional eye.

"M.E. says between midnight and two, give or take," Chandler replied, shifting his weight. "Looks like they were on some sort of prisoner transport. Nobody heard anything. Nobody saw anything."

"That's convenient," Kelly said, standing to circle the vehicle.

He paused at the back door, where something metallic caught the blue strobe of the nearest squad car. A pair of handcuffs lay open and discarded, one bracelet smeared with a dark substance that might have been blood or might have been mud. Kelly pulled a pen from his pocket and lifted the chain with its tip.

Kelly turned to find Detective Simmons approaching, her umbrella doing little to keep her dry as the wind whipped rain sideways. Her dark hair plastered to her forehead, but her eyes were sharp and clear.

"And dangerous, they were transporting a prisoner from that big heist the Feds uncovered the other day." Simmons added, nodding toward the empty holsters visible on the dead officers' belts. "Two missing Glocks. A stolen comms radio. No prints. No shell casings. Whoever took them knew what they were doing."

"Forensics has anything else?" he asked Simmons, who moved to stand beside him, both of them silhouetted by the emergency lights.

Kelly stared down at the scene. "How the fuck did a perp cause this from the back seat? Do we know anything about who he was?"

"Nothing the feds are willing to share. When I asked they said they were sending some of their own down here" Simmons asked.

"Just what I fucking need, a turf war, and I'm thinking we've got a ghost on our hands."

"A ghost?"

"Someone who knows how to be invisible," Kelly said, his eyes sweeping the scene once more. "Someone who can kill two armed officers, take what they need, and vanish without leaving a trace, except for what they want us to find."

The rain was easing now, falling in a gentle patter rather than the driving sheets of earlier. More officials were arriving, the district captain's car pulled up, followed by an unmarked sedan Kelly recognized as belonging to Internal Affairs. The quiet residential street was transforming into a hub of activity, each new arrival adding to the controlled chaos.

The rain stopped now, leaving behind a slick, reflective world that distorted the emergency lights into long, stretching fingers of color. Kelly stood watching as the bodies of the two federal agents were extracted from the vehicle, their forms zipped into black bags that erased their individuality and reduced them to evidence.

"We've got a ghost on our hands," he had said earlier. But as he surveyed the scene one last time, he amended the thought: We've got something worse than a ghost. We've got someone who is good what they're doing and doesn't care who knows it.

And that was the most terrifying possibility of all.

***

Isabel Serrano's sketchbook lay open on her lap, its blank page an accusation. The charcoal pencil balanced between her fingers had not touched the paper in the forty-three minutes she'd been sitting at Gate 59. Around her, LAX Terminal 5 performed its chaotic morning ballet, harried business people checking watches and phones with identical expressions of impatience, families corralling sleepy children and overstuffed carry-ons, airline staff maintaining plastic smiles despite the mounting complaints about the weather delay in Chicago. But Isabel remained still, a point of calm in the human current, her artist's eyes taking in everything while her hands refused to create.

The morning sun slanted through the massive windows, catching dust motes that danced in shafts of light. Isabel found more beauty in their random patterns than in anything she might draw. She wore a simple linen blouse and well-worn jeans, her dark hair pulled back in a loose knot at the nape of her neck. Nothing about her appearance suggested that her fingers had recreated Goyas with such precision, auction houses had been fooled, or that her understanding of pigment chemistry rivaled any museum conservator.

The buzz of early morning travel pulsed with its usual rhythm, calls for boarding, children crying, the static hum of tired businessmen on cell phones. A nearby television mounted on a pillar broadcast CNN with closed captioning, the news crawl reporting stock market fluctuations and a tropical storm brewing in the Caribbean. Ordinary concerns for ordinary people living ordinary lives.

Isabel forgot what ordinary felt like.

For nearly a decade, she lived in a world of shadows and masterpieces, where her talent had been both her salvation and her prison. The Eclipse Consortium discovered her during her second year at the Madrid Institute of Fine Arts, when one of her professors, a man she later learned had connections to the organization, recognized something in her work. Not technical skill, but an almost supernatural ability to inhabit another artist's mind, to understand not how they applied paint to canvas but why they made each brushstroke the way they did.

"You don't copy," he told her over coffee in a small café near the Plaza Mayor. "You channel. That's much more valuable."

The money they offered had been impossible to refuse, her father's medical bills were mounting, and her mother's restoration work struggling to covered the rent on their small apartment. One job, she told herself. Just one forgery, and she would walk away.

But of course, there was never one job with the Consortium. Each successful forgery led to another commission, each payment larger, each risk greater. Before she understood what was happening, Isabel became indispensable to their art trafficking operation, creating works that passed authentication tests and fooled experts, allowing the Consortium to sell stolen originals on the black market while returning her perfect replicas to unsuspecting museums and collectors.

Isabel's fingers tightened around the charcoal pencil as she remembered the last piece she created for them, a mid-period Picasso, one of his less abstract works from the early 1930s. The original had been stolen from a private collection in Buenos Aires, and Isabel had been given three weeks to produce a copy that would pass inspection when the insurance company sent their authentication expert.

She worked day and night in a secure studio outside Valencia, studying photographs and technical analyses, mixing pigments to match the aging and chemical composition of the original paints, even replicating the specific wear patterns on the canvas where it had been exposed to sunlight through a window in its previous location. The work consumed her, as it always did, a total immersion in another artist's vision and technique until her own identity seemed to blur and fade.

When she finished, even she had trouble distinguishing her creation from the photographs of the original. The Consortium handler, a cold-eyed man who never gave his name, had actually smiled when he saw it.

"Perfection, as always," he said, running a gloved finger along the edge of the frame. "You are an artist, Ms. Serrano."

The praise lay in her mouth like bitter lemon peels. An artist creates. She had replicated.

But that was before. Before the FBI raid on the Consortium's Los Angeles operation three weeks ago. Before the international arrests and the assets seized and the names released to the press. Before Isabel helped the organization that defined her adult life collapse like a house of cards.

Inside, there was only silence.

The Consortium was gone, fractured, dismantled, swallowed by its own rot. And with it, so was the part of her that had once thrived in shadows. For the first time in years, she was no one's forger. No one's asset. No one's secret.

The thought made her breath hitch, a small sound that drew a curious glance from the businessman seated across from her. Isabel offered a polite smile that revealed nothing before returning her attention to the blank page before her.

What now?

The question hovered at the edges of her consciousness since all the news reports, since she burned her false documents and contacted her mother for the first time in two years. The answer remained elusive, shrouded in a fog of possibility that was both exhilarating and terrifying.

Her tiny apartment in Madrid's Lavapiés neighborhood was waiting. The sunlight that poured through her favorite window in the afternoon, casting long shadows across the worn wooden floors. The small balcony where she had once kept herbs and flowers before her work with the Consortium took her away too often for proper care. The blank canvases she dared not touch in years, waiting for her own vision rather than someone else's.

But what would she paint? After so long inhabiting other artists' minds and styles, did she even have a voice of her own anymore? The thought sent a cold current of anxiety through her chest. Perhaps her talent had only ever been mimicry, a sophisticated form of artistic ventriloquism rather than genuine creation.

Isabel closed the sketchbook with a decisive snap, sliding the charcoal pencil into the spiral binding. Dwelling on such fears would paralyze her. Better to face the uncertainty head-on, to discover the answer through action rather than endless introspection.

A child's laugh cut through the ambient noise of the terminal, bright and uninhibited, the sound of someone too young to understand limitations. Isabel turned to see a little girl, perhaps four years old, spinning in circles near the window, her pink backpack swinging as she twirled. The girl's mother hovering with the fond exasperation unique to parents of energetic children, ready to intervene if the spinning veered too close to other travelers.

Isabel found herself smiling, a genuine expression, a foreign feeling on her face after so many years of careful self-control. There was something innocent and hopeful in the child's joyful abandonment, something Isabel forgot was possible.

"Now boarding: Iberia Airlines, Flight 684 to Madrid," came the announcement, the voice crisp and professional through the terminal's speaker system. "We would like to invite our OneWorld Emerald members, business class passengers, and those needing special assistance to board at this time."

Isabel gathered her belongings, the sketchbook, a worn copy of García Márquez she'd been carrying for weeks but never opened, a small travel bag containing nothing more valuable than a change of clothes and basic toiletries. No forgery supplies. No false documents. No burner phones or encrypted drives.

Just her. Just Isabel.

She joined the line forming at the gate, passport and boarding pass in hand. For a moment, an old instinct surfaced, the urge to check for surveillance, to scan for Consortium contacts or law enforcement, to ensure she wasn't being followed. But she pushed it aside. That life was over. The woman who lived it was someone she no longer needed to be.

As she approached the gate agent, Isabel caught her reflection in the glossy surface of a nearby advertisement. Her eyes looked different somehow, clearer, more present. The perpetual furrow between her brows softened. She looked younger, or perhaps less burdened.

"Buen viaje," the gate agent said as she scanned Isabel's boarding pass.

"Gracias," Isabel replied, the familiar syllables of her native language a welcome homecoming already.

As she walked down the jet bridge, Her step lightened with each meter she put between herself and American soil. The past was still behind her, lingering in shadows, but ahead? Ahead, there was color. True color, not the matched pigments of forgery but the wild, unpredictable palette of a life reclaimed.

She paused at the threshold of the aircraft, taking one last glance back at the terminal. A final look at the life she was leaving behind. Then, with her first full breath untroubled in years, Isabel stepped forward into the waiting plane.

No aliases. No disguises. And the quiet promise of freedom stretching out before her like a blank canvas, waiting for the first brave stroke of color.

***

The fluorescent lights of the bus station bathroom flickered with the consistency of a failing heart. The woman viewed her reflection appear and disappear in the grimy mirror, studying the stranger that gazed back at her. The red hair, box-dyed earlier in the night in another filthy bathroom, hung blunt around her face, the color harsh against her olive skin. It wasn't flattering, but beauty wasn't the point. Anonymity was. She ran a hand through the unfamiliar strands, noting that her manicure was chipping at the edges. Three days ago, she would have considered that unacceptable. Now, it was another layer of her disguise.

She finished drying her hands on a coarse paper towel, her movements precise despite her exhaustion. Seventy-two hours without proper sleep had left her with a dull ache behind her eyes, but her posture remained impeccable, her senses alert. Old habits. Survival mechanisms.

The bathroom door swung open with a protesting creak as the stepped back into the main terminal. The bus station existed in that liminal space between night and morning, not quite empty enough to be eerie, not quite populated enough to provide the comfort of anonymity in numbers. A janitor pushed a mop across the worn linoleum, spreading the scent of industrial pine cleaner that failed to mask the underlying odors of diesel and desperation. At the ticket counter, a heavyset woman with hair arranged in meticulous cornrows sorted cash with practiced efficiency. Three people waited in line: a young man with headphones and a military duffel, an elderly couple leaning against each other with the comfortable familiarity of decades together.

Ginevra's reflection flickered in the scratched metal of a vending machine as she passed, a tall woman with fitted jeans and a plain black coat that belied its expense and craftsmanship. The sunglasses she slipped on were dark enough to obscure her distinctive eyes, one more precaution in a life built on layers of them. Her fake ID, Sofia Mendez, according to the expensive and near flawless documentation, rested in an interior pocket, close to her body.

She adjusted the strap of her worn leather duffel, feeling the reassuring weight of its contents. The bag contained three changes of clothes, basic toiletries, thirty thousand in mixed currencies, and a leather case of specialized tools that would raise significant questions if discovered. The weight of her other tool, the one nestled in a custom holster at the small of her back, was so familiar she rarely noticed it anymore.

Ginevra moved toward the seating area, selecting a plastic chair with a clear view of both the main entrance and the boarding gates. She crossed her legs at the ankle, her posture relaxed to casual observation but coiled with potential energy that a trained eye might recognize. As she waited, her mind drifted to three nights ago, to the moment when everything shifted.

Now, as she sat in this nameless bus station in a nowhere town, she knew she was both hunter and hunted. The Consortium would assume she was compromised. Standard protocol would call for her elimination. But she had no intention of making it easy for them, or for the federal agents undoubtedly searching for her.

A harried mother struggled through the main doors, wrestling with a stroller and two small children. Ginevra's eyes followed with clinical detachment as the woman navigated the space, noting how her attention was fractured, how vulnerable she made herself with each divided glance. Such observations were automatic, ingrained. Everyone got categorized: threat, non-threat, potential asset, potential liability.

The overhead speakers crackled to life, announcing the imminent departure of the 4:15 Greyhound to Phoenix. The woman checked her watch, a modest Timex that replaced her usual Cartier. It was 4:03. She rose with fluid grace, her movements economical as she gathered her bag.

The true bite of winter never reached this part of California, but she still pulled her coat tight around her body. Not for warmth. For the psychological comfort of a barrier between herself and the world. For the concealment it provided.

"Long ride ahead," the driver said as she passed, his eyes lingering a beat too long on her face.

"I'm used to it," she replied, her accent softened, the crisp Italian edges of her natural speech patterns smoothed into something more ambiguous.

The bus was half-full, passengers distributed in that peculiar way of strangers sharing transport, maintaining maximum distance from one another, territories defined by bags placed on adjacent seats. Ginevra moved down the narrow aisle, her gaze sweeping each occupant with practiced efficiency.

A businessman in a rumpled suit, sleeping with his mouth open. Low threat.

Two college-aged girls sharing earbuds, giggling over something on a phone. Non-threats.

An older man with calloused hands and a worn baseball cap. Potential threat, his posture suggested military or law enforcement background.

A thin woman with nervous hands and bloodshot eyes. Unpredictable. Worth monitoring.

She selected a seat near the back, positioning herself with her back to the wall and a clear view of both the front entrance and the emergency exit. She placed her duffel on her lap rather than stowing it overhead or beneath the seat, another habit born of necessity. Her possessions never left her immediate control.

She leaned her head against the glass, feigning the posture of someone who might sleep through the journey while remaining aware of every movement around her. The bus's engine rumbled to life, vibrating through the worn seat. Through the window, the station receded, the gray concrete and harsh lighting giving way to darkened storefronts and empty streets.

She didn't look back. She never did.

Looking back was a luxury afforded to those with regrets, those who left pieces of themselves behind. Ginevra learned long ago to travel light in all respects, material and emotional. Attachments were vulnerabilities. Sentimentality was a weakness. There was only forward momentum and survival.

As the bus merged onto the highway, heading east toward the still-dark horizon, Ginevra allowed herself to consider her options. The Consortium was fractured but not destroyed. There would be those who escaped the federal net, those who would regroup and rebuild. And there would be scores to settle, loose ends to eliminate. She looked at the window the reflection of El Fantasma stared back. "Ghosts never die." she though to herself.

About the Author

William D. Howell never set out to become an author, but sometimes the best stories begin unexpectedly.

A devoted father, William was inspired to write his first novel when his young daughter discovered the magic of books. Fueled by her excitement and curiosity, he picked up the pen not just to tell a story, but to show her how powerful and joyful storytelling can be. What began as a personal project quickly evolved into a full-fledged novel, blending adventure, emotion, and imagination in a way that speaks to both new and seasoned readers.

When he's not crafting characters or building suspense on the page, William enjoys the rough-and-tumble rhythm of rugby, the satisfying challenge of woodworking, and quiet moments with his wife and daughter, usually with a good book nearby. His writing is driven by a deep love for family, a belief in the power of stories, and a desire to pass that love on to the next generation.

You can connect with me on:

- https://www.wordsofwilliam.com
- https://x.com/wordsofwilliam_
- https://www.facebook.com/wordsofwilliam1